BEAUTIFULLY RUINED

MJ MASUCCI

ISBN 978-1-950175-38-3

CHAPTER 1

Avery

Payne Berne. He was the reason I was in this situation. After he, my new stepfather, swept my mother off her feet, they were married within three months. I guess she was lonely since my father died almost four years ago. Now I was living in what can only be classed as a freaking castle.

Who the hell has a home with twenty-seven rooms for two people? It made no sense. Servants, a chef at our beck and call, and drivers to take you anywhere you want. It was a dream, except it wasn't.

Worse, with Payne's entrance came an evil stepbrother. Gideon Berne was number five in the line of Bernes—a bunch of pretentious assholes. My new stepbrother paraded around the house like he was king of the castle. Berne Manor was built entirely of stone brought over from Ireland in the eighteen hundreds. Your footsteps echoed when you walked the halls, but despite the enormity of the building, it was comfortable.

In a few weeks, I would be out of the safety of my mother and off to Bancroft Preparatory Academy. Gideon was a god there, but it seemed he was a god no matter where he went. Right now, he was holding court in front of the swimming pool with some of his buddies from Bancroft.

The school was full of blue bloods, and I would be thrown in with the sharks in my senior year. I was told that once Gideon and I were settled at school, Payne was whisking my mother away on a belated European honeymoon for two months. It would be sink or swim for me.

My mother refused to allow me to stay with one of my friends for the year while attending Arlington High School. Before she met Payne, my life was perfect. I was cheerleading captain, class president, and in line to be head editor for *The Roar*.

"Avery!" my mother called in a sing-song voice.

I rolled my eyes as I slipped on a long gray t-shirt, preparing for some time at the pool.

"Yes, mother."

My door burst open, not even a knock. I could be naked, but it didn't matter to her. Once she became a Berne, it seemed her entire sense of respect for me went out the window. All her attention was on Payne, and it pissed me off.

"What are you doing?" she asked, her voice stern.

I grabbed a tube of suntan lotion and ignored her while I hunted for my sunglasses.

"Avery, I'm waiting for an answer."

I whirled around to see her standing there, entirely made up and wearing a cute light blue dress with too much cleavage showing. My mother. She transformed the minute the ring went on her finger at the lavish wedding Payne allowed her to have.

Gone was any trace of casual. She expected me to dress for

dinner like we were going out to some fancy restaurant. And to wear jeans was blasphemy. My only solace from her newfound standards was taking the new silver Mercedes my stepfather and mother bestowed on me as a bribe and escaping to my friend Clover's house.

She was my bestie since sixth grade when we landed in detention for sneaking away during recess. Clover came from a rich family, but you would never know it with her antics. During our junior year, she was suspended four times for various infractions, mouthing off to the principal, wearing clothing in violation of the dress code and refusing to change, smoking on campus, and cutting classes.

Clover was a bad influence, but she was fun. I didn't know what I would do without her when I went to Bancroft. I would be drowning without her to keep me sane, especially with Gideon stepping on my head.

"Swimming, mother. I'm going swimming."

She frowned. "You promised to go with me to the club for lunch."

I rolled my eyes, making sure she saw it.

"I didn't promise. I told you I would see if it fit in my schedule."

From her rigid response alone, my mother was practically on the verge of stamping her high-heel-clad foot on the hardwood. I knew she wanted to do it, but she held back. It was a move I'd seen before when we weren't around Payne.

"Your mouth. I do hope Bancroft can do something with you."

My anger fed my insolence, and I poked her because I couldn't help myself.

"Really? I was perfectly fine before you sold me out and forced me to go to your precious Bancroft."

My mother's face grew tight with the same argument we had had over and over again. I didn't understand why I couldn't stay home or with Clover and attend Arlington High for my senior year. I was already part of the popular crowd, and now I would be banished with the bottom feeders: the misfits, the new kid.

"Gideon tells me the school has a wonderful business department. Their classes are advanced, unlike Arlington. Bancroft is in a top five for prep schools."

I snorted. "Now you're looking down at Arlington? My, my, mother, how stuck up you've become in such a short time."

She began to wring her hands. "I've had just about enough of your sass. How about I take the keys to your car? You won't be able to see that horrible Clover."

It was no secret that my mother despised Clover, even before she married Payne. My bestie was well known across town for having committed a few crimes; well, misdemeanors. She was caught drunk at the junior prom, pouring liquid soap into the community pool the day before it opened and spray painting a devil on the front of the firehouse.

"She's not horrible!" I snapped. "I could've stayed with her and finished my senior year at Arlington."

I tried to brush by her, but she grabbed my arm. "I wouldn't allow you to stay with the likes of Clover Delahunt. She has no discipline. Her parents let her do whatever she wants."

I wrenched my arm from her grip, stepping into the hall. "Like Gideon?" I mumbled.

I didn't wait for her reply because I didn't care what she had to say. She called after me, but I ignored her, rounding the corner and almost bumping into Payne. He knocked me off balance but grabbed me before I fell back.

"Are you okay?" he said softly.

I nodded. "If you're looking for mom, she's in my room."

His blue eyes crinkled at the edges when he smiled. "Is she giving you a hard time again?"

"A little," I whispered.

Payne brushed at the non-existent wrinkles in his starched blue oxford shirt. "She wants the best for you."

Behind us, I heard the clacking of my mother's heels as she hurried down the hall. I slipped around my stepfather as I tried to dodge the next barrage of insults. Gideon was still holding court when I emerged through the sliders. He glanced up at me, pulling his sunglasses down his nose before returning to entertain his guests.

I was a speck of dust in his world unless he wanted to torture me with some stupid nonsense. It started as soon as I moved in, and whenever he was around, I was on alert. The best thing for me to do was ignore him.

Wanting to forget my mother, I settled on the lounger on the opposite side of the pool from him and slathered myself with lotion after I removed my t-shirt—stupid move. When I glanced over, Gideon had removed his sunglasses, and his admirers were looking my way. When he rose from his chair, hooking his sunglasses in the waistband of his blue swim trunks, I tensed, wondering what he would do to me.

"Gideon."

Payne's voice was like music to my ears. My stepbrother froze in his tracks and looked toward the giant glass slider. In the cooler weather, the entire wall could open. All the doors were on tracks, but only one was open now, and Payne was standing there in his usual authoritative stance, his stance wide.

"Yes, Dad."

"We're heading to the club for lunch."

"And?" he barked.

"I'm letting you know. Make sure you clean up after yourselves. I don't want to find wrappers and bottles sitting on the table."

In true stuck-up Gideon fashion, he wrinkled his nose. "That's what we have staff for."

"They work for *me*. This is *my* home, and I expect you to

respect it. You don't see Avery leaving garbage all over the place."

I wanted to shrink into the lounger. The worst thing Payne could do was call Gideon out in front of his friends, especially when using me as an example. I could bet my evil stepbrother was conjuring up ways to make me miserable that very second.

"Yeah, fine." He said as he slumped his shoulders.

Gideon waited for Payne to duck back inside, then continued his stroll toward me. I tensed further as he grew closer. Behind him, his friends sat at the table, staring at us with interest. Gideon stopped a few feet from my lounger.

"You're a tasty piece of ass."

I ripped off my sunglasses, sick of his sexual innuendos. "Gideon, why don't you stop harassing me and find something else to do? You can try to shock me, but it won't work."

His lips curled in an evil grin as he sat on the edge of the lounger. "Remember, two weeks."

"Two weeks what?"

"Two weeks, and you're all mine. You won't have mommy to protect you."

Fear curled in my belly, but I stood my ground. "Protect me from what?"

He reached into my space and gripped my knee, squeezing it hard in his hand.

"I run the school. I do whatever I want."

I tried to push his hand away, but he slid it up my thigh, dangerously close to my pussy. I dug my nails into his skin, but he didn't flinch. Inside, I was trembling, and I struggled to keep my voice from breaking.

"Does that include rape? It's a crime. I doubt your precious Bancroft would overlook sexual assault."

Gideon removed his hand. "I won't need to rape you. I'll seduce you until you beg for it."

He fixed his gray eyes on me, and I forced myself not to look away.

"You're so sure of yourself?"

"You'll be dripping with lust when I get done with you. Your body was made for me, Avery. We'll fit perfectly together. I can't wait to have you."

I tried hard not to squeak my reply, "In your dreams."

I swallowed hard and clenched my jaw.

"My dream is to ruin you."

He reached out to touch my face, but I pulled my head out of his reach. A deep laugh erupted from him. Gideon's traveled my body with his gaze, but this time, I couldn't escape before he grasped my belly button ring, tugging at it.

"Stop it," I protested, trying to remove his hand, which displayed my nail marks from when I tried to pry him from my knee.

He let go, rose from the lounger, and looked down at me.

"Darling Avery. Save that pussy for me. I will have you, and it's not an if; it's when."

Once Gideon sauntered away, I grabbed my things and hurried into the house, the laughter of the boys burning in my ears.

"THAT'S WHAT YOU'RE WEARING?" my mother asked.

I plopped into my chair at a table designed to sit sixteen. These little nightly charades of playtime as a family were annoying. Gideon sat next to me as I settled in. I wore what I did on purpose: cutoff jean shorts, a yellow tank top, and a black bra underneath that was very visible.

Mr. Perfect sat beside me, wearing a pair of tan slacks and a white oxford shirt. It was comical to dress for dinner when we never did before we got here.

"I'm wearing it because it's comfortable."

"This isn't McDonald's."

Payne saved me by placing his hand over my mother's. "Renata, it's fine."

My mother gave him a smile dripping with syrup before returning her attention to me. "It's not fine. Gideon dresses for dinner, and I expect her to follow suit."

I forced back a smile, straining hard as my lips threatened to pull back over my teeth.

"It's one dinner," I mumbled.

"Excuse me?" she snarled.

Rather than looking at her, I began eating my salad. Payne engaged her in conversation, and she soon forgot about me. I just wished Gideon had, too. He leaned toward me and whispered:

"I have no problem with those sexy shorts."

"Fuck off," I growled under my breath.

Under the table, Gideon curled his fingers around my inner thigh, close enough to press his pinkie against my cleft. I shifted in my seat, and he snorted, which was followed by a cough. We both glanced toward our parents, looking at us. Gideon gave them a sweet smile, and they returned to their conversation.

"Get off me," I hissed, scratching at his skin.

He yanked his hand back, acting like nothing had happened, and took a sip of water as we were served dinner.

AFTER A GRUELING HOUR of playing make-believe, I was able to retreat to my room. Sitting on my bed, I was texting when my mother burst through the door. I made a mental note to lock my door next time as I threw my phone down.

"Mother, don't you believe in knocking?" I growled.

She slammed the door shut. "Your attitude is horrible lately.

I don't like it. Maybe I should ground you for the next two weeks."

My mouth dropped open. I had plans, which didn't include spending time here so I could be preyed upon by Gideon while my mother gallivanted around with her fancy new friends.

"That's not fair. I only have two weeks left before school starts."

She tapped her chin with her dark cherry-painted nails for a few seconds. "Then Friday night. I know you were planning something with your friends. You'll stay here."

My mother held her hand out at me and curled her fingers back and forth.

I was puzzled. "What?"

"I want your key fob. You won't need it because you're grounded."

"But today is Wednesday. Suppose I want to go out tomorrow?" I protested.

Behind me, my phone pinged twice.

"You can have Watkins take you. Payne is taking me out on his yacht for the day, so we won't be using the limo."

A rock formed in the pit of my stomach. If my mother and Payne were out of the house for the day, I would also need to make plans to be. I couldn't stay here with Gideon lurking around, especially since he seemed to do that a lot more recently.

"Can I use the credit card for some school clothing?"

My mother frowned. Until Payne came along, money was always tight. My father kept us comfortable, but after he died, we discovered he had tons of debt and no insurance. By the time everything was paid off and the house sold, there was just enough for one month's security and two months' rent on the apartment we lived in at the time.

My mother met Payne at a business function; she was helping her best friend cater for the extra money she desperately needed. He followed her as she served appetizers and drinks, telling her he would make a scene if she didn't go out on a date with him. She agreed, and the rest was history.

As he did with Gideon, I was given a credit card—two actually—and allowed to charge things as long as I didn't go overboard. Over the past two months, I hadn't spent a dime. I didn't want to take advantage buying things I didn't need.

"You have uniforms, which you will wear to school every day."

I wrinkled my nose. The knee-length navy skirt, matching jacket with a Bancroft crest, and white blouse along with white knee socks were school high fashion. I almost balked when she showed me a picture. It was absolutely ancient.

"And what about after? I won't be in school after 2 pm. And on weekends."

"You can buy some jeans and a few shirts," my mother said. "I don't want to see your boobs hanging out, or they go back to the store."

"Jesus Christ," I muttered.

"Excuse me?" she said in a stern voice.

"Thank you."

She shook her hand. "I still need your key fob."

Arguing was no use because she would stand here all night or search my room until she found the fob. It was better to give it to her and get back to texting with Clover. My phone had been chiming like a church bell during my talk with my mother.

I removed the fob from my nightstand and held it out to her. Two could play her little game. She took a few steps toward me and, in parental defiance, stood just out of my reach until I got off my bed and handed it to her.

CHAPTER 2

Gideon

The rest of my evening was spent in the pool house playing cards with my bros: Remington, Jaxson, and Xavier. We were the cream at Bancroft—athletes, scholars, and rich beyond belief. Between the four of us, nothing happened without our say-so at school.

Remy slapped down his cards. "Fuckers, you lose again."

His set of cards read a full house, but mine was even better. I put my hand on his arm as he reached out to drag the cash toward him.

"Not so fast."

Remy's eyebrows knitted together. "You can suck my dick. No one is beating my hand."

Xavier and Jaxson tossed their cards on the table—they were tonight's losers with weak hands. They leaned back in their chairs, waiting as I used my cards to fan my face.

"Will you suck my dick if I can beat you? Take it all and swallow when I come?" I scoffed.

Remy grabbed for my cards, but I pulled them away.

"Fuck off, Berne. Show 'em."

"You didn't answer my question," I said as I rubbed my crotch.

He grinned wickedly. "Why don't you get your dick sucked by that pretty little stepsister of yours. If you don't, I might just have to break her in."

Mood ruined; my blood boiled. No one would touch Avery without my say-so. If anyone had her, it would be me. I would ruin her, and these wolves could have the scraps. At least, that's what I told myself. Flexing my jaw, I tossed the cards face up on the table to reveal a royal flush and rose as I grabbed my zipper.

"Ready to suck, Remy?"

"No fucking way!"

He pushed the cards apart amid the fifty and hundred-dollar bills, not satisfied with what he was seeing. Xavier and Jaxson laughed like hyenas as Remy banged the table, and I swept the cash toward me.

"How you like that, Anderson?" I said with dominance.

Remy leaned back in his chair, full of defeat. It gave me great pleasure besting him. I'd been friends with him since we were in nursery school, and of our group, he was the only one whose family could match mine in wealth.

He took a swig of tequila from the bottle next to him. "How about you kiss my ass? You know you want to."

I checked my watch; it was nearing 3 am. "I'm going to bed."

"You gonna give us a chance to win our money back?" Jaxson said.

"You suck at cards. I have no idea why you even bother," I replied.

He picked up a handful of popcorn and paused at my glare.

I shook my head. "You do, and you're dead. My father is

already on my ass not to leave a mess for the staff. Clean this shit up before you leave," I demanded.

The table was strewn with snack wrappers, popcorn, beer bottles, and cups. The floor around it was piled with peanut shells and two empty wine bottles from my father's private stock. I was betting with the thousand bottles he had in his cellar, he wouldn't figure it out.

Leaving my friends behind, I trekked across the grounds, which was as quiet as the house was when I entered. The alarm beeped several times before I punched in the code to shut it off, and then it beeped a second time when I reset it. If the damn thing went off and woke the whole house, there would be hell to pay, and I didn't need a lecture from my father.

Payne was more involved in my life now that Renata was here. He tried to actively participate in my upbringing after my mother died, but his business and dating took precedence. In his place, I got used to the staff babysitting me until I got old enough to take care of myself.

Instead of going to bed, as I did every night since Avery got here, I went through the hidden passage in the closet that connected our bedrooms. There were several, some even my father didn't know about. I used to explore the house from top to bottom after my mother got sick, and I wasn't allowed to visit her.

The particular tunnel I was in opened into Avery's walk-in closet. A magnetic strip held a shoe shelf in place, and its hinges swung open when I pushed. I stepped out and tip-toed to the door, peering out. She was asleep, bathed in light from the colorful light string attached to her headboard.

She was killing me. I wanted her more than I wanted anyone in my entire life. Avery Bedford was the one girl who was totally unattainable. She also hated me, and with good reason. I choked back my feelings because I was afraid of rejection, and I tortured her, angry that she wouldn't give me the time of day.

I relished the few minutes I watched her sleep each night, my eyes always traveling across her ample breasts, usually clad in a tank top. One night, she wore a white see-through top and almost came right there when I saw her nipples.

Avery's full red lips moved in sleep, and I wished I could press mine upon them, share her bed, and try to fuck her out of my system. I didn't think it was possible. I'd never been such a mushy asshole about a girl before, and if anyone found out I was lusting after my stepsister, I would be a pariah at Bancroft.

I leaned against the wall, watching her for a few more minutes before I headed back to my room, making sure I hid my intrusion by checking the seal on the shoe case twice. My dick was straining against my shorts by the time I left, and I tore at them, releasing my length before I came prematurely.

It was always the same vision in my head as I stroked myself; her lips wrapped around my dick, and me holding the back of her head when I got ready to come before shooting my load down her slender throat. It always worked, like now, as I orgasmed, making a mess on my hardwood floor.

Avery was a problem for me. I didn't want to admit my infatuation with her, but I also didn't want anyone dating her, especially the assholes at Bancroft. I would need to formulate a plan to keep the wolves at bay because she was mine.

KNOCKING ROUSED me from a deep sleep. I rubbed my eyes as my father's voice filtered through the closed door.

"Yeah," I mumbled.

"We're leaving, Gideon. Can I come in?"

He doesn't wait for me to answer because the door swings open.

"Hi, Dad."

"Another late night of cards with the boys?" he asked.

"I got in bed before the sun came up."

He looked disapprovingly around my room at all my clothing strewn about, the stacks of books on my desk and nightstand, and general disarray. I refused to allow the staff in here except to change the sheets under my direction. This was my sanctuary, and I didn't want anyone disturbing my things.

"Christ, Gideon, you live like a slob. If you don't want Rina coming in here, you could at least clean yourself."

My father went to my desk, where he unstacked the books I had there and silently read the titles.

"On a Dickens kick this week?" he said, holding up a worn copy of *Oliver Twist*.

I yawned and stretched, keeping the sheet wound around my naked body.

"That stack will take me a few weeks."

"Just make sure you return them to my library."

From down the hall, I heard Renata calling my father's name. They wouldn't be back until tomorrow evening, giving me time to devise new ways to torture Avery. I was sure she was anticipating my attention since there was nothing to stand in my way with our parents gone.

"When will you be back?" I asked even though I knew.

"Friday evening, but maybe Saturday afternoon. It depends on how nice the water is."

And how open Renata is to let you fuck her on the many decks of The Gale.

I found it cringeworthy that rather than selling the yacht my father named after my mother, he chose to take his dates and now his new wife out on her. I once caught him one July 4th screwing his latest girlfriend on the helipad, the highest point on the yacht. I was fourteen, and we were sailing around New York harbor for the holiday.

It was after the fireworks when most of the crew had gone to bed. I couldn't sleep, so I overindulged on the spread the chef laid out for the few guests my father had invited on board when I heard them. After listening to their moans, I slinked away.

"Can you let me know?" I asked.

My father narrowed his eyes at me. "Gideon, this will not be party central with your buddies while I'm gone, and ease up on Avery."

Ease up? I want to press her to the wall and sink my dick in her.

I was happy the sheet was over me because just the thought of her caused me to become aroused. I casually moved my hands between my legs, just in case.

"If you think what I give her is rough, just wait until she needs to tread water at Bancroft. They won't be nice to her. She's new. It's a rite of passage, one she couldn't take as a freshman."

He cocked his hip. "And you're her stepbrother."

Renata showed up at the door. "Payne, we have to go."

He turned and moved to put his arm around her waist.

"Remember what we discussed," my father said as they walked away.

"Close the damn door!"

My father ignored me, so I yanked the sheet off the bed to wrap around my waist. As I started to close the door, Avery passed by, and I dropped the sheet. The look of shock on her face as she viewed my semi-erection was priceless. I slammed the door, grabbed my sheet, and hopped back into bed.

With our parents gone, I could sleep until late afternoon and repeat the day before. I knew Jaxson and Xavier were looking to take me down at the card table. Each week we played, I cleaned out their allowances, causing a deficit in their party money. At one point, Xavier cashed in a bond, and Jaxson conned his sister to lend him cash.

Remy, however, didn't give a shit since he had unlimited funds. His parents gave him unfettered access to part of his multimillion-dollar trust fund last year, and he was good at poker. Where I took about seventy-five percent of Xavier and Jaxson's cash, Remy took the other twenty-five.

In another two weeks, late-night poker games would be a thing of the past. Bancroft had a strict no gambling policy, and the basement room we used for debauchery was now stuffed with new sports equipment. I would have to figure something out because I wouldn't live by Bancroft's strict rules.

CHAPTER 3

Avery

"Fucking Christ," I mumbled.

Gideon was a pervert if he thought he shocked me. Well, he was wrong. This wasn't the first time I'd seen a penis. I've had boyfriends before, and even though I'd done things with them, I was still a virgin.

I wouldn't have sex with someone until I loved them, and my former boyfriends didn't fit the bill, if that makes sense. Unlike Clover, who had started sleeping with her boyfriends a couple of years ago, I planned on waiting until it was right.

My dopey stepbrother was hot, but I could never fall for a guy like him. He took what he wanted and worked on intimidation. His group of friends were gorgeous, and it might be fun to poke him by messing with one of them. Maybe.

Shaking the thoughts away, I smirked at a new one. Little did my mother know that my gum-cracking bestie would sleep over tonight. What made the idea even better was that I heard her talking to Payne this morning about staying an extra day on the yacht. With Clover around, I would be safe since she was my ally.

~

I WAS SITTING by the pool just before 10 am when Clover showed up wearing a long blue t-shirt, multicolored flip flops, and her red hair in a tight ponytail. I jumped up as she dumped her duffel bag on the pool deck.

"I thought you wouldn't be here until noon." I hugged her in a tight embrace. I needed her support now more than at any other time.

"Where's Satan?" she said in my ear.

"Probably still in bed. I saw him naked this morning."

She laughed. "Get out of town! Why do guys think if they show us their dicks we'll spread our legs?"

It was a relief to have her here. Gideon would shred me without support. Since day one, he was itching to tear me down, and without our parents here, he smelled blood in the water. No matter what I did or said, he found something wrong. He was just plain mean.

"I don't know."

I led her to the lounger beside mine, where she plopped down. "This is some spread. Look at this place. I thought our house was big."

I grabbed her arm. "I'm so glad you're here."

"What would your mother say if she knew?" she asked with a smirk.

I screwed up my face. "I don't give a shit. Do you know she now wants me to dress up for dinner? Can you imagine?"

She cracked her gum several times. "She *really* loves the good life."

"And she fits right in. I'm sure Payne is showing her off to all his friends."

Clover pulled a long string of gum from her mouth, tilted her head, and sucked it back in. She was crude, but I loved her.

"It's mutual satisfaction. She gets a rich husband, and he gets arm candy."

I sighed. "I wish you were going to Bancroft. I just can't."

"Get kicked out. I can give you some pointers."

I laughed sarcastically. "I'm the stepchild to Payne Berne. He donates a ton of money to that place. They wouldn't expel me no matter what I did!"

She raised an eyebrow. "Suppose I go there?"

My heart skipped a beat. To have Clover at Bancroft for support would be a dream. However, the registration period had passed, and my mother reminded me endlessly that the school had a quota for new students.

"I'd love that, but I don't think you can."

Clover leaned over to me. "My father can work wonders. We might not be this rich, but we still have some pull."

"If you could…." I trailed off in hope.

"If she could do what?" Gideon's obnoxious voice interrupted.

I looked up at Gideon standing nearby. He was up earlier than normal.

"Is that him?" Clover whispered.

"Shhh," I told her before adding, "Mind your own business," at Gideon.

He stalked toward us dressed in a pair of Hawaiian swim trunks and a plain white t-shirt. I didn't want him sitting with us, poisoning Clover's opinion of him when he began oozing his usual honey and sugar that his shallow friends seemed to eat up.

Gideon ignored me and fixed his stare on Clover. It was no secret that she was pretty with her long, wavy red hair and light brown eyes with gold flecks in them.

"Gideon Berne," he said as he offered his hand.

My stepbrother was full of phony, but Clover wouldn't be fooled. She didn't take his hand and, instead, slipped her sunglasses from the collar of her shirt and put them on. Gideon pulled his hand back and wiped it on his shorts as if they were sweaty.

"This is Clover," I said because I knew Gideon wouldn't give up.

He smirked. "The Clover your mom hates? *That* Clover? The one she doesn't want you to see?"

My best friend didn't flinch. She was well aware of my mother's dislike of her. However, with this knowledge, I couldn't deny Gideon would have more firepower to hold over my head. I could just imagine what horrible plan he was formulating. My stepbrother's mind was always going.

"So? Are you telling her?" I challenged, despite feeling uncertain.

He crossed his arms and puffed out his chest. "Maybe, unless you do something for me?"

Like what? Get down on my knees and suck your cock in front of your friends?

"Don't try to blackmail me. If you want to tell my mother, tell her. I have a few tidbits of my own to tell Payne."

I had little to hold over Gideon because his father didn't care what he did. But I knew my stepbrother was sneaking bottles of Payne's expensive wine. I found the bottles in the pool house once when I went to the bathroom. Curious about why they'd be there, I looked up the labels online and found out they were worth four hundred dollars apiece. Even if Payne let Gideon get away with some things, I doubted he'd be amused by Gideon and his friends downing his wine collection.

"Like what? My father knows everything."

"Not everything," I muttered.

Clover yawned. "It's a pleasure listening to you two argue

over nonsensical bullshit, but Gideon, I just met you, and I can tell you're not very nice to my girl here."

"Is that the best you got?" he jeered.

"For now," she dismissed. "I'll be spending the night, so give me time. Maybe you can introduce me to some of your friends."

For the time being, she put him in his place. I thanked God I had the foresight to invite her over if only to enjoy the show she was putting on. Gideon mumbled something incomprehensible as he walked away, heading to the pool house. He would probably spend the entire day playing cards, drinking, and talking about how horrible my friend was once his friends arrived.

Although amused, I told Clover, "I'm sure I'll pay for this after you leave, or Gideon will save it all up for Bancroft."

"You're really making me think I should ask my parents if I can go. I worry about you, kid."

"I've been holding my own," I defended, although how convincingly I wasn't sure.

"Yeah, but for how long?"

"OH MY GOD! Who the hell is that hot piece of ass?" Clover whispered.

When I glanced where she was looking, I spotted Xavier sauntering over to where Gideon was now sitting. My stepbrother's friends never asked to come over; they just did. Even though I didn't like how Gideon's crew would follow him around like little puppies who would do everything he told them, I could admit they were all beautiful.

Xavier was hot and dreamy with his short dark hair and almost black eyes. His beard was so thick that a shadow was still on his face even when clean-shaven. If I didn't hate them so much, I could see myself falling for any of them.

"Xavier Toscano," I answered.

"Mmm, a hot Italian. Look at that tight ass."

"Wait until you see Remy and Jaxson."

"I love how we can watch them, and they don't know. Sunglasses are a dirty girl's best friend."

This wasn't the first time I'd heard Clover say this very statement. She loved to say things for shock value and never sugar-coated anything, not for anyone. It was probably the reason she ended up in detention all the time.

I snorted. "Trust me, they know. Every single one of them knows they're the center of attention."

Gideon was used to the attention, and it not only came from girls on campus, from what I'd heard about and seen, but guys who wanted to be in his inner circle. It wouldn't happen because my pretentious stepbrother had standards that included a list of requirements to be part of his crew. It was nauseating.

When I went on a forced tour of the campus, teachers and administrators alike were fawning all over Gideon, who was a student advocate. Everyone thought he was the perfect little gentleman, but I knew differently.

"Where are the others?" Clover asked.

"Give it a few minutes. Where one is, the other two won't be far behind. They love sucking up to Gideon."

Clover sucked in her breath when Xavier removed his shirt. All four boys were the perfect physical specimens, molded by hours in the gym and on fields. They all played football in the fall, but Gideon and Xavier also played baseball in the spring, while Remy and Jaxson played lacrosse.

"Holy fucking hell," Clover whispered.

"Don't be fooled. They're evil assholes wrapped in pretty paper."

Gideon followed suit, removing and tossing his t-shirt over one of the pool chairs. Even I had to admit that he had the body of a Greek God with chiseled abs and sculpted arms. If I didn't hate him so much, I might be attracted to him.

"I can't believe you live with him," Clover said.

"Unfortunately."

I settled back on my lounger, closing my eyes as I looked up at the bright sun through my sunglasses. Clover nudged me.

"Are you taking me on a tour of this castle today?"

"In a bit. It's no big deal."

"Says you. This place is too big for four people, let alone two."

"I'm sure my mother will manage. It's not like she has to clean the place."

Before we moved here, it was my job to keep our apartment clean because my mother worked one full-time job between side gigs her friend gave her when she was short on a waitress for her catering company. I didn't mind cleaning because the place was small.

"She has plenty of help," I growled. "She doesn't lift a finger."

"Damn, Bedford, are you still not getting along with your mom?"

We used to be like best friends until my mother no longer considered my feelings. She didn't ask my opinion on switching schools or if I was comfortable wearing a uniform. Before her marriage, we would spend one night a week sitting around and watching romantic movies while stuffing our faces with popcorn and Skittles.

"She doesn't care about me anymore," I muttered.

We were interrupted when the rest of Gideon's crew arrived. Remy and Jaxson were whooping it up when they arrived, flashing wads of cash for an all-night poker game, no doubt.

Clover gripped my arm. "Please tell me the tall blonde is not attached."

"That's Remington Anderson. He's Gideon's best friend and has just a smidge less money. The dark-haired guy is Jaxson Curran."

"They're a pretty picture to look at. I'd love to be the filling of a hot guy sandwich."

"Eww, that's gross!" I hissed.

She laughed. "If you didn't know what a bunch of assholes your stepbrother and his friends were, would you find them hot?"

Sure, I was attracted to them, but just the outside. Gideon wasn't the only one who gave me a hard time; they all did when they had the chance. If he made a joke or called me a name, they would join him.

Across from where we sat, it was clear they were staring at us now, gesturing like we couldn't see them. Since we had an audience, Clover chose this time to go for a swim.

She rose and yanked off her long shirt to reveal the tiniest thong I'd ever seen. It was shimmery silver with a scrap of cloth over her mound, and her top was made up of two tiny pieces of fabric over each breast, all held together by string, leaving everything in full view. Clover gave a sweet smile and a little wave to the guys, who were now fixated on her every move.

She slowly strolled to the edge of the pool, positioned her feet on the edge, and dove in, barely making a splash. Everyone but Gideon stood up and clapped, screaming out the number ten for her performance—everyone, again, but my stepbrother. When I glanced his way, he had removed his sunglasses, and his eyes were fixed on me.

CHAPTER 4

Gideon

Avery's brash-talking friend was making a spectacle of herself. I did have to admit her ass, and tits were spectacular, and if this were any other time or place, I would take her ten different ways. But I didn't want Clover the way the other guys did. I wanted Avery, and I wanted her to want me.

I was disgusted with myself because I'd never acted this way toward any girl, even if I was the only one who knew about my behavior. Girls existed for my amusement. I could have anyone I wanted at Bancroft. I had a phone full of contacts and knew of a bunch of ways to sneak girls to my room or leave campus to rent a hotel room.

Clover swam the length of the Olympic-sized pool before walking up the stairs on our side and squeezing the water out of her long red hair. Remy was the first to reach her, wrapping a towel around her shoulders.

"Thanks!" she said as she glanced over at Avery.

My conquest was sitting on her lounger, disinterested in what was happening on my side of the pool. It irked me that she didn't even look our way. It was the same shitty attitude Avery had when she first moved in. It wasn't my choice to have her here, even though I went through the motions during the wedding to be cordial.

Remy pulled out the chair he was sitting in and gestured for Clover to sit down, which she did.

"What's your name?" Remy asked.

I wanted to backhand him. We didn't invite random girls to get involved with us unless we had a purpose.

"Clover."

He plopped down next to her, and she reached over to pluck Xavier's sunglasses from his face. I wasn't amused that my bros were acting like thirteen-year-olds at their first middle school dance—like they never had a girl before.

My chair squealed against the pavers as I forced it back and stood up. Avery was heading for the house, and I planned on confronting her about this problem. I followed close at her heels as she got inside, but I grabbed the slider before she closed it behind her.

"Get away from me," Avery said.

I slammed the slider hard enough for the glass to rattle in the frame.

"I want you to tell your slutty friend to leave mine alone."

Avery looked out the window. All three of my friends were crowded around Clover, jockeying for top position and the chance to get her into bed.

She clenched her fists. "Don't you dare call her that."

She yanked open the refrigerator and pulled two bottles of Pellegrino, ignoring me. Once she placed them on the counter, I grabbed her wrist, squeezing to get a response from her.

She yelped. "Let me go, asshole!"

I pushed her against the cold stainless steel of our restaurant-sized refrigerator, then pressed my body against hers. I curled my other hand around her hip and stroked the bone with my thumb. She gasped as I inched it up under her t-shirt, which caused her to dig her nails into my hand. I gritted my teeth as they bit into my flesh.

"Behave, or I'll make your life worse than a living hell when you get to Bancroft," I whispered in her ear.

As I pulled back, I focused on her smoke-gray eyes. There was fear but also defiance. Her breasts pressed into my bare chest, and my dick began to swell. How I would love to bend her over the counter and fuck her from behind, but I had a feeling once would not be enough.

Avery arched her back, trying to push me away, and when she did, her pelvis bumped my partial erection. She gasped, and her face wrinkled with disgust.

"Oh my God! This is turning you on?! Is this your thing? You force a girl to do what you want?"

I immediately let her go and backed away. "No! I don't have to force anyone to do anything. But if I want to get you on your knees, I will."

She slammed me in the chest with the palm of her hand, but it didn't hurt as much as she probably wished it would. I loved how her nose crinkled when she was angry. Tonight would be torture with the guys staying over because I wouldn't be able to sneak into her room and watch her sleep.

"Fuck!" she screamed, shaking her hand.

I laughed at her as she cried out in pain to cover up how all I wanted to do was take her in my arms and soothe that pain away. My dick was at full mast now. Maybe I really was a sick fuck who enjoyed someone else's misery. Either way, I would have to handle this problem before stepping outside.

Avery's yells of 'asshole' rang in my ears as I ducked into the nearest bathroom to relieve my problem. By the time I came out, she was no longer in the kitchen, but through the slider, I noticed her sitting on the lounger, sipping her water as if nothing had happened. She'd removed her t-shirt, and I thought I might need to return to the bathroom as I viewed her tanned body.

IT TURNED out Clover was good at poker, maybe better than me. She'd already won several hands, and the stack of Remy, Xavier, and Jaxson's money in front of her was growing. On the other hand, Avery could barely keep up and was almost out after only playing a few hands.

I wanted to help her, but once she was out, I could go for blood. With her sitting at the table, she was a distraction, and I couldn't concentrate as well as I usually did.

"It's just you and me, Berne," Clover said.

"What about Avery? She's not out yet," Remy said.

Avery folded her cards and nervously tapped them on the green-felt table. I was surprised she agreed to play with us, but Clover prodded her on. In the time that I'd known her, Avery didn't seem like the extroverted type, so it surprised me that she was popular and captain of the cheerleading squad.

Avery hadn't revealed any of this to me, however. I found her yearbook when Renata took her shopping. I paged through it, finding many pictures of her at various events. The book was cram-packed full of signatures, and anything I didn't find in the book I found on two collages of photos glued to backer board she had hung on her bedroom wall.

It was in my nature to know everything about my opponents, as well as the girls I wanted to take to my bed. But with Avery, I just wanted to know her, and she never gave me that chance. Her defenses were up the minute she met me, so I knew I had to break her first.

"I don't have the money," Avery eventually said. "I think I'll fold."

Jaxson smirked at her. "Perhaps you can put something else in the pot to satisfy your contribution."

Avery narrowed her eyes at Jaxson, and I stiffened. Clover waved her hands to interrupt him.

"I can lend her some cash."

"You can't do that! It's against the rules," Jaxson protested.

Clover snorted. "What rules? You never said we couldn't lend cash. I know Avery is good for it if she loses."

"We don't lend cash during the game," Jaxson persisted. "You can use something else."

Avery looked around the table. "Like what?"

"Clothes," Jaxson said.

She bit her lip. "Why aren't we just playing strip poker then?" she said sarcastically.

I stopped the conversation, snarling out, "We're not playing this game for anything but money."

Even if Avery had agreed to strip, I wouldn't have allowed it. I was the only one who would see her naked. I wouldn't share that delight with this bunch of animals. I made a mental note to pick Jaxson's pockets clean once the girls were out. I would drain every penny from him for even suggesting it.

"Then I'm out," Avery said.

She plunked her stacked cards face down on the table and leaned back in her chair with a look of defeat. I raised, and Clover matched me. We kept going back and forth until everything we had was in the pot.

"I call," I said.

There was no way Clover would beat my full house. She placed her cards on the table, one by one. Once she was finished, four threes stared me in the face.

"Son of a bitch," I said as I tossed my cards onto the table to reveal my full house.

Clover threw her head back and laughed. "Thanks for the cash," she said as she dragged the pot toward her. Avery hugged her and pressed a kiss to her cheek.

"You showed them who was boss," Avery said.

Remy massaged Clover's shoulders as she counted the cash. She cleared over five grand of our money.

"Let's drink!" she yelled, picking up the empty champagne bottle sitting on the floor and holding it above her head. "Hey, Berne, you got more of this stuff?"

"That's expensive stuff, and I can't take too much, or my father will know."

Clover picked up the cash in front of her and waved it. "How much will this buy me."

Avery tugged at her arm. "We can't stay."

"Come on, Bedford," Clover returned, "Don't be so boring."

She frowned at Clover and rose from her chair. "I've had enough," Avery protested. "I'm leaving."

The boys laughed at her.

"Don't be a baby," Remy said, backing Clover.

I noticed he was working on Clover's bikini top, running his thumbs over the strings as he massaged her shoulders. Back at Bancroft, we shared girls, sometimes a couple of us together, but I had no intention of partaking in anything involving Clover. I rubbed at my temples.

"I think I'll go to bed," I voiced, standing at the same time Avery began to move.

Everyone looked at me like I was crazy since it was barely midnight. I hadn't been lying. I had a headache, and it wasn't getting better. For the first time in my life, I didn't give a shit about the money I'd lost. And if Clover was getting it on with my friends, I could enjoy my favorite part of the night without drawing attention—watching Avery sleep.

"Clover, you know where your room is when you're done here," Avery said harshly.

"Hell no," Clover said, pushing Remy's hands away. "I'm not staying here if you don't, and I'm not sleeping alone in that big room."

My heart dropped because my plans would be ruined if they shared a room. She rose, grabbed her stack of cash, threw her t-shirt over her shoulder, and followed Avery out.

"God dammit," Remy cursed. "I almost had her. Thanks for fucking me over, Berne."

As Xavier and Jaxson chimed in, I laughed. That girl wasn't letting any of them have her. She was a tease to the nth degree. I'd encountered them at Bancroft plenty of times. They would act all prudish and proper until we were alone, and I made sure to get them alone. Once they were, it was game on. They would drop their panties as if they were on fire. I never begged; just waited because my reputation preceded me. They knew what they were getting when they had sex with me, and I made it more than worth their while.

But the minute I laid eyes on Avery, I knew she would be a challenge. I wouldn't say I was in love; it was more like lust. Once I got between her legs, it would be over. That's the way it always was once I achieved my goal. I grew bored because the chase was over. Only, she was proving to be a tough customer, so I was sure that once I got her onto my playing field, it would be easier to bed her.

I also knew I wasn't scoring points by acting like a dick, but she brought it out of me, especially with her smart mouth. Deciding to call it a night, I began to walk toward the door of the pool house as Remy continued bitching about Clover.

"That's it, Berne? You're leaving us high and dry?" he called out.

"Fuck off, Anderson. I'm not your pimp." I turned back to them. "Make sure you clean this shit up, and if you sleep over, don't set off the damn alarm," I ordered harshly.

I wouldn't be held responsible for the mess they left, and if it weren't cleaned up by the morning, they would all catch beatings from me.

~

IN THE HOUSE, I paused at Avery's door, listening to the muffled voices through the heavy wood. Clover was inside with her, so I wouldn't take the chance tonight. It didn't matter; I convinced myself. My head was pounding like a drum solo, so instead, I stripped naked and fell into bed, hoping the three dumbasses did what I told them.

Two hours later, I woke from a bad dream. My heart was slamming so hard against my chest that I felt it in my throat. It was always the same dream: my mother, her body unmoving and cold. I rubbed my eyes to try to push the image from my head. Her death still disturbed me.

My head was still pounding when I got up to search my bathroom for a bottle of aspirin. There wasn't any, so I would have to check the cabinet in the hall bath, which usually was stocked with everything. I wrapped a towel around my waist and entered the darkened hallway.

I froze as I heard voices. Avery's door was still closed, but the voices belonged to a guy and girl. Over their exchange, the sound of flesh slapping together, followed by moans, erupted from down the hall. Forgetting the aspirin, I continued my trek to find the hall bath door ajar. Just beyond it, Remy stood between Clover's legs with his shorts pooled around his ankles.

"What the fuck!" I yelled.

Neither one of them reacted with embarrassment. Rather, Clover answered with a loud moan, and Remy grunted before he grasped the door's edge and slammed it in my face. It wasn't as if I'd never been in the same room with Remy while he was having sex. Hell, we'd shared the same girl before, taking turns fucking her. What bothered me was that he didn't respect my home.

Scoffing as I headed back to my room, I froze when Avery opened her door.

"What's going on?"

I couldn't help traveling her body with my eyes, and she tugged at her long t-shirt to ensure it was covering her panties. I took a step toward her, gripping the knot in my towel.

"Your slutty little friend is fucking Remy," I snarled.

She licked her full lips with the tip of her tongue, and at that moment, I wanted to pin her against the wall and slam my mouth on hers.

Avery shrugged. "It was bound to happen," she said as if everything was okay. "He spent the past two hours in our room. He also doesn't act like an asshole when you're not around."

I took another step toward Avery, gently tugging at the knot in my towel. She stood her ground, rocking back and forth on the balls of her feet, waiting for my next move.

"He does what I tell him to do." Another tug, tug. The towel was now so loose around my waist that it slipped down my hips. Avery's eyes flicked to the cuts in my hips, which excited me to finally get her attention.

"Is he a robot?" she challenged anyway.

Clover let out a screech from the bathroom, followed by Remy's loud grunt. Their moans stopped, which meant they'd both just climaxed.

"Remy is a follower," I clarified. "He won't help you."

At that moment, my towel fell away from my hips, and I held it in my fist as I debated whether I should let it fall to the floor and give her a full view. Avery's eyes widened, but she stood there watching me.

"Let it go. You think it's the first dick I've seen," she said with defiance.

I didn't let it show, but I was disappointed at the realization that once I got her in bed, I wouldn't be her first. I might not be, but I would make her remember me. I slid the towel down enough so the top of my trimmed pubic hair showed. Avery kept looking at my hand or the bulge under it, and I decided it was enough.

"Too bad," I replied. "But remember this: when I fuck you, it will be unforgettable."

She laughed sarcastically. "You'll never get the chance," she shot back.

We both turned to look down the hall as the moaning and grunting started again.

"Fuck," I muttered.

"What they're doing is none of our business. What, are you jealous?" she asked.

"Not in the least."

Avery stepped back into her room, and for the second time in three minutes, a door was slammed in my face.

CHAPTER 5

Avery

I put my back against the door and took a deep breath. My lungs burned as oxygen-filled them. The entire confrontation with Gideon brought up so many emotions, but the one I was unsettled about was my arousal. He was a neanderthal, a rude asshole with no respect! How could I possibly be attracted to him?!

I turned the lock before I went to bed. If Clover planned on sleeping in here, she would have to knock. But if I knew my best friend, she would find a free bedroom and spend the night with Remy. It didn't matter to me. I slipped back into bed and shut off the light, trying to ignore the annoying throb between my legs.

The furthest I'd gone with a guy was giving head this past year, but I'd been masturbating since I was fourteen when I had my first sexual experience granted by the water jets in Clover's jacuzzi. The feeling at the time was indescribable, but I soon realized I could just touch myself to repeat the process.

After over half an hour of tossing and turning, the throb had not abated. With the door locked, I knew I had privacy to get myself off. I moved to my back and slipped my hand into my panties, sliding my finger over my swollen nub. I was soaked, and as soon as I touched my clit, I shivered at the sensitivity.

I shifted my hips in rhythm with the movement of my finger, and as my breathing and heart picked up, a low moan escaped me as I grew close. My climax came in less than a minute, and I remained still with my hand in my panties, trying to catch my breath, when a knock at the door made me jump and quickly fix myself.

"What?" I said, trying to hold my voice steady.

"Why is the door locked?" Clover responded.

I rose from the bed and popped the lock, pulling open the door. Clover looked disheveled with just-fucked hair and pink cheeks.

"I thought you were staying with Remy."

She grinned. "I'm in the guest room, so I wanted to let you know. I think I'm in love."

I rolled my eyes. "You're in lust, you dirty girl."

She nodded. "I am. He's good."

I plugged my ears and began to sing softly. "I don't want to hear anything about his dick size or what he can do with it."

Clover pressed a kiss to my cheek. She smelled like sex and Remy's cologne. As she headed down the hall, I noticed her panties were missing as her t-shirt swished around. I shook my head as I closed the door. It was just before 3 am.

I WAS the first one up just before 11 am. I didn't expect Clover to come up for air until the afternoon, and when I passed by

Gideon's door, it was still closed. Except for the maids and chauffeur, the chef was given a few days off, so we were on our own for food.

I rummaged around the refrigerator to find some fruit salad and yogurt. Twenty minutes later, I glanced up at Gideon, who wandered into the kitchen looking like shit. His hair was a mess, and his gray eyes were bloodshot. As I went back to eating, he spoke up.

"Where's your whore of a friend?" he growled.

I slammed my spoon on the table. "Why do you always have to be such an asshole?" I screeched.

"If you wanted something creamy, I could've helped," Gideon said, nodding at my yogurt as he grabbed his crotch.

"You're a disgusting pig."

My chair scraped the tile as I pushed back from the table, took my leftover cup of yogurt and a half-eaten bowl of fruit salad, and dumped them in the garbage. Gideon scratched at his balls and watched me stamp out of the kitchen.

"Wait until you see what I am when we get to school!" he called.

Shivers danced up my spine. By the threat in his voice, I knew he wasn't joking. My stomach churned the food I had just eaten, and an overwhelming urge to vomit came over me. I swallowed it down as angry tears welled in my eyes. I hated Gideon with such a passion. I never expected my life to take such a turn, and worse, my mother was oblivious to my distress. Now I knew how the misfits at my school felt, eating lunch by themselves and being picked on. Not by me, of course. I would never bully anyone like Gideon.

Gideon clearly relished in my misery, but I was pissed that I got aroused by him last night. He was a horrible person! I knew if I complained, my mother would somehow sugarcoat it and say I was mistaken by Gideon's behavior. But I knew what I knew.

CHAPTER 6

Gideon

Holy hell! I couldn't get the sound of Avery's tiny moans out of my head. Like some pervert, I took a risk last night and stroked my rock-hard cock as she masturbated. Christ, she was beautiful, and I wished I could see what she looked like beneath those lacy panties I knew she liked.

One day, I would find out; I was sure of it. But right now, my focus went back to tormenting her. It surprised me that she agreed to play cards with us the night before. Avery usually acted like she had something to prove, but it was apparent she didn't have a clue about poker strategy.

I could've wiped her out within the first fifteen minutes, but I wanted her to stay, even if it meant her obnoxious seductress of a friend was with us. Hell, I folded a few times just to let her win, and I made sure the boys followed my instructions to let her win. The plans I had for Avery once we were away from this place meant she was as good as mine.

Upon deciding to check in on the guys, I found the pool deck a mess of cans, bottles, and wrappers. A towel was hanging off the diving board, making me wonder if they followed my instructions and cleaned the pool house. The pavers were warm as I walked out of the slider. Barely steps beyond the house, anger bubbled in my chest when I found not only a condom wrapper but a used condom thrown near the table.

"Crap!" I screamed.

The pool house was a bigger mess than when I left it last night. Another bottle of my father's expensive champagne was lying on its side, empty. Crumbs littered the floor, and I found Xavier and Jaxson asleep on the sectional with some girl I'd never seen before.

I kicked Xavier's foot, and he opened one eye.

"What's up, my good man?" he asked through a groan.

I crossed my arms. "You fucking tell me," I hissed.

Jaxson stirred and yawned, but the girl stayed asleep. I wondered what they gave her and when.

"We had a little party," Jaxson said.

"Who the fuck is that?" I asked as I pointed to the girl.

Both Jaxson and Xavier started laughing.

"What's funny? Is it this place? Because it's a fucking joke," I growled.

"You don't recognize the help?"

I frowned with confusion. "What the hell are you talking about?"

"This is Laura, one of your maids," Xavier said.

I scrubbed my face and looked closer at the girl sleeping in between Xavier and Jaxson.

"You diddled the maid? What the hell did I tell you two assholes about fucking the help?"

"We tag-teamed her, and she didn't seem to mind," Xavier said.

I gritted my teeth. "Clean this place up and get her home. And I want all that shit by the pool cleaned up."

They both stared at me blankly before I turned and walked out the door. Avery was sitting on a lounger at the other end of the pool. She wouldn't look at me, but I didn't expect her to. I debated whether I should antagonize her further but decided against it.

~

AVERY AVOIDED me like I was the plague. When she saw me by the pool earlier, she went inside and locked herself in her room. It was a personal joke because I could access her space even if her door was locked. Of course, she had no idea, and it was a fact I would keep to myself—maybe even never reveal to her.

Clover claimed Remy and fucked up our foursome card game. She was also on the outs with Avery, from what I saw. I was sure the reason she was here in the first place was for protection from me.

"Gideon!" my father thundered several minutes after I heard him arrive home.

I had a hangover of monumental proportions since I spent yesterday by the pool downing a bottle of tequila with Jaxson and Xavier. I strolled into the kitchen from the library, where I was trying to sleep off my headache. I loved to read, and the scent of books and leather soothed me.

"Hi, Dad."

He was tapping his foot, looking tan and, despite his frustration, somehow satisfied. It made me wonder which surfaces of the yacht he and Renata defiled.

"Don't 'hi, Dad' me. What did I tell you before I left?"

I clenched my jaw, trying to stem the pain in my head. "Keep the place clean."

He tapped his foot. "And?"

"Everything is clean."

He slapped the granite island and pointed out the sliders. "Then why is there broken glass by the diving board."

Fuck. It sounded like the first thing my father did when he arrived home was to check everything to see if I followed instructions, even though he should know I never did.

"I thought I got everything."

"Didn't I tell you not to bring glasses out by the pool? People walk out there with bare feet."

"I'll ask Henley to clean it up," I said.

He bounced the tip of his index finger off the stone. "No, you won't. You will clean it up, and I want it done now. We're having guests by 2 pm."

I perked up. "A party by the pool?"

"You're not invited. I have a business meeting, and he's bringing his wife."

I resisted the urge to roll my eyes and felt like asking why he didn't take the guy on his yacht—anything to close the deal and increase the Berne Industries empire. I didn't want any part of it, but I was a Berne, and any escape was futile. My father had been grooming me since I was twelve to take over the company my great-grandfather started.

"Well, excuse me," I said with gritted teeth.

"Just get out there and clean it up. The last thing I want is a lawsuit from someone getting cut. Where's Avery?"

I shrugged. "I'm not her keeper."

"Don't get smart with me, Gideon, or you won't take your car to Bancroft this year."

I clapped my mouth shut. The sleek silver Bugatti Chiron my father promised for my eighteenth birthday was being prepped at the dealership. I would receive it just before I left for Bancroft.

"I'm sorry," I mumbled.

"I don't want apologies."

It took an effort to look up at him because of the pain behind my eyes. Aware of where things were heading, I waited for him to launch into his "You're a Berne, and you have responsibilities" speech.

"You're a Berne; you have responsibilities to this family and your legacy," he began on cue, his voice hardening. "Enjoy the last days of your freedom because I expect you in the office next summer with me."

I stifled a groan. The last thing I wanted to do was wear a suit all day and learn the business. I had a trust fund, which was mine when I turned twenty-one, but I was also aware that if I wanted to access it, there were stipulations. The largest one was that it required that I graduate college, preferably from an ivy league school.

The Bernes had a long line of legacies at Yale, and I was admitted early and even offered a spot on the football team. Remy would probably be joining me since he was a legacy, too.

Another thing I wasn't looking forward to was how I would also need to put my summers into learning the business through college so I could take a junior executive position once I graduated. If I failed to follow these requirements, I wouldn't get access to my trust fund until I was twenty-five.

It was a bitter pill to swallow, but I had no intention of spending my life as a working stiff or taking on the helm of Berne Industries. I would go through the motions until I could run to freedom.

"You're dismissed. Get that glass cleaned up," my father said before he headed out of the kitchen.

I scrubbed my face before getting the broom and dustpan from the oversized pantry. When I came out, Avery had the door to the refrigerator open, where she was plucking grapes from a bowl and sucking them into her mouth. Seeing the green fruit pass through her full, ripe lips was erotic enough to make me freeze.

She spied me watching her at some point and mumbled, "Asshole," as she shut the refrigerator.

I approached her, but she backed away and hurried from the kitchen. Watching her retreat made my brain spin. I would be leaving for Bancroft in a few days since I needed to start practicing for football. I also had a few administrative things to handle when I got there—things that involved Avery.

CHAPTER 7

Avery

The day Gideon left for Bancroft was a celebration for both him and me. Payne ordered the chef to make a beautiful spread of all Gideon's favorite foods and create a chocolate cake for his upcoming birthday. Lunch was over the top occasion, with Payne and Gideon joking around.

I'd be happy, too, if I got a four-million-dollar car for my birthday, but it was to be expected since Gideon received whatever he wanted. After lunch, I went upstairs to my room. I didn't feel the need to give him a fake goodbye when I really wanted to bust him in the mouth with my fist.

"What, no goodbye?" Gideon's voice growled from behind me.

I looked up as I put my panties and bras away that one of the maids dropped off. I allowed them to wash my clothing but not invade my privacy by putting it away in the drawers. Gideon eyed a lacy thong that had dropped on the floor too long for my comfort. I swiped it up, balling it in my fist.

"I want to start my week without you as soon as possible," I said, trying to remain unbothered.

Before I could act, he stepped into my room, closed the door, and pinned me against the wall with his body. His face was so close to mine I could smell the mint on his breath.

"Know this, darling Avery. Once you leave here, you're all mine. I will make your life a living hell. You will be the ultimate new girl. Nothing will save you."

My heart sped along, and bile rose in my throat, which I forced down. Tears threatened to spill over my lids, but I fought them away, not wanting to give him the satisfaction.

"Why do you hate me so much?" I cried.

He grabbed my face and pressed his lips against my ear. "Because you're the girl I love to hate. You don't belong, and you never will," he whispered.

He kissed me on the cheek. Then it was over, and he backed away, his chest heaving as if he'd run a marathon. Of everything that had just happened, I found that peculiarly disturbing.

He waved his arm too casually. "Until we meet again, darling Avery. Be prepared."

His retreating footsteps were a relief to me. I would finally have the entire house to myself and not worry about his verbal assaults or sexual innuendos.

"Avery!" my mother called. "I want to talk to you."

I was sitting by the pool, enjoying my last days at home. I pulled my sunglasses off as she came toward me.

"What's up?"

She put her hands on her hips and tapped her Manolo

Blahnik clad foot. "I was told you had a house guest while we were gone last week."

Tap, tap.

Gideon. I knew that bastard would rat me out.

I decided to play innocent. "A house guest?"

My mother's face was tight with anger. "I told you I didn't want that girl here. She's a menace."

I avoided her gaze. "Yeah, she's a menace," I mumbled.

"What did you say?"

"I said, yeah, she's a menace."

She crossed her arms in an attempt to make me believe she meant business. "What exactly is that supposed to mean?"

I was getting sick and tired of my mother and Payne overlooking Gideon's behavior. He could do no wrong, but if I did one thing, it was addressed immediately.

"It means Gideon does whatever he wants, and if I do anything you don't like, you give me a hard time."

Between Gideon's abuses and my mother's blindness, I was ready to explode.

"That's not true. Payne got on his ass about the glass."

"Mother, do you know why I had a house guest?" I screeched, unleashing what I'd been holding in for the past few weeks.

She set her mouth in a hard line before she replied, "Because you like to defy me. I think Bancroft will be perfect for you. You need to re-learn manners you seem to have forgotten."

I rose to meet her face-to-face. She was slightly taller than me, but I wouldn't be intimidated.

"No! Because your stepson has been making my life miserable! He abuses me, *mother*," I said as I clenched my fists.

Her face twisted with surprise. "Gideon?"

"Yes, Gideon," I mocked.

"I refuse to believe your brother would do anything of the sort."

"Of course. Take his side," I spat as I stamped away.

"We're not done!" she screamed.

I was done. I couldn't take her bullshit any longer. Once she got back from her yachting trip, she had promised to give me my key fob back, but here we were days later, and she was still holding it over my head. She could shove the car up her ass for all I cared.

"Tough!" I yelled back as I entered the house, leaving the slider open.

I ran up the curved stairway and down the hall to my room, slamming the door and engaging the lock. Voices in the hallway told me she was speaking with my stepfather, and a minute later, she was banging on the door.

I slipped my earbuds in and clicked on my Spotify playlist, flopping back on my pillow. Over the music, I could hear her banging on the door, and then it stopped. I breathed a sigh of relief, but it was short-lived as she burst into my room with a key in her hand and Payne right behind her.

"Shut the music off!" she yelled.

I sat up, clicked off my playlist, and removed my earbuds.

"Tell Payne what you told me."

Payne sat on the corner of my bed. "Has Gideon been giving you a hard time?"

I nodded and burst into tears. My mother sat on the other side of me and put her arm around my shoulders. With how she reacted earlier, I was amazed she gave a damn about how I felt. I know she loved Payne and wanted their marriage to work out, which is probably why she didn't want to even think about feuding children ruining the illusion.

"I'm sorry; I thought I could handle it," I explained through shaking sobs. "I didn't want to say anything."

"Once we're done here, I'm having his car towed back here," Payne replied.

I gripped Payne's tanned arm. "Please don't," I begged.

"He needs to be taught a lesson," he insisted.

I squeezed his arm tighter. "Don't."

"What do you suggest I do?" he questioned.

"Nothing. Doing something will make it worse."

Payne sighed. "I won't take his car away, but I will have a talk with him. I'm afraid I've given Gideon too much leeway since his mother died."

It wasn't what I wanted, but now that I had revealed what Gideon had been doing, I tried to reason that the least Payne could do was talk with him. I was sure it would make my life harder, but how much harder could it get beyond what Gideon had done?

"I'll call him now," Payne reassured. "Don't worry; it will all work out."

Payne was a fool if he thought Gideon would let it go. Once he was gone, my mother focused on me.

"About Clover," she started. "I'll give you a pass this time, but next time you have a problem with Gideon, you need to let us know."

"I didn't want to get him in trouble."

"Try to get along with him," she urged. "You have a whole year before you graduate. Have you decided what schools you want to apply to?"

"You know I want to go to Columbia. They have a good business program."

She stroked my hair, taking me back to a time before Payne came into the picture.

"You could do an internship with Payne. You're part of the Berne family, so you might as well take advantage."

"I want to do it myself."

She laughed. "Payne won't make it easy for you if that's what you're thinking."

"Can we watch a movie and eat snacks the way we used to?" I asked.

My mother tensed. "Can you take a rain check? We're having dinner at the club with the Fitzgeralds. Payne has a deal with James Fitzgerald."

Disappointment washed over me. I was once again let down by my mother, but this was her new life, and I learned a while ago that I wasn't her top priority any longer.

I pouted. "Fine."

"We'll fit it in before you leave, I promise. Just you and me."

A grin broke out on my lips, but it wasn't genuine. I didn't want to hurt my mother's feelings even though she'd hurt mine repeatedly.

"Let me know."

"Why don't you see your friend, Sara?" she suggested.

I huffed. "Mom, Sara moved to Minnesota in the middle of last year."

"Oh. Well, you haven't seen any of your old friends. Why don't you make a date?"

"Because they're all on vacation."

After my father died, I was one of the few people who weren't well off in my circle of friends. My mother and I were left with tons of debt, and by the time the estate was settled, there wasn't much money for anything other than necessities. I wasn't treated differently by my friends, but gone were the winter break ski trips, shopping sprees, and summers in another country.

Now, I could run rings around them in the financial department. Payne was a billionaire, and as his stepdaughter, I fell into the same category. My mother wasn't aware that I knew about her prenup, too. For every year of marriage, she would get several million dollars and a home of her own if they ever divorced. Even more, would be provided if she had a child. If they ever were separated, I could go to her for financial help.

My mother was forty, and I doubted another child was in her future, but I heard them talking about it before they were married. Having another child would attach me to the Berne family for the rest of my life, and though Payne was kind, I didn't think I could tolerate seeing Gideon on holidays.

"Then order a pizza and binge on some television," she encouraged.

My mother kissed me on the cheek and rose from the bed. I knew that would be the end of any further discussions.

~

"YOU'RE WEARING THAT?"

I looked down at my cut-off jean shorts and a pale pink t-shirt that rested just above my frayed waistband.

"Mom, it's move-in day," I replied, obviously. "I can wear my uniform on Monday. Besides, the handbook said we can dress casually after the school day is over."

She sighed. "Fine. Payne will have your bags brought down to the car."

I was amazed Payne, and my mother allowed me to take my car to school. I thought they would say no after all the drama my mother and I had over it. I was a ball of nerves, and the toast and coffee I had consumed an hour ago were churning uncontrollably in my stomach. Despite partially being related to the move and my new school, it was more because I was going to be on my own with Gideon.

After Payne made the call, Gideon promised his father he would lay off me and make sure I was taken care of when I arrived at school, but I knew differently. By now, he had almost a week to plan new ways to torture *and* command his henchmen to assist. I was walking into the snake pit.

On the way to Bancroft, I pulled over to vomit. Yeah, it was that bad. When I pulled into a parking lot at school, it was filled with parents and their children. Although Payne had ensured everything was packed for me, he and my mother were too busy entertaining one of Payne's clients to join me on my check-in. Steeling myself, I followed signs that directed me to the Adwell Hall parking lot. This would be my new home for the next year.

Before I could drive further, a man dressed in a bright yellow vest holding two orange flags stopped me. I opened my window for him as he stepped up to me.

"You can't park here," he said.

"But this is my dorm," I whined.

He pointed at my windshield. "You don't have a parking sticker. If you park here, your car will get towed. You need to go to administration. For now, you can park in the visitor's lot."

The man gestured to a lot next to Adwell Hall. I was annoyed because Gideon could've told me I needed to get a sticker before I arrived, but then again, why would he make my life easier?

I parked in the far lot and trekked to Adwell Hall with a small duffel bag on my shoulder. I would bring in the rest once I received my room assignment and key. The campus was full of kids heading back to school, and I'd never felt so alone. The only people I knew wanted to make my life a living hell.

The buildings on this campus were obviously old, fashioned from stone and brick, with high archways and wide low steps. The line leading into Adwell Hall was short as I stepped through the heavy glass doors, and a woman at the desk waved her hand a minute later so I would step up.

"Name?" she asked.

"Avery Bedford."

She typed my name into a tablet, her pink-painted nails clicking on the screen. She waited a moment and then looked up at me. "Your dorm has been switched. You're now in Beckley Hall, a coed dorm."

I frowned. "But I never got a letter or an email about the change."

She was curt as she said, "You would need to speak to administration about the change."

She called the next person, and I backed away. On the end of the table was a campus map I grabbed, checking for where Beckley Hall would be located. It was on the other side of campus. I didn't mind if the dorms were coed or single-gender. Living with Gideon had already taught me I would probably see things that wouldn't shock me.

I made my way back to my car, hefting the duffel bag into the back seat before I turned on the car. According to the map, Beckley Hall was the biggest dorm on campus, with five floors. By the time I got over there, the parking lot was jam-packed with expensive cars, even a few Bugatti's like the one Gideon drove.

After I parked, I grabbed my duffel bag again and headed inside the stone building. There were a few guys playing football on the lawn in front who I hoped wasn't any of Gideon's friends. As I waited in line, I heard my name and shuddered.

An arm draped around my shoulder, and Gideon's familiar cologne filled my nose.

"You finally arrived, little sis." His sugary sweetness scared me.

I knew I would pay for tattling on him, certain he had a few things in store for me. I pulled away from Gideon and stepped to the table, trying to ignore him. He stayed behind me, his band of idiots probably not far behind.

"Avery Bedford," I said to the man behind the desk.

"Darren, she's in room 502, right?" Gideon asked confidently.

The man smiled at me before fishing an envelope from a clear bag. On it was stamped the number of my room, along with a key and a welcome packet. I couldn't get away from Gideon fast enough as he curved his arm around my neck and pulled me close as he turned me.

"Don't think I haven't forgotten what you did," he whispered.

"Why can't you leave me alone?" I whispered back.

He walked me away from the table and over to the side of the room.

"Imagine my surprise when they put you on the same floor as the boys and me. Well," he added smugly, "actually, I had something to do with the change."

My mouth dropped open, and I gaped at him. "You did this?" I hissed.

"I sure did."

I pushed at him and slipped under his arm, hurrying away. Gideon was fast on my heels, and by the time I hit the sidewalk, Remy fell into step with him.

"Come on, Avery, we'll help you with your bags," Remy called.

They snickered and kept following me. Once I got to my Mercedes, Gideon waited at the trunk.

"I don't need your help, assholes," I snapped.

Remy guffawed like a donkey. "Get a load of her."

Gideon elbowed him in the ribs. "Shut up, Remy."

Once I popped the trunk, they yanked out my bags. I wanted to push them away and tell them to leave me alone, but it was futile. Gideon was an evil shithead who never listened. A few guys I didn't know walked up to us and stopped to talk to my stepbrother and Remy.

"Is this her?" One of the guys pointed a thumb at me.

"You've been telling your friends about me?" I demanded.

Gideon's lips curved into a wicked sneer. "Of course, darling Avery."

I tried to pull the suitcase Remy held from his hand, but he tightened his grip. My stepbrother kept talking to his friends as if I wasn't there, and in frustration, I turned on my heel and walked away. If he wanted to make me into a cruel joke, I wouldn't stand there like a fool.

"Darling Avery!" he called.

"Fuck you," I muttered as I kept my head down and hurried into Beckley Hall.

My stomach threatened another exit of food though I didn't think there was anything left. The elevator was discharging passengers, so I hopped inside, jamming my finger on the number five, breathing a sigh of relief for a moment away from Gideon. Upstairs, the hall was busy with students walking around in various states of dress. By the looks of things, the girls had one half of the floor and the boys the other, split by a lobby area.

I followed the directions down to my room. On the door was a sign with *welcome* and my name. The room was larger than I expected. There was an attached bathroom in one corner, two beds, and two desks—one on either side—with a large closet and a six-drawer dresser next to it.

Since I only saw my name on the door and two names on the others, I concluded that I wouldn't have a roommate. I was happy because I wouldn't put it past Gideon to have poisoned every girl's opinion of me at Bancroft. I had gone from popular to the school pariah. What a wonderful year this will be.

As I pulled up the shade, the door slammed behind me, and Gideon dropped my bags on the floor.

I tried to keep my voice steady when I asked, "Where's Remy?" but it came out just above a whisper.

Gideon took a step toward me, scolding me like a child as he said, "Bad, Avery. You embarrassed me in front of my friends by walking away."

I sighed and gritted my teeth. "You know what I don't understand about you?"

"What's that?" he growled.

"Why are you doing this to me? You never give me an answer."

"If I remember, I did give you an answer. You don't fit in.

You're not one of us."

I put my hands on my hips. "If I have to act like a nasty asshole, then I don't want to be one of you." With the knife inserted, I decided to twist it, adding, "Remember this, dear stepbrother, I'm now part of the Berne family whether you like it or not."

"You'll never be," he said with a sneer. He then shook his head and strode toward me, pushing my body against the window. "You're not really. Your blood is not blue, and it never will be."

Gideon turned away and sat on my bed, leaning against the wall with his sneaker-clad feet hanging off the side.

"You can leave," I growled.

"We have a few things to discuss, starting with you telling my father about how I treat you. I almost lost my car."

I lifted one of my suitcases onto the opposite bed and unzipped the top.

"Maybe you should stop acting like an evil fuck," I retorted.

"I decided your punishment will be for you to suck me off," he said crassly. "I haven't had a good blowjob in a while."

I dropped the stack of shirts I had lifted from the case and whipped around. Gideon was on his feet, and his fingers were paused on his zipper.

"There is no way," I snarled, looking over his shoulder at the closed door.

"On your knees, darling Avery or I'll put you there."

Unable to process what was happening, I began to cry fat tears that dripped down my cheeks, and for a moment, through my blurry vision, I saw a flicker of sympathy from him, but it quickly passed.

"Oh, for fuck's sake!"

I put my hands over my face and cried harder. The next thing I heard was the closing of the door. For the moment, I was safe.

CHAPTER 8

Gideon

"What's your next move?" Xavier asked.

"As far as what?" I asked.

We were sitting in my room right down the hall from where Avery now lived. My plan worked after I conned Dean Carlyle into changing her dorm assignment. I needed to be able to watch Avery, so I used the excuse that she required my help transitioning as she was new and my stepsister.

It didn't hurt that my grandfather and father donated money to Bancroft every year. The library was named after my grandfather, and one of the other buildings was dedicated to my mother.

"Darling Avery," he joked.

I jammed his shoulder with the heel of my hand. "Only I can call her that."

Xavier narrowed his eyes at me. "What are you sweet on her?"

I quickly changed direction because if any of the guys knew of my feelings for Avery, they would make my life miserable.

"Hell no." I denied. "I'll ruin that dirty little slut once the time comes."

"And when is that?" he said, goading me.

"When I say it is. It has to be right. My father is on my ass for treating her like shit, and I need it to die down. Once they leave for Europe, Avery won't have a prayer."

Xavier flopped back on my bed. Like Avery, I had a shared room, so I pushed the twin beds together and covered the crack between the two with a thick mattress pad. While I was comfortable, the other slobs I was friends with had to sleep in narrow beds in their rooms and listen to the snoring of their roommates.

Avery had a private room because I wanted her to. There would be a night when I would share her bed. The dorms at Bancroft were old and solid block, meaning you could barely hear the person next door, which I needed that way because when I fucked Avery, I didn't want anyone to listen to her moans.

And she *would* moan. She would not only be dripping wet when I slid my dick inside her but begging for it. I swore she would do anything to have me fuck her, and I couldn't wait. I was growing hard just thinking about getting in her pants.

"You really hate this girl," Xavier said, pulling me from my fantasy. "What is the point of hate fucking her?"

"Because it will give *me* pleasure to defile her. She doesn't belong even though she thinks she does. Avery can pretend the big house, expensive car, and offers of work at Berne Industries make her part of the family, but it doesn't."

Xavier sat up. "I'm surprised to hear you say that."

"Why?"

"Because for the longest time, you talked about wanting a sibling."

I'd known Xavier since middle school, when I met him the year before my mother died. I had wanted a sibling back then, but once she passed, I no longer had the desire to share my father with anyone else. Renata was bad enough, but now Avery was trying to grab his attention, too.

"Not a step," I shot back. "I wanted a sibling who shared my blood."

"What if Renata and your father have another child?"

"It will be only a half, and that's not good enough."

Xavier eyed me. "How can you live with that woman? She's hot as hell, and I would always be thinking what it would be like to claim that hot little ass of hers."

I glared at him. "Watch yourself," I growled. "That's my father's wife."

He snorted. "So you have absolutely no sexual feelings about Renata at all?"

When my father brought her home to meet me for the first time, I thought about what it would be like to seduce her, but now, no way. Not her, anyway. There were a few young female teachers I could charm. It wouldn't be the first time. Last year, Remy and I double-teamed our accounting teacher. She left after the first quarter, and I would assume it was our fault.

I sat on my bed and picked up a football from the floor to spin on my palm.

"No way. She's not my type. Do you want to get your dirty shoes off my bed? I sleep there."

Remy and Jaxson barged into the room without knocking.

"What the fuck is going on?" Jaxson said as he hopped on Xavier, causing him to howl as his balls got crunched.

"Fucking idiot! I need my balls," Xavier complained as he massaged them.

"You two are ridiculous," I said as I flipped the football at Jaxson's head.

Remy spun my desk chair around and straddled it. "I got a date tonight."

We all looked at him.

"With who?" I asked.

"Tessa Lawrence."

We all gaped at him. Tessa was the daughter of Bancroft's president. Remy tried to fuck her in his black BMW SUV after he brought her home from the movies one night, but President Lawrence came out to see why Tessa was late for her curfew. Remy had to pull his shirt over his erection, which was already out of his pants and encased in latex.

Jaxson tried to kick at Remy's thigh. "Trying to finish what you started? Don't get caught with your cock out of your pants this time."

"We're not going anywhere but a suite at The Wyatt. We'll get room service and then get naked."

I began to laugh. "You think she'll drop her panties just like that?"

"Tessa is hot for me, so I have no doubt, and President Lawrence and his wife will be out at the Welcome Dinner."

"Shit, I forgot about that. Avery has to go," I said.

They all looked at me with confusion, and I rolled my eyes.

"It's my chance to embarrass her in front of the new students. She'll be an outcast," I said with a wicked smile.

Making Avery's life miserable—even though I wanted her—had nothing to do with emotion. I just physically desired her, and when I got done, she would follow me around like a puppy dog. As pretty and hot as she was, no one would be her friend, or they would have to deal with us.

I would make sure she would eat alone, spend her weekends alone, study alone, and just be alone. Once she was broken down, I would move in and seduce her until she did anything I asked.

I yawned. "Can you assholes get out of my room so I can nap?" I asked.

Xavier kicked Jaxson off the bed, and he fell on the floor, cursing at his teammate. Sometimes they were like a bunch of children. I waited for them to file out and locked the door behind them.

~

Another snoozefest. Glancing around, I spotted President Lawrence at the head table, and he gestured me over. The room was full, mostly of freshmen and transfers. I hunted the room for Avery and eventually found her standing in the corner with a cup of red punch in her hand.

When we had our welcome dinner, Remy spiked the punch with a bottle of gin he sneaked out of his father's liquor cabinet. It wasn't enough to make everyone drunk because of the size of the bowl, but you got a pretty good buzz. The president, however, realized what was going on by the end of the night, and we were all interrogated.

I sauntered toward Avery, and her eyes grew wide as she saw me coming. It looked like she wanted to fade into the wall.

"Go away," she growled.

My tone was sweet and dripping with honey. "Don't be like that."

"Fuck you, Gideon," she hissed.

"In due time, darling Avery."

Her face turned sour. "Never. You can try all you want, but it will never happen."

"Then this will be the worst year of your life. You see the people in this room?" I asked, glancing out as if proving a point. "None of them will be friends with you when I get done. Your popularity meter is down to zero. This isn't Arlington."

Avery's shoulders slumped as I faced her, and I slipped a

silver flask from the inner pocket of my navy sports jacket. I took a sip as she stared at me with wide eyes.

"Hey, baby!" a grating voice suddenly burst out nearby.

I whirled around and almost spat my whiskey on the floor. Clover Delahunt was walking toward us. Her skirt was way too short, and her blouse had one too many buttons opened, revealing her ample cleavage. Avery pushed by me, bumping my arm and sending the flask to the floor. It hit with a clatter, and I quickly swept it up before someone saw it.

"Oh my God!" Avery cried in a high-pitched voice. "You go here?"

They hugged, and it instantly pissed me off that Avery would have an ally—one who might try to tease Remy into turning against me, though I doubted it would happen.

"Damn right," Clover responded confidently. "You ruined my chance to rule the senior class at Arlington, so don't ever say I never did anything for you."

Clover gave me an evil grin, and I wondered how she managed to get into Bancroft on such short notice.

"Miss Delahunt, how are you?"

We all turned to see President Lawrence coming toward us. He took Clover's hand and covered it with both of his.

"How is your father?" he continued. "I haven't seen Samuel since our Harvard reunion a couple of years ago."

"He and mom are well," Clover relayed in the most suck-up way. "They give their regards and plan to visit during parent's weekend."

"I'm so glad you're here. I hope you like your room."

"It's lovely. I appreciate the privacy."

President Lawrence leaned in and lowered his voice. "It's a pleasure to do a favor for a close friend. I must get back to my wife."

He nodded at Avery and me as he turned and headed back to his table.

"Fuck a duck," I cursed. "How did you manage to get in here?"

"My father and the president go *way* back," Clover emphasized. "It wasn't hard, and I did it to show your lame ass up." Clover then put her arm around me. "Don't even think of pulling some shit on my girl. I have some power too, and if you think you can beat me, just try."

Fuck. Clover would be a more formidable opponent than I anticipated. Even if I had tried to tell myself not to worry about his flipped allegiances, I might have to employ Remy's charms to keep her occupied. If I were to exact my plan to isolate Avery, I would need to separate her from Clover. I watched as they walked away with their elbows hooked.

Restraining my anger, I started to follow them when one of the sophomore transfers stepped in front of me. The tag on his left breast indicated his class and first name – David. His bangs were plastered to his forehead, making him look like Moe from the three stooges.

"You're Gideon Berne, right?" he said, pointing at me.

"Yeah, who are you?" I asked harshly.

"David Penner," he answered, undeterred. "My brother played football with you last year."

Benji Penner was a blowhard. He was a loudmouth writing checks his ass couldn't cash on the field, which resulted in a dust-up with him during practice before the last game of the year. He accused me of not throwing him the football enough. He was a shitty receiver who often dropped the ball.

Remy had also punched him in the thigh so hard he couldn't play the last game, leaving a big purple and black bruise the size of Remy's fist that stood out when he pulled off his practice uniform. I guess Benji never told David that story. We weren't friends or even buddies, so I was confused why David was talking to me now.

"Yeah, football," I said as I craned my neck to look for Avery.

"He said to look you up when I got here."

I couldn't see Avery or Clover anywhere, so I turned my attention back to David.

"Look, your brother was a dick. We weren't friends, we were teammates, and he wasn't very good. I hated throwing him passes because he usually dropped them. He sucked."

David's face turned sour, and he took a couple of steps back. I wasn't in the mood to entertain some transfer who thought he would find a way to the promised land by sucking up to me. I didn't feel good about what I said, but if I continued to engage this kid, he would never leave me alone. I didn't mean to burst the kid's perception of his brother; it was apparent he looked up to him.

"He said you were a jerk," David stuttered out.

I smirked and patted the flask in my pocket. I needed a drink after this conversation and what transpired between Avery, Clover, and me.

"Then why talk to me?" I asked.

"I-I-I thought I would introduce myself."

"What you thought was that you would get in good with me an make your transition to this school easy. Let me give you a piece of advice, David. Keep your head down and your mouth shut. It's not happening. You won't be part of the popular crowd even when I leave here."

David glared at me before he turned on his heel and hurried away. I was in a foul mood as I turned toward the wall and fished my flask from my pocket. Taking a swig, I then popped a mint in my mouth and went to mingle. My job as a student advocate was to welcome the new students, not to make friends with them.

I was only doing this because it would look good on my college application, not that I needed to worry since I was already locked in as a legacy at Yale. And I wanted to stay on the good side of President Lawrence. For the next hour, I flowed around the room, answering questions about the campus and school.

Once it was over, I pasted a fake smile on my face and shook hands with President Lawrence and his wife before I hightailed it out of Clarke Hall. Beckley Hall was two buildings over, and as I walked across the quad, I polished off the whiskey from the flask.

"Berne!"

I looked around to see who was calling me and spotted Jaxson standing by the stone statue of Sutherland Bancroft, founder of our school.

"What's up?" I asked, switching direction over to him.

His backpack rattled as he removed it from his shoulder.

"What the fuck is in there?" I asked.

Jaxson cracked a wide grin. "My parents are somewhere in the Caribbean, and I made a trip home. This bag contains six bottles of the most delicious elixirs."

I chuckled. "You raided their liquor cabinet?"

"You know it. You think I'm spending my weekends sober?"

"Come to my room; we have a situation."

"A situation?" Jaxson asked.

CHAPTER 9

Avery

I couldn't stop hugging Clover. Not only was she attending Bancroft, but she was living in the same dorm.

"Why would you want to come here?" she said after the door was closed to my room.

I scowled. "Are you fucking kidding? I didn't want to come here. I would've had a beautiful senior year at Arlington, but my mother insisted."

Clover kicked off her heels. "This place has a bunch of stuffy rich assholes. I haven't been here for a day and can tell already. We should shake this place up."

I shook my head. "Hell no! I just want to keep a low profile and graduate."

"With Gideon on your ass, your profile will be anything but low. Have you seen Remy?" Clover's voice became dreamy.

"Stop thinking about your own satisfaction. You're here to help me."

She plopped down on the bed opposite mine. I hadn't yet pushed them together because I didn't have linens big enough to cover two mattresses. I never expected to have a single.

She chewed at her thumbnail, painted with chipping pink polish. "All I'm saying is he's a good fuck. I'm not in love with the guy."

"I hope not. I need you to have a clear head. Tell me how you convinced your parents to let you go here."

She rolled her eyes. "They're so easy. I just whined to them about how you were at Bancroft and how I would miss you. My father's told me a million times about President Lawrence and how he runs this place, so it wasn't hard."

I threw my pillow at her. "Why the fuck didn't you tell me?"

"I wanted it to be a surprise. You were complaining about this place so much, and once I met Gideon and his band of dopes, I knew I had to save you. These assholes would eat you alive by yourself."

"I could hold my own," I insisted.

"Bullshit. You're too nice, Bedford."

I grinned. "You know you get more flies with honey than vinegar."

She laughed. "Sometimes, you need to dump vinegar on the flies to keep them away. Fuck these dimwits. I'm going to run this place. You let me handle it. Your nasty stepbrother won't know what hit him."

I frowned. "What are you going to do? THEY run this place. Everybody loves them, especially Gideon."

My stepbrother wouldn't loosen his hold on Bancroft. When he walked the halls, everyone parted like the red sea.

"You let me handle it," she reassured. "I'll start with Remy. He'll be easy to turn since he loves my pussy so much."

I inserted my finger into my open mouth, making vomiting noises. "Gross."

"His dick is magic."

"Just don't be seduced by that magic."

Clover rubbed her hands on her thighs. "Not possible. I'm sure there are plenty of hot guys here, not just Remy."

"Yeah, but if you want the cream, you've already met it. I'm sure Gideon is fuming now that you're here."

She looked around my room. "Maybe I should request a room switch. I could move up here."

I clasped my hands together. "You would do that?"

"Sure. I'd like to piss your mother off."

My jubilance faded away. I had completely forgotten about my mother. Once she found out Clover was here and my roommate, she would work to get us separated. And Gideon would be a force since he disliked how Clover didn't fawn all over him like everyone else.

"Fuck, I forgot," I said, deflating.

She yanked a long string of pink gum from her mouth and sucked it back in.

"That's nasty," I chided.

Clover cracked her gum several times before she blew a big bubble. "Should I call the president to get my room changed?"

"I think you would need to speak to the dorm director, and if she said no, then go over her head. Gideon probably bought her a new car or some shit like that."

As if summoned, Gideon's voice sounded in the hall like he was talking to someone. I froze, but Clover got up and yanked the door open. My stepbrother was standing there with a shit-eating grin on his face with Jaxson in tow.

"Want to get fucked up?" he asked.

"Fuck off, Berne," Clover spat. "Don't try to charm me. If you want to get on my good side, apologize to Avery."

Gideon's face went stoic. "Who the hell do you think you are?" he said through clenched teeth.

Jaxson looked ready to burst into laughter, but he held his tongue. I was willing him to let loose to break the band of tension stretching tighter by the second, but he did nothing as Clover and Gideon were caught in a standoff, glaring at each other.

"Someone with more clout than you," Clover replied. "I know the president, and he would do anything for me."

Gideon jutted his chin out. "You dirty little cunt," he snarled. "*I* run this school, not *you*."

She shot him with a finger gun and blew at the tip. "Looks like there's a new sheriff in town, pardner," Clover said with a western drawl.

For the first time since I got here, I was enjoying myself as Gideon met his match. Jaxson stood behind him, looking on with amusement. I cracked a grin, and if looks could kill, I would be dead from Gideon's acid-dripping stare.

"Bitch, you couldn't play on the same court as me," he retorted.

Clover closed the distance to my stepbrother and ran her nails over the stubble on his cheek. "Sweetheart, I not only can play but run rings around you. You don't want none of this," she said, sliding her other hand down her body.

Gideon ignored her and looked over Clover's shoulder at me, his voice full of venom as he said, "This just got worse for you."

I shivered.

"Touch her, and you don't want to find out what I'll do," Clover growled.

"Whore, please."

"Is there a problem?" a voice called out.

We all looked toward the person in the hall. Our floor advisor, Daniel, was standing there with a look of concern. When no one answered, he asked again, "Is there a problem?"

"No, Daniel," Gideon spoke up first. "I was just having a disagreement with my stepsister."

Daniel didn't look convinced. "I suggest you keep the colorful language to a minimum, and if you have any issues, my door is always open."

Gideon looked as if he wanted to pour some of his charm on but thought better of it and kept his mouth shut. Daniel stood there until Jaxson and Gideon backed out of my doorway and headed down the hall.

Once we were in private behind closed doors, we made plans to have Clover move into my room. Even though it was late, she called President Lawrence, who said he would personally handle the change.

"This is so easy," Clover said smugly.

"What is?" I asked with confusion.

"Getting under Gideon's skin. He really is full of himself."

I moved some clothing to one side of the closet while we talked.

"He's a fucking God on this campus," I corrected. "Did you see how people were looking at him during the dinner? They love him."

"He's a façade. You can get to anyone if you know their weakness."

I snorted and plopped down on my bed. "And you know his?"

Clover clucked her tongue. "You lived with him for several weeks, and you haven't figured it out? I had the guy pegged in five minutes."

I knitted my eyebrows together. "And?"

"Losing. He doesn't like losing. Did you see him when he lost a hand at poker? I thought his head would explode."

I sighed. "I wish I had your confidence."

She unzipped her small duffel, spit her gum in the garbage can, and pulled out a bag of M&Ms. She threw one in the air and caught it in her mouth. For as long as I could remember, they were her favorite candy—but not any other variety—just the regular.

"You want one?" she said as she shoved a handful from the large bag into her mouth.

"No, I prefer Skittles."

Clover flicked her finger, momentarily pointing at me. "Right. How could I forget."

"I still can't believe you're here."

She yawned. "I needed something to do for my senior year. Arlington wouldn't be the same without you."

"But you were at the top of the food chain in that place. Why would you want to start over?"

She chuckled, crunching down on another handful of M&Ms. "Silly girl! I told you I like a challenge. Let's give these snobs a run for their money."

I laughed. "Literally."

Clover spread her arms out to her sides. "Of course, this place is nothing like my bedroom at home, and the bathroom could use an upgrade, but at least it's private."

She threw a yellow M&M at me, and it bounced off the wall and rolled under the bed.

"Don't do that! We'll get ants," I said.

"This place could use some excitement." Clover rose from her bed, zipped the closure on the M&Ms shut, and tossed the bag on her desk. "I have to get my suitcase and pillow from my old room. Will you be all right for a few minutes?"

I sighed. "Clover, we'll be separated sometimes. You can't protect me every second of the day."

She stuck her multicolored tongue out at me before she exited the room. While I was looking for a t-shirt and shorts to wear to bed, the door opened. I didn't bother looking at who it was.

"That was fast," I commented. "Did you hold the elevator?"

When a body pressed against mine, I knew I was in trouble. Gideon's breath, laced with alcohol, stung my nose as his arm slipped around my belly and held me to him.

"Darling Avery, you keep slipping from me but not this time."

I dug my nails into his arm, but he didn't flinch. "Gideon, please. Clover will be back in a minute."

"That's where you're wrong. Remy is keeping her occupied. It seems his date didn't work out the way he wanted, and he's all fired up," he taunted.

"She won't sleep with him again."

Gideon hooked my hair around my ear and ran his tongue over its shell before he kissed my neck. "Do you know what tomorrow is?"

I squirmed in his grip. "Sunday."

"It's the day our parents leave for their honeymoon. I'm sure they won't be happy if you call them and report my bad behavior. Your mother was quite distressed at the lies you told about me."

"They weren't lies!" I choked out, finding it hard to breathe.

He ground his pelvis against my ass and wrapped his free hand around my throat.

"Admit it, Avery, you like what I do to you."

"I don't," I insisted.

"I think you do. And you know why? Because you were the queen at Arlington. You were a guy's wet dream, and you loved having them pant after you. And you like to get me going."

I clawed at the hand around my throat even though Gideon wasn't squeezing—it was more like resting despite his strength.

I could smell cologne on his skin and the scent of laundry detergent on his clothing. He released my throat and ran his hand down to my hip, where he paused at my upper thigh.

Taking my chance, I escaped from his grip and whipped around to face him, jamming my black cherry-painted nail in his chest. "I *was* a queen, and your father fucked it up! I could be enjoying my senior year, not putting up with your bullshit."

"My father will tire of your mother soon enough," he sneered. "He likes variety. Frankly, I'm surprised he married her. His usual M.O. is to date until he uses them up, and then he moves on. Renata hit the jackpot. I must applaud her for her golden pussy."

"How dare you!" I snarled.

My blood began to boil as he disrespected my mother in the worst way. I raised my hand to slap him as hard as I could muster, but he caught my wrist in his grip and yanked me forward, biting the heel of my hand. I yelped as his teeth sank into my flesh, expecting something worse to follow, but then something weird happened.

He released his bite, closed his eyes, and pressed his nose against my skin before he kissed the indentations he'd made with his teeth. Uncertain about what I just saw, I couldn't pull away in time before the veil came back over him, and he stepped away, dropping my hand.

"I can't wait to have you, darling Avery."

"You marked me, asshole," I argued, looking at my hand.

"It won't be the last time," he replied darkly.

He turned, opened the door, and left it ajar as he walked down the hall. I closed my fingers over the teeth marks, which had begun to fade. The scent of Gideon's cologne hung in the air, but it wasn't the only thing I was aware of. I was aroused. There was a dull throb between my legs.

What the fuck is wrong with me?

I hated Gideon Berne, and I cursed the day his father came

into my mother's life, so how could I be turned on? He was an abusive asshole threatening to take what I wasn't offering or willing to give.

I sank to my bed and stared at the wall behind Clover's bed. A few minutes later, she breezed in with her belongings. Her cheeks were pink with activity, and a smile was pasted on her face. I knew what she was already up to.

"What the fuck took you so long?" I screeched.

"I had to check the room," she said, turning her back to me.

"Bullshit," I accused. "You were messing around with Remy."

"I wasn't."

"It was enough time for Gideon to come in here and bully me!"

She whirled around, a stern look on her face. "What do you mean he came in here?"

I held my hand up for her to see the fading teeth indentations in my hand. "He bit me."

Clover grabbed my hand and ran her thumb over the bite marks. "Fucking bastard."

She dropped my hand and headed for the door. I jumped up and grabbed her by the hem of her shirt.

"Don't."

She turned to me. "This doesn't only concern me. Remy was in on it, and that makes it personal."

I let her shirt go, and she stalked out of the room. I followed as she hunted for the door that had Remy's name on it. When she found it, she burst in and revealed a naked Remy in the middle of changing. A surprised look came over his face, more so when she rushed forward and grasped his balls and squeezed.

"Clover, it's not what you think!" Remy cried.

"Avery, close the door unless you don't want to see this," she growled.

I kicked the door closed, and it slammed, echoing down the

hall. I couldn't stop from noticing Remy had a big dick, one that was growing despite his precarious position.

"Did you use me so Gideon could get to Avery?" Clover interrogated.

"It's not like that," he said again.

She squeezed harder, and Remy gritted his teeth.

"Tell me how it is," she ordered.

"It had nothing to do with him!" he tried to reason. "I wanted to see you."

She laughed sarcastically. "You wanted to fuck me. There's a difference. If I find out you used me at that evil fuck's say so, I'll slice your balls and dick off, then feed them to the birds."

"I didn't, I swear!" He sounded scared as his face was twisted in pain. I wondered how hard Clover was squeezing.

"So it's a coincidence that Gideon was giving Avery a hard time while you had me bent over the desk? Doesn't that seem convenient?"

"Clover, please," he nearly panted.

I bit my lip to stop myself from laughing. She let him go, and he swallowed hard, probably to stop himself from vomiting. She smelled her hand.

"You should shower; your balls smell like my pussy."

Remy took a deep breath. "I like that smell."

"You pull this bullshit again, and you'll never go near it again."

"Let me take you to lunch tomorrow," Remy begged.

She smirked. "I'll think about it."

CHAPTER 10

Gideon

Clover was a problem for me. Again. Remy could only distract her from hanging around with Avery for so long. And because she was here for the year, it was creating a boldness within my stepsister that I thought I had previously eliminated. With her best friend here, her confidence had returned. I recognized it from when I first met her and realized I would need to knock her down a few pegs.

Jaxson pulled up the window and sat on the windowsill, removing a joint and a lighter from his shirt pocket. He lit it and held the smoke. I didn't smoke weed as it wasn't my drug of choice. I preferred alcohol.

"You gotta smoke that shit in here?" I questioned. "Why don't you go to your room?"

"Because Xavier will smoke this shit up, and I don't feel like sharing."

"Then go out to the quad."

He checked his watch. "It's almost curfew."

Jaxson took another hard pull on the joint, holding the smoke as he stubbed it out between his thumb and index finger. He slipped it back into his shirt pocket along with the lighter and headed toward the door, punching me in my non-throwing arm before he hurried out the door.

"Fucker!" I yelled as he ran down the hall.

I kicked the door shut with my toe and went to close the window. It was still August, so the air conditioning was on. I took a deep breath. Being so close to Avery earlier still had me hot and hard. My balls ached as I flipped the lock on the door, pulled down the shade, and jerked off, coming quickly like a kid having his first orgasm.

I took a fast shower, and even though there were muffled voices in the hall, I shut out the lights and climbed into bed. There would be no more nightly visits to Avery through the secret tunnel until we got home for the holidays. Until then, I'd already spread my instructions over the campus, sending out emails and texts about Avery. She was to be isolated. I wanted her to become so lonely that she begged for my attention and begged for me to take her V card.

It wasn't hard to pump information from people who attended Arlington, and her last boyfriend was a plethora of details. It was how I found out she was still a virgin, but it still bothered me that other guys had touched her in sexual ways. I wanted to be the only one. In the meantime, I was enjoying breaking her down. Once I had her on her knees for more than one reason, I would build her up and make her mine.

"HERE, HERE!" Xavier screamed as he waved from the end zone.

I fired the ball downfield, and he jumped up and caught it

before he was hit by Jaxson and knocked to the ground. Coach Ramsey blew the whistle.

"Curran!" Coach thundered. "These are no contact drills."

"Sorry, coach!" Jaxson yelled as he came back to the line.

"Fucking idiot," Remy said.

Coach tossed me another football, and I spun it on my palm.

"What's the big deal?" I asked.

"Xavier is our best receiver. If he gets hurt, we're fucked."

I shook my head. "You think I give a shit? No one on this field is going to a Division One school. We all have trust fund money and don't have to worry about paying for college. Who would bother getting their head bashed in at the college level?"

He snorted. "As opposed to getting your head bashed in at the high school level?"

"Shut up, dickhead."

The coach blew the whistle and called out a play. We got into formation, then Xavier ran the pattern, catching the ball at the twenty-yard line. The truth was, there was no other team in our division that could match us. We hadn't lost a game since I was a freshman, and we finished the year with eleven wins and one loss.

Remy bumped me with his shoulder. "What are we doing tonight?"

"Nothing. We have class tomorrow and practice in the afternoon."

He lifted his helmet to wipe the sweat from his face. "I was just asking because *I* have something to do."

"Remy, don't fall for her."

"For who?" he asked.

"Clover. I need your head in the game."

"Oh, so it's all about you and what you want?" he asked lowly.

Coach Ramsey blew the whistle and ended practice. I was exhausted after two hours in the hot sun, and I didn't sleep well the night before. I was getting progressively angrier about my situation with Avery. I thought it would be a cake walk and that I would have her in my bed by the end of September, but with Clover cock blocking me, it wouldn't happen. I would need to work harder and smarter.

Xavier slapped my helmet. "Nice pass. Are we heading to Preppies for lunch?"

Preppies was a place in town that catered to the students of Bancroft. It had been there for over fifty years, and my father used to eat there when he went to Bancroft. They sold upscale burgers with toppings like truffles and bleu cheese. At the mention of the place, I suddenly had a craving for the filet mignon burger with a thick slice of Jarlsberg on top.

"I guess. Ask Jaxson if he wants to come."

"What about Remy?" he asked.

I was still annoyed at my best buddy because I could see he was getting seduced by a tight pussy and big breasts.

"Ask him yourself," I growled.

"You pissed at him?"

"What gave it away?" I retorted as I ripped off my helmet.

I wiped sweat from my face with the hem of my jersey, stopping by the sideline to slurp down a cup of orange Gatorade before I went inside to shower.

PREPPIES WAS PACKED when we arrived since it was just after noon. The hostess on duty, who I had slept with the year before, was the daughter of the owner. She was three years older than me and a great lay. I nodded at her as we entered, and she winked at me before escorting us to a table right away.

We got a booth in the back corner, but my attention was on one across the restaurant. I was surprised Avery and Clover would come to Preppies. It was mainstream, and my thought was that my stepsister wanted to keep a low profile. Taking advantage of the moment, I studied her. She was wearing a tank top and cutoff jean shorts.

I poked Xavier. "Look," I said, pointing to Avery.

Jaxson looked up from his phone to see what I was talking about.

"Should we pay them a visit?" I added.

"Are we sharing?" Xavier asked.

I ignored him because the answer was no. Avery would not be one of the girls we shared. Over the past two years, we had shared girls, and they let us because of who we were. There were also times they came to us. Bancroft was a prep school with a lot of naughty things going on behind its walls. Some of the bad behavior would probably die down once we graduate. The four of us were some of the wealthiest students to pass through Bancroft, so it didn't take a genius to figure out the amount of leeway we got.

I rose from the booth with Xavier and Jaxson behind me. Neither Avery nor Clover saw us until we sat down next to them. Jaxson grabbed an empty chair from the table across from us and sat at the end of the table.

"What the hell are you doing here?" Avery squeaked.

"We're here to have lunch with you," I answered in a cheerful voice.

"Cut the crap, Berne," Clover said. "What do you want?"

"Is it so hard to believe I want to have lunch with my stepsister? I'm the only family she has in the states now that our parents are off to Europe."

I draped my arm across Avery's shoulder, and she immediately tensed up. Her skin was so soft as I stroked her shoulder with my fingers, which only caused my dick to stir in my shorts. She shrugged off my arm, and I used it to cover my lap. Our legs were almost touching, and while I bantered with Clover about our presence, I slid my hand up Avery's thigh.

The muscle in her leg flexed as I rested it just short of her crotch. The heat from her pussy emanated through her shorts, and my dick became painfully hard. I shifted in my seat for relief and gently kneaded her inner thigh. Her breath stuttered, and I wondered if she was growing aroused by my actions.

Snap, snap.

I must have zoned out for a minute because when I looked up, Clover was snapping her fingers at my face.

"Pay attention, Berne. You didn't answer my question."

I raised an eyebrow. "And that was?"

"Where's your fourth wheel? What happened to him?"

"He's taking a nap. The sun got to him."

The fact was, I didn't want Remy to come with us, so when he asked for me to wait while he showered, I left. I was just letting him know how pissed I was that he wasn't following the plan I mapped out. Xavier and Jaxson both looked at me as I spoke the lie.

"The only one I can tolerate," Clover mumbled.

I smirked. "That's what you're calling it?"

Avery hadn't said anything other than to ask why I was there, so I continued to gently knead her thigh. When I glanced over, she had her eyes closed and her lips slightly parted.

Was this turning her on?

For some time, we all bantered back and forth except for Avery, who remained quiet. I noticed her chest barely rising and falling as if she were holding her breath. If this were all it took, I would be fucking her within the week.

"Hey, Bedford, what's the matter? Is your headache back?" Clover asked.

The spell was broken when Avery discreetly pushed my hand off her thigh. She popped open her eyes and looked at Clover.

"I'm tired," Avery croaked.

"You were mumbling in your sleep last night," Clover said.

Avery looked around the table and her face pinked with embarrassment. Lucky for her, we were interrupted by the waitress who took our orders. I took a deep breath as I tried to will my erection away and caught Avery's scent. I didn't know if it was her shampoo, skin cream, or something else, but it was intoxicating. I knew I was tottering dangerously close to showing my cards.

Once more, I pressed my leg against Avery's, and she again closed her eyes. I wasn't doing myself any favors by touching her because my balls were aching with need, but in the moment between us, I waited for Avery to push my knee away, yet we both remained quiet, and she never did.

Xavier and Jaxson were going off script and deviating from the plan as they joked with Clover and tried to engage Avery, who was stoic. She barely touched her meal, and part of me hoped she wasn't sick. It was either that, or I'd broken her already.

CHAPTER 11

Avery

I spent lunch cursing myself and my appetite for the cheese omelet I anticipated eating before it left me. I ended up picking at it while Gideon's knee rubbed against mine. When he had his hand gently kneading my thigh, I was undeniably turned on. The guy I hated, who tortured me from the moment I met him, was turning me on.

Clover drove my Mercedes home, and I stayed quiet, looking out the window at students lounging on the lawns and soaking up the late summer sun.

"Are you feeling okay?" Her voice broke the silence.

I didn't look at her. "I'm all right."

She came to a stop at a red light and touched my arm. "Look at me."

I turned. "What?"

"You were fine until they came over to the table."

Glancing away, I said, "The light is green."

Clover put her foot on the gas. "What's up? You barely ate anything. Did Gideon do something to you under the table?"

I coughed. How could I tell her he touched me just an inch from my most intimate place, and it turned me on? I hated Gideon, but I also hated myself for how I felt. My emotions were so jumbled and confused, and it didn't help that tomorrow was the first day of class, and no one would talk to me.

"No," I lied. "I'm just worried about tomorrow; plus, Payne and my mother are traveling today."

"Yeah, on the freaking company plane. Must be nice."

"I guess it comes with the territory. They said we could go away for Christmas."

She turned into the Beckley Hall parking lot. I had found a parking sticker in my welcome packet and pasted it on my side window earlier. While we walked back to the dorm, a few guys whistled at us. I guessed they had no idea who we were, or they would have ignored us under Gideon's orders that weren't so secretly kept.

"I think I'll take a nap," I said.

"If you are, then I'm going to explore the campus," Clover said.

"We were supposed to do that together."

"Then come with me."

I shook my head. "I said I'm tired."

"Fine. Here's your key, " she said as she tossed it to me.

Clover turned and walked in the opposite direction of our dorm, leaving me lonelier than I had felt in my entire life. A few people were in the lobby when I entered and pressed the elevator button, but none of them even looked at me. When I got upstairs, I stepped onto my floor and looked toward the boys' side.

I don't know what I was thinking, but a surge of determination swept over me as I headed in the direction of Gideon's room. They left before us, and I had seen the Bugatti in the parking lot. A couple of guys passed by me as I paused in front of Gideon's door, and just before I knocked, he opened the door.

His eyebrows flew up in surprise. "What do you want?" he growled.

I put the palm of my hand on his bare chest, pushed him back and closed the door. It shocked me that Gideon didn't push me away, but after the way, he acted in the restaurant, I decided to turn the tables. I moved my hand from his chest to his cheek, cupping it.

"You want me, and it doesn't have anything to do with trying to control or assault me," I said knowingly.

He laughed, and his voice dripped with sarcasm, "Get over yourself."

"Kiss me, Gideon."

His gray eyes met mine. "For what purpose?"

"Just do it."

I wasn't prepared for him as he slammed his mouth on mine or to have his tongue thrust between my lips and probe for my own. One of his hands tangled in my hair while the other supported my body as he tipped me back. I stroked the muscles of his arms feeling them ripple as he held me.

My heart was thumping in my chest as he pushed me against the bed and cupped my ass. His dick was hard; I felt it against my belly. My moan brought Gideon back to Earth, and he tore his mouth from mine, backing away.

"Fuck!" he shouted as he ran his hands through his thick hair.

I reached out, but he wouldn't let me touch him.

"No."

"So this is what it's all about?"

He sat down on his bed, absentmindedly rubbing his erection through his shorts. Gideon wouldn't look at me. "What are you talking about?"

I decided to push him by straddling his thighs. He didn't move me away as I began to dry hump his cock. He groaned and cupped my ass, moving his hips in rhythm with mine. I froze, and he finally looked up at me.

"*This* is what I'm talking about," I pointed out. "You just want to fuck me."

His face twisted in pain. "It was a game," he croaked. "A stupid game."

I put my hand under his chin and brought his face up. He looked into my eyes.

"It wasn't a game. Whose idea was it to send me here? I want the truth."

Gideon turned me so quickly that in a split second, I was underneath him, and he hovered above me with his hands on either side of my head.

"Why did you have to be so damn beautiful?"

I smiled and reached up to touch his face. "Why did you have to be so damn mean?"

"Because I'm Gideon Berne. I don't date. I fuck."

I ran my hand down his throat, chest, and belly, stopping just before the waistband of his shorts. "Is that what you want from me?"

"I want to ruin you, own you, make you beg for what I have," he growled.

I removed my hand from his stomach. "I don't beg."

"But I want you to. I want to drive you crazy."

I slipped from under him, and he moved to a sitting position. I rose, kissed his cheek, and headed for the door but stopped and turned my head. "I won't beg, so you're out of luck. We could've been, but what you're asking is to control me, and I won't let that happen."

Gideon didn't look at me as I opened the door and slipped into the hall. There was a deep ache between my legs and breasts. I passed Xavier as I headed to the girls' hall, and he tapped my shoulder, but I didn't respond.

"Avery?" he called after me.

"I'm fine," I said.

But I wasn't fine because once I got behind closed doors, I started to digest what had happened. The entire day was eye-opening. Despite how evil he was toward me, I suspected Gideon was attracted to me, but what he said made me believe his attraction went beyond it, bordering on obsession. I also had a feeling that now that I knew his secret, he would ramp up his bad behavior.

CHAPTER 12

Gideon

"Fuck," I whispered. "Suck my dick."

I fantasized about holding Avery's head and ramming my cock down her throat, moving my hips relentlessly, not giving her one ounce of mercy. I wanted to empty everything I had down her throat. My balls tightened, and I arched my back as I came in thick ropy jets which coated my stomach and chest.

I wanted it to be Avery so badly. I wanted to fill her mouth with cum and run the head of my dick over her beautiful lips, coating them with my semen. I wished she was with me. I almost had her, but it was on her terms, and that was unacceptable to me.

Now that she knew my secret, I would need to double down. She still needed to be broken. I would just need to try harder to do it. I wiped my chest and stomach before I sat up, tossing the shirt I used into the laundry bag near the bathroom.

Avery had me so hyped up that during a quick shower, I jerked off again, stroking with a soaped hand and visualizing it was hers. I promised myself when she moved in that I would hold off sleeping with anyone. I wanted her to be my next conquest, but now I couldn't wait.

There were any of a dozen girls who would be willing to sleep with me without attachment. Bancroft was full of students not interested in relationships. They were the elite—wealthy and privileged. Most would attend ivy league universities, and if they didn't, they would live off trust funds. I planned to do both.

As far as attending Yale went, I'd already been accepted through early admission, but I kept that information quiet. I was also asked to play football, but it would be one more thing to distract me from my other pursuits.

The room was cool when I exited the bathroom and slipped under the sheets, falling into a deep, satisfying sleep.

WHEN I WOKE, I was bathed in sweat, disturbed by my bad dream. I never told my father about the demons that tortured me at night. He seemed to have moved on from my mother after her death as if he didn't care. He was back to business within four days of her funeral and dating three months after she died. I sometimes wondered if their relationship was broken long before she was gone, and it never helped that my father refused to talk about it.

The clock told me it was barely 5 am, and I had a class at 8 am, so I figured it was a perfect time for a run. Despite my party-hard exterior, I enjoyed the solitude of early mornings. The dorm was quiet, and I nodded at the night guard at the front desk as I exited the building. Outside, the air was cool, but the humidity was thick.

I began to run and suck in the soupy air as I headed toward

the football fields. In fourteen hours, I'd be there in full practice uniform, preparing for our game on Saturday against Philips Academy. I had no doubt we would trounce them.

As I neared the field, I ran at full speed up the walk lined with boxwoods, each squared off and perfect. My head was down because I'd run this path so many times I could do it blind. When I finally look up, it's too late. I ran into a girl, and we both went sprawling to the ground. She cried out as she fell, and when I recovered, I crawled toward her prone form. Her scent was familiar, and I knew the curve of her yoga pant-clad ass before I saw her face.

"Jesus Christ, Avery, what the hell are you doing out here?" I yelled as I rolled her over.

Her eyes fluttered open. "Gideon?"

I took her in my arms and pulled her onto my lap, ignoring my scraped and bleeding knee. "Why are you out here?"

"I couldn't sleep because of you," she said as she struggled out of my arms.

I let her go, and she slipped from my lap onto the hard pavement.

"Why?" I pressed.

Avery slid her hand over a tear in her yoga pants, sliding her finger inside the rip. "I don't get you."

My eyebrows knitted together. "What don't you get?"

"You hate me; you love me," she snapped.

I was about to answer her when she used the hem of her shirt to dab at my bleeding knee. It stung as sweat from my thigh leaked into the wound. I brushed her hand away.

"Don't. It will stop."

"You need a bandage," she replied.

I sucked in a deep breath. "I don't hate you."

She set her mouth in a hard line. "Are we having this out now?"

I shrugged. "Do you want to?"

Avery sighed in frustration. "I won't let you control me. I promised myself I would never let a man do that."

I narrowed my eyes. "Did you have a boyfriend like that?"

If she told me, someone physically hurt her, I would go apeshit. But she was right about one thing: I did want to control her. My life was all about control. But Avery was a free spirit in contrast, and she kept insisting she wouldn't let me cage her.

"No. My mother did before Payne."

I clenched my fists and realized I had scrapes on the heel of my hand. "Did he hurt you?"

"No. I spent a lot of time at Clover's house when he was around. My mother finally dumped him, and a month later, she met your father."

I rose from the pavement and helped her up. There was a hose near the snack bar that we could use, and I held her hand as we walked over. Once there, I let her sit down so I could turn on the hose and wash off the blood from my knee. The wound was oozing, but the bleeding had stopped. Avery took off her t-shirt, revealing a gray sports bra underneath. She gently pressed it to my wound.

"It's okay," I muttered.

When she stood up, I couldn't resist stepping closer and kissing her. Not a bruising kiss like the night before, but a sweet, gentle kiss that I hadn't realized I was capable of giving. Once I broke from her lips, Avery hugged me.

"Where do we go from here?" she said into my chest.

"I'm not sure. This is new ground for me."

She looked up at me. "You didn't answer my question last night."

I frowned. "Which one?"

"Were you the one who talked my mother into sending me here?"

I sucked in my bottom lip, biting down on it, tasting my salty skin. "I had to."

"Why? I was perfectly happy at Arlington."

I smirked. "Prom queen, class president, breaker of hearts."

I knew everything about Avery. What I didn't know from her former classmates, Renata supplied before they moved into my father's home.

"I don't break hearts, but I think you do," she returned.

I let her out of my embrace. "I don't break hearts because I don't date."

"And *I* don't have casual sex."

Wanting to hear her say the words, I asked, "Are you a virgin?"

She knitted her eyebrows together. "Does it matter?"

"You seemed pretty willing to give it to me last night," I taunted. "I was just wondering."

Avery backed away. "I wasn't willing. I was teasing, but I wanted to know something. If I didn't give in, would you have forced me?"

The seriousness of her words made me realize my behavior implied that I would have forced and brutalized her to get what I wanted, but I would never. My plan was only to seduce her until she gave it to me willingly.

"No. Never. I know it seemed that way, but I feel like shit if I did that to you."

She took my hand and ran her finger over the scrapes. "Why didn't you just talk to me? Do you do this to all the girls you want to sleep with?"

I sighed. "It's getting late, and this conversation will take way too long to have with the time we have."

"Then when?" she asked.

"Tonight."

Avery bit her lip. "I'm not sure I can get away."

I threw my head back and laughed. First, she avoided me, and now that I wanted to have a civil conversation, she couldn't get away.

"I could get Remy to occupy Clover."

She gave me a sour look. "It's not funny. This is your fault."

"I know."

The sun was rising, and the morning mist was beginning to fade away as I cupped her face and kissed her again, this time with more passion. She pushed away from me, her chest heaving.

"You make no sense."

I grinned. "I try my best."

"We should get back. I have a class at 8 am where I'm sure everyone will ignore me."

"I'll fix it, I promise, not that the boys will listen. I see how they look at you."

One last time, I pulled her into my arms and kissed her before she walked ahead. It was on now.

CHAPTER 13

Avery

"What the hell happened to you?" Clover asked as I entered my room.

Gideon was not far behind me but, instead, heading down the other hall.

"I fell up by the football field."

She strolled around in a short pink silk robe as she prepared her uniform for school. I hated wearing a uniform, but at least we didn't have to worry about shopping for school clothes.

"What were you doing up there?" she asked with suspicion.

I shrugged. "Walking. I couldn't sleep."

"I'd stay away from there, especially since everyone on the football team are Gideon's puppets. You never know who you'll run into up there."

I pulled off my shirt, and Clover must have seen the blood on the back from when I wiped Gideon's cut because she screeched, "Where the hell is that from?"

Since I had no visible cuts, I had no choice but to lie. "From my nose."

Clover narrowed her eyes. "You don't get bloody noses. Tell me the truth. Did someone hurt you up there?"

"Clover, no one was out this early. I'm fine, and I do get bloody noses. The air at the manor is dry. I've had a few of them lately."

She seemed satisfied with my explanation because she went back to choosing her clothing, and I internally exhaled. Just as I prepared my own things, I raised an eyebrow at Clover, who pulled out a red lace bra and panty set from her drawer.

"You're wearing those?" I asked.

"This shitty uniform is ruining my flow," she replied nonchalantly.

At Arlington, Clover pushed the envelope with her outfits. She wore skirts and dresses a centimeter below what was outlined in the school handbook, so that they couldn't get her on a technicality. Her shirts, however, usually showed too much cleavage, and she liked to wear white shirts with either black or red bras. There were several times she was sent home for inappropriate dress. But you had to love her enthusiasm.

"Well, get used to it since it's all we can wear until after class or on the weekends," I pointed out.

She smirked. "We should go to your house this weekend."

I bit the corner of my lip. "Why? No one is home."

"Exactly, and you have servants and a chef."

"*And* a stepbrother who could come home at any time and give me a harder time than before."

What I'd just said wasn't true. Based on how he'd treated me earlier, I thought Gideon was possibly done with making my life miserable. I anticipated our talk later this evening and hoped I could get away without being noticed or followed.

"Fuck him," Clover stated. "I'll be starting my campaign against him today."

I started laughing. "How, by seducing the boys with your silky bra strap?"

"You'd be surprised how excited a hard-up guy gets when he sees a bra."

"Okay, that takes care of the guys. What about the girls?"

Clover gave me a lopsided grin as she removed her robe, revealing she was totally naked underneath. I cringed and put my hand in front of my face.

"Bitch, please," Clover teased. "It's not like you haven't seen me naked before."

"I'm taking a shower. When you're finished prancing around naked, come in and talk to me."

I grabbed a fresh towel and headed into the bathroom, shutting the door behind me so the steam wouldn't escape. Clover entered as I slipped inside the shower stall, closing the glass door with a clang. For a prep school, the bathrooms were smaller than I would have liked but still nice. I expected the dorm rooms at college wouldn't be as accommodating.

I was washing the shampoo from my hair when Clover propped herself up on the sink. Through the glass, I noticed she was only half dressed in her white blouse and red underwear, a large cross dangling between her cleavage.

"Unbelievable," I said with a laugh.

"What? This?" Clover said as she held up her cross. "It's a nice touch."

"You know they'll make you button up your shirt."

"Unless it's a male teacher," she replied with a smirk.

I scrubbed myself with the purple poof I had attached to the shower wall with a suction cup. "You're perverse. No teacher will look at you like that."

"Mr. Callahan did."

I scoffed. "He was a dirty old man."

"A little cleavage goes a long way. I got an A in accounting."

I stepped under the spray to wash the soap off my body. "Tell me your plan again?"

Clover turned and wiped off the fog from the mirror to apply her makeup, going heavy on the mascara. "Intimidation. These prep school bitches will fold like cheap lawn furniture. It'll be so easy."

"You think?" I asked as I shut the water off.

Clover handed me my towel when I opened the door, surveying my body.

"You look good. I'm not sure any of these guys will be able to follow dickhead's instructions. They'd be stupid not to want you."

I don't want them; I want Gideon, I immediately thought. *My fucking stepbrother, who as mean as he is to me, is a major turn-on.*

I wrapped the towel around me. "I'll find out. Today is the day."

"I need to get my schedule. President Lawrence said to check my school email."

I rolled my eyes. "It's almost 7:30. Don't you think you should do that?"

She hopped off the sink and sashayed out of the bathroom. I was brushing my hair when she ducked her head back inside.

"What is your first class?" she asked.

"English—Mr. Dornan."

"And second period?" she continued.

I worked on a knot in my hair. "Accounting."

"Third period?"

"Chemistry," I replied. "Why?"

"Because I have the same classes, though I'm sure I'll need that beautiful brain of yours to help me make it through chemistry."

I quirked an eyebrow. "Get the hell out of here. How did you manage to get the same classes as me?"

"President Lawrence."

"I have art fourth period and then a study period or gym depending on the day," I added.

"My sixth is trigonometry, seventh is Spanish 3, and eighth is history."

I slipped on a pair of pink lace thong and a matching bra I left on the vanity. The only class we didn't have together was Spanish because Clover chose to take German as a freshman before deciding to switch languages. I thought I could survive on my own for one period.

When I finished dressing, I put my hair in a ponytail and went light on the makeup except for lip gloss. I loved glossy lips. We were ready by 7:45, and our first class was in the building next door, so it was a short two-minute walk.

By the time we stepped into the elevator, the tension was obvious between us and two girls from our floor. They practically hugged the back wall like we were diseased. Clover glanced at me, then turned around and stepped toward them. In the shiny steel on the front wall, I saw their expressions turn to fear as they stared at my best friend.

When we hit the main floor and the doors opened, Clover kept standing there staring at them but suddenly made her move.

"BOO!" she yelled, throwing her arms up.

She didn't wait for a response as she turned and fell into step with me as we walked out of the car. I started laughing uncontrollably once we were out of their sight.

"That was fucking hilarious!" I exclaimed.

"Did you see their faces?" Clover asked. "I like this place."

I turned to see the girls weren't behind us. They were probably trying to calm down. If Clover pulled that shit at Arlington, the girls would've told her to fuck off. But some of these kids weren't from New York—they were blue bloods from all over the country, and there was no way of knowing what rumors they believed about Clover to have reacted like so.

Kids of privilege like them usually had no idea what preparing a meal or doing their own laundry entailed. Bancroft had laundry service as well as maid service. Even though Payne and my mother were providing me with plenty of spending money for the services, I preferred to clean my own room and do my own laundry.

My first class was small, with only about fifteen people. It was a big change from my last public school, where you would have almost thirty kids in a class. And there were no individual desks. The class was held at a large rectangular conference table with comfortable leather chairs. The teacher sat at the head of the table, and everything was done on tablets, which were ours to keep for the semester.

"Can you believe this place?" I whispered toward the end of class.

"I know, it's insane," Clover responded.

Mr. Dornan looked up at us. "Do you two have a question?"

The entire class looked our way, and I nudged Clover under the table.

"No, sir," she replied. "We just thought it's nice to have everything on a tablet."

The boy next to Clover raised his eyebrows. "You didn't at your old school?"

She pointed at him. "Dear, what's your name?"

"Eric."

"Dear Eric," she repeated insincerely, "not all schools have the financial capacity to offer tablets to everybody."

"I guess," he said as he looked away from her.

The bell chimed then, indicating class was over in two minutes. Mr. Dornan assigned us a chapter to read and dismissed us. So far, no one was unkind to me, but the tension was still there with how they wouldn't directly address me unless necessary. Gideon would need to do some damage control if he ever wanted to get me in his bed.

~

GIDEON AND JAXSON were in our trigonometry class. Gideon gave me a subtle smile when I walked into class. Unlike English, this class had assigned seating, and because our last names were close together, I was placed next to Gideon. Clover was sitting next to Jaxson, who was on the other side of Gideon, and all together, we were two seats from the teacher.

"Will you be all right sitting next to him?" Clover asked behind their shoulders.

I nodded silently. *I want to be next to him. I want him to touch me.*

As mean as Gideon had been all summer, I couldn't exactly explain why I was this excited by his presence. After I settled in my seat, he immediately put his hand on my knee and slid it up to my inner thigh. I bit my tongue to keep from moaning. As before, he gently kneaded my flesh, causing me to grow wet.

The only difference between yesterday and today was the barrier. Yesterday I was wearing jean shorts; today, the only barrier between his fingers and my slick clit was a thin piece of lace. If he touched me there, I would burst into flame right here in front of the class.

Once Mrs. Ordonez started to speak, I fixed my eyes on my tablet, trying not to draw attention to myself, but Gideon's fingers shifted and drew closer until they were pressed up against the panel of my panties. Clenching my jaw, I was sure they were soaked since the ache between my legs had become unbearable. I shot him a cautionary glance, but he didn't pay attention.

When his pinkie stroked upward, I almost cried out as my tablet slipped from my hand, clattering on the table. Everyone looked at me, and my face grew red—my heart thumping in my chest.

"I'm sorry," I said.

Clover leaned forward and stared at me. I shook my head, and she went back to concentrate on her tablet. Gideon took that moment to press harder, moving his pinkie back and forth in steady swipes. If he continued, I would come in front of our whole math class. Trying to control my breathing, I pretended to bend down and scratch my leg as I slipped my hand under my skirt to grip his wrist.

Gideon doubled his efforts, even with me trying to stop him before we got caught. He was much stronger than me, and not taking a hint; he continued to stroke me. I was thankful his hand was hidden by my skirt because as he sent me closer to the edge, my desire blanked out my efforts. Letting out a breath, I spread my legs a little wider, allowing him better access. Once I removed my hand, I almost passed out when he snaked a finger under the panel.

He groaned at my wetness and covered it up with a cough. Speeding up the movement of his finger, he flicked and then pressed harder until, right in front of the class, I broke apart. I gripped my tablet so hard I thought I would break it. As I came down, I tried to discreetly glance around us. No one at the table seemed to have a clue that Gideon just got me off.

He slowly pulled his hand out, pretending to bite his nail as he tasted me from his finger. While I recovered, he spent the rest of the class with his finger near his nose, inhaling my scent.

I wasn't a stranger to getting off. I had boyfriends before and even shared classes with them, but they never touched me during them. Gideon was expectedly bold, and I was powerless to stop him because I wanted him to keep touching me. He might have weakened me, but I had to remind myself that even though things were complicated, I couldn't let him control me.

"THAT WAS A DIRTY TRICK," I hissed as we rose from the table.

Gideon smirked at me and stepped away to talk to Jaxson while I turned to Clover.

"Will you be okay by yourself?" she asked.

"You mean in Spanish?"

"Yeah?"

"And suppose I'm not? You can't come with me."

She nodded. "You're right. But if anyone tries shit, you let me know." She flicked her eyes to Gideon.

"He won't," I whispered.

"I have to get going, but something fishy is going on here. I don't know what, but I'll figure it out."

I laughed weakly. "You're so suspicious."

Following behind a small group, I walked out of the building and spied Gideon, surrounded by a few people, including several girls. A pang of irritation struck me at how they tried to press up against him even though I didn't know why I was jealous because he wasn't mine, and if he didn't follow my rules, there would be no us.

I kept my head down, passing by them as I headed for the building next door. My seventh class would be Spanish, and then one more class with Clover would finish out the day. I was sure I could manage by myself for this one. I hurried to the bathroom to wipe myself dry before then. It likely wouldn't have mattered since my panties were probably too soaked to be salvaged. When I came out of the stall, Gideon stood against the wall near the door.

I ignored him as some girls leaving the bathroom yelled at him to get out. After I washed my hands and looked up into the mirror, Gideon was standing behind me.

"You're so sweet. I can't wait to put my mouth on you."

I sucked in my breath. "You can't be in here."

"I locked the door, and if we had time, I would fuck you."

I wiped my hands on my skirt and turned to him, our chests nearly touching. "I wouldn't let you, and who said I'm giving you my V card? You think I would want to lose it in a dirty bathroom?"

Gideon laughed and kissed the tip of my nose. "You will give it to me, and that's a promise."

"Are we still talking later tonight?" I asked, bypassing his 'promise.'

His seemingly regretful expression told me he couldn't.

"I have a weight session with the trainer. I won't be back until after eight."

"Why can't we talk then?"

"We'll see."

The bell giving the two-minute warning sounded as I went to reply, but he cut me off as he pressed his mouth against mine and tugged at my ponytail. He groaned before he pulled away.

"Time for class."

"But, Gideon," I pouted, feeling lightheaded.

"We'll be late; now go."

I grabbed my backpack from the floor, turned the lock on the door, and slipped out. I sat in my chair just as the second bell went off. Gideon hurried in the door shortly after.

"Nice of you to join us, Señor Berne," Mrs. Dolan said.

He gave a sheepish look as he took his seat on the opposite side of the table from me. I was thankful he wasn't near me because I didn't think I could handle another public orgasm.

CHAPTER 14

Gideon

As the day drew on, Avery's scent faded from my fingers. I took a chance with getting her off in front of the class, but it was well worth the risk to give her some pleasure. I had a lot to make up for after what I did to her.

Once classes were over, I went back to the dorm to change for practice. By five, I would be back here, take a quick shower, nap, get dinner, and then weight train. I wanted to talk to Avery, but it would probably turn into something physical if she let me.

My phone rang as I dropped my backpack on the floor.

Checking the ID, I picked up, saying, "Hey, dad, how is Paris?"

"Beautiful. How are you settling in?"

"Fine. Football is fine, classes are fine."

"And are you treating Avery with respect?" he asked, his voice a warning.

I toed off my shoes, rolling my eyes. *If by respect you mean getting her off in math class, then yes.*

"Of course. I told you I would."

"I hope so," he replied. "Avery was very upset with your behavior, and so were your stepmother and me. I don't want *any* problems, Gideon."

"Dad, I get it," I emphasized. "We're getting along fine. I have to get changed for practice."

I shrugged out of my jacket and unbuttoned my shirt with one hand.

"How is football?" he asked.

"Great. No competition this year."

"Have you considered playing at Yale?" he continued.

"No. I want to devote my time to studying."

No matter how much he asked, I wanted a life, and college football would consume too much of my free time. Once early November came, I wouldn't be playing football ever again. I wanted to date, hang out, and enjoy what college had to offer. My father didn't get that.

"You can do both," he kept going. "Think hard."

"I will. I have to go. Tell Renata I said hello, and enjoy your honeymoon."

"Thank you."

Our conversation exhausted me. My father always wanted to push me into activities I wasn't interested in pursuing—just like how he tried to force me to eventually work for him. Each time it was brought up, I didn't know if I wanted to or do something on my own.

My door burst open, revealing Avery with the doorknob in her hand. I smirked as I stood up and tossed my shirt on the bed. She slammed the door shut as I worked on my belt.

"That was a dirty trick you did today. How embarrassing!" she cried.

"It was dirty, but I'm not sure how much of a trick it was."

I slowly unzipped my pants and pushed them down my hips. Avery licked her lips and fixed her eyes on the bulge in my underwear.

"Did you come here to yell at me or for something else?" I asked smugly.

She swallowed noisily. "To yell at you."

"Are you sure?" I said.

I hooked my fingers in the waistband of my underwear and slid them down a couple of inches.

"I've seen it before," she tried playing off but failed.

Lowering my voice, I said, "Avery, that was nothing. Just wait. You'll scream when I give it to you. I want to hear you as you take every inch. And another thing, I won't be gentle."

She visibly shuddered and leaned against the door as I divested myself of my underwear. My dick was big without an erection, and as she stared at my crotch, I stirred.

"Go before I forget practice and make you wish I went."

She turned and grasped the doorknob. "Are we discussing things tonight?"

"I'd rather fuck you."

Avery whipped around. "Why do you always feel the need to shock me?"

I winked at her. "Because I can."

"Asshole," she mumbled as she slipped out of my room.

"Lift, I got you," Drake said.

I arched my back and pushed hard, lifting the weights out of the cradle. I did several pumps before my arms became like Jello, and I dropped the bar back down. I was at the end of my session and maybe looking forward to leaving.

Drake patted me on the shoulder. "You did well."

"I'll sleep like a baby after two hours of practice and this."

"We could've done this later after you had some rest."

I shook my head. The room was almost empty except for a guy from the soccer team working his legs.

"It wouldn't work with my schedule," I complained. "I have homework already."

He pursed his lips. "Already? It's the first day of class."

"That's Bancroft—preparing us for the future."

Drake sat down on the weight bench across from me while I removed my weight belt and wiped the sweat from my face.

"You thought anything about playing at Yale?" he asked.

I barely kept from rolling my eyes. "Who told you to ask? My father?"

"He thinks you can be successful at a higher level."

I wrapped my small towel around my neck. "He wants a lot of things. I don't want to be bogged down with sports in college."

My father would keep pushing until I agreed. I know he spoke to Coach Martin at Yale about a possible starting job at quarterback. The guy they had for the upcoming year was a senior graduating early in December.

"Some guys change their minds when they get to school," Drake replied. "They miss the competition."

I stood up. "I'll have enough with classes. The answer is no, and I would appreciate it if you wouldn't champion my father's cause."

He rose and slapped my arm. "I'm just asking. I didn't mean to upset you."

"I'm out. I have a bunch of things to do tonight."

I threw my weight belt over my shoulder and walked out of the training facility that could rival a college program. Bancroft spared no expense for the blue bloods of the world, and it reflected in our tuition. Once I got in my car, I blasted the air conditioner to ward off the heat of the evening.

It was almost September, but the hot summer temperatures

persisted. The campus was busy with students hanging out on the lawns or blasting music from their rooms. By eight, it would be quiet as study hours kicked in. I planned to shower, eat dinner, and talk with Avery. What I really wanted to do was fuck her, but the dorm was no place for what I desired to do now that Clover was her roommate.

My bed looked inviting as I stepped inside, but I had a schedule to keep. I wasn't worried about homework since it was my senior year, and I was already accepted to Yale. I wished I could move ahead a year and not put up with this bullshit, especially when football was losing its luster.

I stripped my sweat-soaked clothing off, dropping them on the floor before I turned the shower on. Stepping in before it warmed, I soaped up, thinking of a breathless Avery this afternoon in trig class, which made my dick grow hard. I stroked myself, wishing she was kneeling before me so I could coat her face and neck with come.

She still didn't have an idea about what was in store for her. Our sex life wouldn't be as simple as gentle fucks. I wanted to tear her in two. Tying her to the bed and teasing her until she screamed also wasn't out of the question.

Thinking it over, my father and Renata's bedroom was on the other side of the house, but even if they were home, they wouldn't hear Avery. And back when she moved in, I used the excuse of her being new to the area and house as to why her room needed to be next to mine. In the end, her room near mine turned out to be better than I had originally planned.

My real reason was the pass-through. The minute I met her, I knew she had to be mine. I wouldn't let anyone else touch her, and when I brought up my plan to the boys, they thought it included them. It didn't. Avery Bedford was mine, and I wouldn't share the way I'd done with others.

I grunted her name as thick jets of cum shot from my cock, slapping the shower floor with a thwacking noise. As I finished,

I stabilized my shaky legs by propping my body against the tiled wall. Once it passed, I shut off the water and wrapped a towel around my waist.

I was pulling on a pair of shorts when a knock at the door disturbed me.

"What?" I called out.

Remy shoved the door open so hard the knob hit the wall. He was drinking from a silver flask.

"Are you out of your fucking mind?" I demanded.

He laughed. "It's apple juice," he said.

I lowered my voice. "Yeah, probably spiked with vodka."

Remy kicked the door closed and jumped on my bed, taking another swig of whatever the flask held.

"It's a school night. I had a shot of tequila, but that's it."

I was irked by his intrusion. I wasn't interested in his musings of the day. Remy had a way of annoying me with his impeccable timing when it came to ruining my plans. Sometimes it felt like all he wanted to do was one-up me.

"Why drink at all?" I argued. "We have a long season ahead."

"Something to loosen me up. I had a rough day."

I snorted. "By pretending to have a cramp in your calf?"

He frowned. "I needed a rest. You were fine with Cranston."

"Cranston sucks as a lineman. If it were a hitting drill, I would've been slammed to the ground three times," I snapped.

Remy sat up. "You need to get laid. I think your lack of sex is going to your brain. Why wait for *that* hot little pussy when you can have any girl here?"

"Because I need to finish the game." *And I need to fuck her like I need air to breathe.*

"When do we get a taste again?" Remy asked.

I wanted to crack him in the mouth. He was constantly sucking off my leftovers as if that made him a big man.

"When I'm finished?" I challenged. "Aren't you fucking around with Clover?"

He tipped back the flask and finished what was inside, wiping his mouth with the back of his hand. "I need something to occupy my time until I get my chance with Avery. Besides, Clover is a kinky little bitch. I might just give up waiting and keep her."

I smirked, swallowing my anger. "You finally decided to date someone?"

"She isn't like the stuck-up vanilla sex girls we have here," he explained. "All they want is to have me lead. Clover takes charge, and I like that."

"Why don't you do me a favor and keep her occupied tonight?"

He narrowed his eyes. "Why?"

"Avery."

I didn't need to elaborate. Remy knew it was a critical time for me to set the wheels in motion for playtime since our parents were in Europe. What he didn't know was that I already had a foothold in her bed. I'd already got her off and addicted.

"You know you're bordering on a stalker behavior," he said.

"Maybe, but she ain't telling anyone. So will you help me out?"

"When?"

"Now, I guess. Take Clover to your room so I can pay Avery a little visit."

He capped the flask and got up. "I could use a little pussy tonight."

"Then pussy away."

He bounced out the door, and I grabbed my phone to text Avery.

Care to talk?

A: Clover.

Remy will take care of her. I can come to you.

A: Are you fucking crazy? Suppose she comes in and sees you?

Then come to me and wear something sexy.

A: We're just talking. I'm not fucking you.

I SMILED EVEN though Avery couldn't see me. What she didn't realize was that if I wanted to fuck her, I would seduce her until she asked me to do it.

I promise not to touch you unless you ask.

A: Idiot.

Does that mean you'll come?

A: As soon as I can.

I RAN around the room to straighten it up, tossing my workout clothes into the hamper I had in the corner. Next, I smoothed the covers on the bed and adjusted the air conditioner, so the room wasn't as cold. I would never go through this trouble with any girl other than Avery.

Five minutes later, she was knocking at the door. I opened it and pulled her inside, flipping the lock before I buried my face in her hair. She smelled of freesias and lavender. I wrapped my arms tighter around Avery, pulling her against my chest. She didn't struggle.

"We're just talking," she murmured against my skin. "I thought you had weight training. It's only seven."

I held her tighter. "I skipped dinner and trained right after practice."

Avery gently pushed against me, and I let her go.

"You can't skip dinner," she lectured gently. "You'll get sick.

I chuckled and led her to the bed. "I thought you hated me."

We sat down, as she replied, "I don't hate you. I hate your behavior. I hate what you did to me," she said harshly.

"Did you hate what I did to you this afternoon?"

She ducked her head down and wouldn't look at me. "If I say I did, I'm stupid."

"Avery, why would you say that?" I stroked her back.

"Because I let you do it."

I leaned closer to press my mouth against her ear. "And you liked it. You spread your legs for me."

"If you were anyone else-" her voice trailed off.

I finished her sentence, asking, "You would report me for sexual assault?"

"No."

I moved away and placed my back against the wall while Avery sat up near my pillows.

"Because I'm your stepbrother?"

"Should that matter?"

"I guess not."

"I wouldn't because I wanted it. I thought you were sweet until you weren't."

Once more, I closed the distance to her and took her hand. "Darling Avery, I'm anything but sweet."

My heart was pounding in my chest, and despite the coolness of the room, I was sweating like a freshman on their first date. I was never like this—ever.

She fixed her gaze on mine. "But you will be with me, right? I decided to go home this weekend. I'm leaving after the game."

I quirked an eyebrow. "My game?"

"Yes. I don't want to spend my birthday here."

I frowned. "Wait, what?" I squeezed her hand and pulled her closer to me.

"My eighteenth birthday is on Saturday."

That pissed me off. Our parents must have known her birthday was on Saturday, and they couldn't wait a week before they left for their honeymoon. At least I got a cake and a car from them before they did.

"Jesus Christ," I spat out. "You're going home to spend your birthday alone?"

She shook her head. "Clover is coming with me. My mom might hate her, but she can't say anything about it because she's across the pond."

"I'm coming with you," I insisted. "I'll have the guys come with me, and we'll celebrate."

Avery shook her head. "No, if you come, I just want you and Clover."

I threw my head back and laughed. "How is that going to work? Clover hates me, and if I'm home with you, she'll keep me away from you."

She put her head on my shoulder as if resigned. "Right."

"We'll figure something out," I reassured. "I might have to bring *Remy* home with me to keep her busy."

"She likes him."

I kissed the top of her head, and then she lifted her face, offering her lips. I pressed mine to hers, my stomach in a knot, and pulled her under me as she gave in. I thrust my tongue into her mouth, and when hers met mine, I grasped her hair tightly to keep her from pulling away. In response, Avery dug her nails into my skin. I broke from her lips and made a wet trail to the hollow in her throat.

"I didn't come here to fuck," she whispered.

I hovered over her. "Avery, I want to give you a birthday present this weekend."

She shuddered under me. "What is it?"

"I'm taking your V card."

Avery reached up to pet my cheek. "Shouldn't that be my decision?"

"Do you want to give it to me?"

"Do you deserve to take it?" she quickly returned.

I pecked her lips. "I promise to make up for my shitty behavior. All of it."

"That's a lot of stuff to make up for."

I pursed my lips. "I know, and I'm sorry. Would you like a little preview?"

"Gideon, you gave me a preview this afternoon, but do me a favor; don't do that again."

Ignoring the order, I dipped down and kissed her cleavage, sliding my tongue between her breasts. She gasped, and I moved to her left breast, sucking her nipple into my mouth through her shirt.

She pushed at my face. "Don't. I can't walk down the hall with a wet shirt."

"Then let me see them."

"You're already hard," she noted. "I don't think you need to see them and make it worse."

I put my weight on her, moving my hips so she could feel my cock against her belly. "I'm already there."

Without pause, I kept gyrating my pelvis against hers before sliding lower until I hit the right spot, my cock against her clit. I thrust hard, and she cried out, exciting me further.

"Gideon," she panted.

"Avery, you want to come. Say it. You're thinking about what I did to you this afternoon."

She whimpered and mewled. Her eyes were shut tight, and her hands were on either side of my hips, gripping tight.

"Tell me, darling Avery. Tell me you want to come, or I'll stop."

Her lips moved, but no sound came out, and I stopped.

"Nooo," she protested.

I grinned wickedly. "No, you want me to stop, or do you want me to continue?"

"Dammit, Gideon," she said through gritted teeth.

I slowly slid against her, and she once again cried out.

"Tell me before I pull off your shorts and eat your pussy until you scream. Everyone in the dorm will hear you," I threatened. "The walls are not as thick as you think."

Her eyes flew open and widened. "You wouldn't."

I shrugged. "I don't want to because I want to wait until this weekend when we have plenty of privacy."

She didn't speak, and as much as I wanted to stay where I was, I began to shift to kneel between her legs.

"Make me come," Avery whined.

"Make yourself come. I want to see you do it. I want to hear your moans and see your beautiful face when you come without fourteen other people in the room."

"Bastard," she growled.

I ran my fingers over her soft thighs. "Darling Avery."

"Why do you call me that?"

"Because it suits you."

"It's kind of creepy, but I like it."

I chuckled. "Are we done?" I leaned back against the wall, occupying my previous spot, and she sat up with a dissatisfied look on her face. I was sure she was as hot and bothered as I was. There was no doubt she would be in my thoughts as I later relieved myself of the gigantic set of blue balls I had right now.

"Creepy?" I asked.

"Not in a bad way?" she tried to explain.

Dismissing that, I instead kept my mind on one thing. "Make yourself come, Avery."

A crimson blush crept up her neck. She was beautiful, with her cheeks pink with embarrassment. She averted her gaze from mine.

"No."

"Why not? Should we do it together?"

Her eyes immediately shot up to mine. "Together?" she questioned.

Excitement charged through my chest. How erotic it would be for her to get off while I did. When I watched her touch herself that night at home, I finished in my bedroom, but here we would be fulfilling my fantasy of doing it together. I would be able to see her every expression and gauge her emotions as I stroked and came.

"Yes," I said as I hooked my fingers in my shorts.

Avery once again averted her gaze. She was playing a cute little game with me because I could tell she was curious. Of course, she'd seen my dick before in passing because I had been setting her up for this moment. But it was no longer a game of back and forth. I wanted her in a much more intimate capacity.

"Together?" she repeated.

"Do you want me to help like I did this afternoon?" I offered.

The crimson grew deeper on her cheeks as she thought about what I'd done—what *we* did in front of everyone. Her fingers twitched, and she paused on the button of her sexy cutoffs, which had framed her beautiful ass.

"Maybe we should wait."

Disappointment bubbled in my chest as I realized there would be no mutual satisfaction tonight. It would have to wait for this weekend. I removed my thumbs from the waistband of my shorts.

I tried to keep the dismay out of my voice by consoling myself with the upcoming weekend. I *would* get what I had craved for the past three months. Her. It wouldn't only be a birthday present for her, but a late one for me.

"Kiss me," I ordered.

Avery obediently got up and crawled over to me. It was almost too much to bear to see her on all fours as visions of my dick buried inside her danced in my head. What a wonderful sight it would be when it happened.

She pressed her lips to mine, and I pulled her onto my lap by wrapping my arms around her. Everything about her turned me on down to the tiny moans she made when I thrust my tongue into her mouth and roughly cupped her breast in my big hand. She was perfect in every way.

CHAPTER 15

Avery

"Why does he need to come home?" Clover asked, clearly unconvinced.

I folded a shirt and shoved it into my duffel bag. "Because he wants to celebrate my birthday. It will be me, you, Remy, and Gideon. The whole house to ourselves."

"Then we should invite some people from Arlington; remember, your friends?"

"I live on the other side of town," I argued weakly.

She frowned and put her hands on her hips. "So? I'm not understanding what your problem is."

The problem was the more people who came to my birthday, the less time I would have with Gideon. It would take hours to get everyone out, and even though my eighteenth birthday was a milestone, I wasn't in the mood to share it with too many people.

"It's not my house. I don't want people running around and

making a mess. Four people is enough."

Clover threw some clothes in her bag. "Invite Duncan."

"Dunc?" I choked out.

Duncan Jennings was the last boyfriend I had at Arlington. It ended just before I moved and switched schools because he got pissed that we wouldn't be sharing our senior year together. During the summer, he called and texted. I always kept the conversations light because he hurt me when he broke it off. He was the first guy I let go down on me, and even with his mouth, he was nothing compared to Gideon's hands.

"Yeah, Dunc," she mimicked. "Let him see what he gave up."

"He already knows. He wants me back, but I'm not interested. He dumped me simply because I was moving to the other side of town."

She shrugged. "He's still hot, and you're not getting any from the guys at Bancroft."

"I don't want any from the guys at Bancroft."

Except for the one guy who's my evil stepbrother and makes me wet every time he touches me or gives me one of his smoldering stares.

She chuckled. "I do."

"Ugh, you're impossible. I think you have Remy wound around your finger already."

"I had him the first time he kissed me."

"Was your hand on his dick?" I deadpanned.

Clover smirked. "I resemble that remark."

I finished packing and closed my duffel bag. My mother had purchased a set of Louis Vuitton suitcases before I left for school, but I much preferred my duffel bags. They were easy to pack and throw over my shoulder.

"Yeah, you do."

She threw a ball of socks at me, and I slapped it away. "So, remind me why we have to go to the football game?"

I tried not to react to the fact that I had to lie—again.

"Because I promised my mother I would. She wants me to play nice with Gideon."

Clover snorted. "Oh, like he plays nice with you? He's an asshole."

He will play nice tomorrow when he gives me his birthday present.

"Can we not?" I asked. "I don't want any arguments this weekend. I want to enjoy my birthday."

"Then invite some people over and get with Dunc."

"Not interested."

"Do we *seriously* have to wait for the end of the game?" Clover asked.

It was the third quarter, and Bancroft was beating Philips Academy by thirty-five points. I promised Gideon I would stay until the end of the game, and then we would leave for the two-hour trip right after.

I nodded.

She shoved some popcorn in her mouth and pretended to cheer when Gideon threw a pass to Xavier for another touchdown. My stepbrother raised his hands in the air and looked up into the stands. I liked to think he was searching for me, which was why I didn't want to leave early.

Over the past few days, we had shared some stolen kisses, but he stayed away from me for the most part and didn't touch me again in trig class after Monday. I guessed he was building up anticipation for the weekend—tension that kept my stomach in flip-flops.

"Can we please go?" Clover whined.

"Oh God, you're such a pain in the ass. The answer is no."

She huffed. "I wish I brought my own car."

"I promise my chef will make you anything you want when we get back."

Before she could respond, I cheered when Jaxson intercepted the ball as the third quarter ended. One more quarter to go. By the time the game was over, it was nearing 10 pm, and I wanted to get home before midnight. I expected Gideon would be home even later.

"Let's go," I said, nearly vibrating.

The crowd began to head toward the exits, and we pushed our way through until we hit the field level. Gideon was walking by the fence as he headed for the locker room. Catching his gaze, I winked at him, and because Clover wasn't paying attention, he puckered his lips in a kiss.

My core tightened, and I let out a soft moan, but no one heard in the crowd. Clover pulled me along, and we hurried to the furthest parking lot, where I parked before the game. We practically ran to the car once we broke from the crowd and were onto the main road before most of the traffic.

Although I wasn't used to driving in the dark, I wasn't afraid. I was more worried that Gideon would be exhausted by the time he left and would fall asleep as he drove. He promised to let Remy drive if he felt sleepy, but knowing him; he'd probably refuse to anyway.

Clover played with my Sirius Radio by pressing the track indicator over and over to try to find some top 40 stations she liked.

"Hey, you're gonna break it," I finally cut in. "Choose something."

"There's nothing on."

I laughed. "It has hundreds of channels."

Clover cracked on a piece of gum she'd unwrapped at the start of the ride. "Not the kind I like."

I sighed in frustration. "Find something," I said through gritted teeth.

Despite claiming that the music was important, Clover fell asleep about twenty minutes into our ride, leaving me with my thoughts. My birthday was tomorrow, and my stomach was already in knots. I expected my mother to call me to wish me a happy birthday, which just reminded me of how angry it made me that she couldn't wait a week to go on her honeymoon. It wasn't every day your daughter turned eighteen!

And besides my mother and Payne, I didn't want to celebrate my birthday with anyone other than Gideon. I was falling for him, and it was probably stupid of me since he owed me for his horrible treatment. Several times it crossed my mind to ask him why. He didn't even know me, and he treated me like I was trash.

My cell rang, and Jonathan popped up on the screen. I'd put Gideon's phone number under that name because I didn't want anyone to know I was talking to him. If Clover knew, she would try to talk some sense into me, but I didn't want that. I wanted him. I let the call go to voicemail since the car was set for Bluetooth-connected calls. He called once more, and again it went to voicemail.

"Where are we?" Clover asked as she woke and rubbed at her eyes.

"About ten minutes from my house."

She yawned. "Do I get my own room?"

I put my blinker on and got into the exit lane.

"I thought you wanted to sleep in my room."

"You snore."

I was indignant. "I do not!"

She chuckled. "You talk in your sleep."

"Liar," I said as I stopped at the bottom of the exit lane. "What's the real reason?"

"Remy is sleeping over."

I slapped her arm before I turned onto Charles Avenue.

"You would take him over your best friend?"

Rather than answering, I watched Clover look at her watch and started counting down out loud from ten, nine, eight....

"Happy birthday!" she screamed.

I jumped in my seat. "Oh my God, don't do that!" I yelled as I realized the clock on the dash had changed to midnight.

Calming down, we turned down my road and onto the long driveway which led to Berne Manor. Even though I hated how big the place was, at least it was much quieter than the dorms.

"Are you hungry?" I asked as I pulled up to the gate and punched in the code.

Clover yawned. "Fuck food. I need a long nap before Remy gets here."

I shook my head as I drove up the circular driveway to park in front of the house. Since Gideon and I were the only two home, I decided to skip the garage.

A KISS on my cheek woke me, and before I opened my eyes, I knew it was Gideon. His citrusy cologne filled my nose, and I felt the heat of his body against mine. My lids fluttered open to find him kneeling by my bed with a giant grin on his face, illuminated by my Arlington Tigers nightlight.

"What time is it?" I mumbled.

He kissed me again. "1:30 am. I just got home. Remy is with Clover."

I turned on my back, and the sheet pulled away, revealing the lacy white thong I purposefully put on earlier in the day. Gideon sucked in his breath and ran his fingers over the fabric.

"I wanted to be the first one to wish you a happy birthday," he said in a lazy drawl.

I smiled up at him. "Clover beat you to it."

"Shit. I wanted to be first."

"Is that why you called earlier?"

Lowering himself, he latched onto my ear and sucked the lobe, his hot breath fanning down my neck. "I called to find out if you were okay. It was cloudy tonight, and the road was dark. Why didn't you answer?"

"Clover. I didn't want her to hear our conversation."

Gideon moved his hand up to my exposed stomach and began to draw little circles on my skin, sending shivers down my spine. Since it was my birthday, I wondered if he was planning on giving me my gift now or in the evening.

"Avery, I'd like to sleep with you."

"I'm tired," I teased.

He brushed my hair off my cheek. "I didn't say sex; I said sleep."

The closest I'd come to sleeping with a guy was Duncan. His parents weren't home, and I had told my mother I was spending the night at a cheerleader's sleepover, which I was supposed to go to later anyway, and we ended up fooling around in his room.

In the end though, we fell asleep in his bed, half-naked, where his mother almost caught us at 2 am. Just before she could, I ended up sneaking over to my friend Debbie's house, where the sleepover was happening, and slipped through the basement window.

"Suppose Clover comes in?" I asked, breathless.

"She won't, I promise. Remy is keeping her occupied."

Too tired to imagine Clover might barge in, and after having my sleep interrupted, I just wanted to sleep and agreed. "Fine."

Gideon rose and removed his t-shirt, tossing it on my desk chair. He climbed over me and pulled the sheet over us. I turned on my side, and he rested his hand on my hip while tucking his head on my shoulder.

"Darling Avery, I hope you're ready for tonight," he purred. "I have plans for you."

Even though I'd been hit by a rush of ideas of what we might do seconds earlier, a sudden anxiousness crept into my chest, and I found it hard to breathe. I swallowed hard.

"What plans?" I whispered.

He bit my earlobe and then licked the rim. "So many. I expect you will follow what I tell you to do."

"Don't hurt me," I almost cried.

He rolled away and pushed me to my back. "Avery, I would never hurt you. I promise you'll love everything I give to you. Don't be afraid."

Gideon pressed his lips hard to mine, bruising them. One of his hands roamed my body, brushing over the peaked nipples of my breasts, tickling my belly, and resting on the waistband of my panties. I held my breath, but he went no further as he rested his head on my shoulder.

"Go to sleep, darling Avery."

I didn't protest. Even though I was so physically turned on that if he asked to fuck me, I might've said yes, I was still trying to force myself to relax.

~

WHEN I WOKE, Gideon was no longer in bed with me. It had been a long time since I slept so well. I lazily rose and checked my phone, looking forward to the last day of August. The weather was going to be beautiful—sunny and in the eighties. I entered the kitchen to find Remy, Clover, and Gideon sitting at the table eating pancakes, bacon, and biscuits.

"Thanks for waiting for me," I huffed.

"Stop griping; there's plenty for you," Clover said.

When she and Remy went back to their plates of food, Gideon pinned me with his stare and seductively licked his lips.

"I hope you're not having any of your shitty friends from Arlington over," Gideon said.

Right away, I knew it was an act. He was playing a role in throwing Clover off the scent. I had no idea if Remy knew what was really going on between Gideon and me, but if he did, he wasn't saying.

I took my seat by Clover and, matching his tone, replied, "Shut up, Gideon. Why do you always have to be such a jerk? Maybe you can be nice as a birthday present to me."

He shoved a mouthful of pancakes in his mouth and smiled. Gideon didn't say anything else to me during breakfast and instead rambled about the football game. The only time he acknowledged me was to run his bare foot up my leg under the table, causing my skin to break out in goosebumps.

"Are we partying today?" Clover asked.

"If by partying you mean spending time by the pool, then yes," I responded, trying to keep my voice level.

"No, I mean having a party," she corrected.

"I said no," I replied more strongly. "I just want to relax and spend the day sunning myself."

Clover bit her lip. "Don't be mad at me."

I frowned, and Gideon looked up from his plate.

"Why?" I snapped.

"I invited a few people over," she said sheepishly.

I stopped eating. "*What* people and *how* many?"

"A few girls from the cheerleading squad and some of your guy friends."

There weren't many people I wanted to see from Arlington since many people I used to hang out with were pissed. I left like it was my choice. I wanted to stay, but I felt betrayed they would treat me that way, and Gideon didn't make it any better when I got here.

"Ten," Clover clarified. "Come on; we'll have fun."

"Yeah, Jaxson and Xavier are coming by. I'm sure they'll love to meet some of your cheerleading friends."

I pushed my plate away, no longer hungry. I was just about to stalk off, but my cell rang.

"Hi, mom," I said upon answering.

"Happy birthday, Avery!" she shouted in my ear. "I'm sorry we couldn't be there. I'm sure you'll have fun with your friends at school."

I rolled my eyes, annoyed that she was probably trying to make herself feel less guilty for leaving me.

"I came home," I said. "I needed a break."

"You're home? By yourself?" she said with surprise.

"No," I bit out. "Gideon is here with his friend Remy."

Clover waved her hand and pointed at herself, but I shook my head. If I told my mother she was here, she would flip. Eventually, she would not only find out that Clover was at Bancroft, but she was my roommate. I couldn't wait for that conversation.

"I wanted to sit out by the pool and relax," I explained. "Bancroft is hard."

"If you want to attend a good school, you need to get used to working hard," she said, not catching my point.

Our conversation was getting too deep, and it was too early to discuss it.

"I get that," I said a little harsher than I meant to.

"Don't take that tone with me," my mother growled.

"Mom, can we talk about this when you get home?"

She hesitated. "I guess so. I should go. Payne is taking me for tea."

I looked at the peeling pink polish on my fingernails. All she seemed to care about was her good time.

"Well, enjoy," I replied blankly. "I'll talk to you later."

"There's a gift for you in Payne's office on his desk," she added. "I hope you like it."

"Thank you."

"I love you, Avery. Payne says happy birthday."

"Thank him for me," I said stiffly, feeling empty as the call disconnected.

"What did she say?" Clover asked.

I took a final sip of my orange juice. "I don't want to discuss it."

"Damn. Well, we're heading to the pool."

She rose from the table, kissed the top of my head, and walked off to the pool with Remy following her like a little puppy dog. My birthday was turning into shit. Wanting to get it over with, I wondered what she got me, but before I rose from the table, Gideon's hand shot out and grabbed my wrist.

"I'm sorry," he said knowingly. "Parents can be crappy."

I pulled away from him. The chair scraped on the Terrazzo floor as I got up and went to Payne's office—a place I normally didn't venture into. It was set up to be typically fitting of my stepfather, with plenty of leather, bookcases, and a large mahogany desk. Approaching, I found a small box wrapped in colorful birthday-themed paper on the desk with a card underneath it.

Before I could read it, I heard the door click and turned around to find Gideon standing there with a grim look on his face. He said nothing as he approached and embraced me.

"I don't want you to be sad," he said gruffly.

I pressed my face against his bare muscular chest, inhaling his fresh-from-a-shower scent.

"I'm angry," I muttered.

"Don't be. I've learned I'm not their priority, and I can deal with it. You'll get used to it." Gideon kissed my head, and I stroked the muscular planes of his back.

"Gideon?" I prompted.

"Hmm?"

"Why were you so mean to me when I got here?"

He tightened his hold on me. "You want to have this conversation today?"

I did, and I didn't. I was afraid of the answer. I feared his behavior because he'd made it clear so many times before that he thought I would never be good enough, but now I wasn't sure if it had been an act or if he believed it.

Settling on a decision, I replied, "Not really."

"Then let's have it another time. I promise to tell you the truth."

"When do I get my birthday present?" I asked, switching topics to distract myself and hopefully him.

He gently pushed me back and caught my gaze. "You already know what it is."

"And it seems like it's more a present for you than me," I leveled.

"You'll thank me after it's over, trust me."

I giggled nervously. "You're so sure of yourself?"

"I've had plenty of practice, darling Avery."

I bit my lip. "What about the begging for it part?"

"You will."

I trembled, thinking of all the possibilities for how he would manage to get me to beg.

CHAPTER 16

Gideon

I could positively kill Clover Delahunt. At noontime, the buzzer on the gate started going off like a church bell. She invited fifteen people for Avery's birthday, and my stepsister was none too happy. I didn't want to share this day with other people, and neither had she.

I wanted it to pass with a meal, a cake, and seduction. Putting on a front on her default politeness, Avery made the rounds with snacks and tacos Chef Hawkins prepared.

Everywhere Avery went, I tracked her. On her ankle, she wore the thin rope chain her mother and Payne bought her for her birthday, which had factored into my plans the second she put it on. I planned to strip her bare until it was the only thing she wore.

Jaxson, Xavier, and I were sitting at poolside table in the corner, shaded under an umbrella, while Remy frolicked in the pool with Clover. The more he hung out with her, the bigger disappointment he became because it looked like he was falling for her. The boys didn't fall for women, though it hadn't taken me long to figure out how easily I could fall for Avery. I was a hypocrite, but no one knew.

My hackles rose when two *boys* entered the pool area, one tall with sandy hair and the other short and stocky. The tall one approached Avery and kissed her on the cheek before sitting on the lounger next to her. She fidgeted, which I knew the action to be her anxiety rising, and looked in my direction. I couldn't see her eyes, but it was apparent she was uncomfortable.

From what I gathered, Avery had some sort of relationship with him. The other guy jumped into the pool and tried to talk to a group of cheerleaders leaning against the side, but they ignored him. I assumed he was meant to be a wingman, but a poor one at that.

"Who's that fucking guy?" I said to no one in particular.

"The one with Avery?" Xavier asked.

I focused on the guy's every touch, every laugh, and every motion he aimed at my stepsister. She was mine, and I wouldn't let anyone get in my way, but I couldn't play my hand yet.

"Jaxson, go over there and find out who he is," I demanded.

"I was gonna jump in the pool," he whined.

"Stop being a dick. Do some recon for me."

He huffed. "You worried you got some competition?"

I laughed. "No one is my competition. I don't want interference."

Jaxson's chair scraped on the pavers as he rose. He was indignant, but he headed over to where Avery was sitting. I watched as he extended his hand to the guy, and they shook, then he sat down on the end of Avery's lounger.

"Who do you think he is?" Xavier asked.

I clenched my fists, and my finger slipped across my skin from the sweat. "Some wannabe boyfriend or an ex. Look at the way he's touching her arm."

"Could be. All these people are from Arlington?" Xavier asked.

"Yeah. I don't know any of them," I said.

I took another sip of my drink in an attempt to relax. The chef had mixed up a punch with fruit, non-alcoholic, of course, but I slipped in some vodka in my own drink. As much as I tried to distract myself, the guy was pissing me off each time he moved. I wanted to go over there and rip his arms from their sockets each time he put his hands on Avery.

"Look at Remy," Xavier said. "What a sucker."

Remy was holding Clover in his arms and spinning in the water. Eventually, he would probably be lost to me. I'd never seen him like this before. Usually, he was like the rest of us, sleeping with girls but not getting involved with dating.

"Yeah, he's done," I voiced. "She must have a golden pussy or something going on."

"You ever think what we do is shady?"

I elbowed him. "Are you fucking kidding me? We own Bancroft; girls come to us. They want to be with us, and guys want to be part of our group. Xavier, don't go soft on me. I need you."

"Are we sharing Avery?" he asked, almost challengingly.

The fuck I was sharing Avery with him or anyone else. She was mine, and besides, I didn't think she wanted to be with anyone else. My stepsister was different from the girls at Bancroft. She didn't grow up with tons of money, though from what I'd heard, her father kept the family comfortable until he died.

She was also different from any girls I'd ever known. Sure, her beauty was what drew me in, but her stubbornness was what intrigued me the most. If anyone was going soft, it was me. I took another sip of my drink and turned my attention back to continue watching Jaxson interact with Avery and the guy. A few minutes later, he bumped knuckles with him and came over to us.

"Well?" I asked, on edge as I waited for Jaxson to tell me who he was.

He plopped down in his chair and took a sip of the same vodka-laced drink I had.

"He's an ex. His name is Duncan. He was her last boyfriend."

"He's flirting with her."

"Yeah, he is. I think he wants her back."

I sat up from my slump. "If Duncan thinks he's horning in on my territory, he can go fuck himself."

"Asshole told me he was nominated for prom king," Jaxson added with a scoff. "I think he's a big deal at Arlington."

I snorted. I was prom king every year I'd been at Bancroft, and this year would be no different. I was also class president and student liaison to President Lawrence. Duncan couldn't match my success in high school, but I had higher aspirations and had no plans to peak in high school.

"And that's all he'll ever be," I thundered. "Guys like him won't be successful in life, and they'll relive their high school years."

"Sounds like you're making a case for Avery," Jaxson said.

I gave him a stern look, lifting my sunglasses. "I don't need to make a case. She already knows who I am."

"And she hates you," he reminded.

"She won't once I make her come," I said smugly.

"She will still hate you, especially her," Xavier said.

I frowned. "Why do you say that?"

"Because she ain't like other girls. An orgasm is physical, but mentally and emotionally, she'll still hate you. Any sex you have with her is a hate fuck," Xavier explained.

"Bullshit," I argued.

"It's not," he replied. "My prediction is that if you get her into bed, it won't happen again."

I didn't believe that would be the case. I'd been grooming Avery for the past week, and it wouldn't be long until she was entirely mine. Sex with her would be epic, more so because I would be her first. I watched as Duncan tried to kiss her, and she pushed him away. It made me smile. She didn't want him.

"See what I mean? No competition," I said.

~

I WAITED for my chance to get Avery alone, and it came when she got up to go to the bathroom an hour later. I followed her into the house under the guise of refilling my drink. The house was empty except for Chef Hawkins and a couple of maids who were busy cleaning.

Just as she stepped into the bathroom on the first floor, I pushed my way inside and crowded her against the wall once I closed the door.

"Who the fuck was that guy?" I barked.

She put her hand on my cheek, seemingly undeterred by my tone. "Are you jealous?" she scolded.

I grasped her hand and bit the heel of her hand. She yelped.

"He put his hands on you," I stated.

Avery tried to yank her hand away, but I held it to my mouth.

"I don't want him," she returned.

"Where has he touched?" I pushed.

"Just my arm and hand."

I bit her hand again, this time a lot gentler. Her eyes were questioning and confused.

"No," I began again. "How much of you did he touch when you dated?"

She once again tried to yank back her hand, and when I wouldn't let go, she slapped my chest with her other.

"Let go," she growled. "It doesn't matter how much he saw or touched. I don't want him."

"How much?" I demanded.

She averted her eyes from mine, and I let her hand go.

"We did oral," she confessed quietly.

"Fuck."

"We didn't do that," she said, this time more snappily.

"Don't joke, darling Avery."

I tipped her chin up and pressed my mouth to hers, slipping my hands around her back and fingering the tie on her orange bikini top. I wanted to open it, tease her breasts with my fingers, make her beg for me to fuck her, and then deny her.

"Do it," she murmured against my mouth.

"No. If I do, you won't be back to your friends anytime soon. You'll just have to wait."

"Give me something," she whined. "It's my birthday, and you haven't given me a present."

"Your present is tonight. I'll worship your body, and I want you in nothing but that anklet."

I planned to drive Avery crazy until then. Based on what was happening now, things were on track. She would never want another guy ever again, and she would beg me to give her what I had over and over. I was so sure of myself that I pressed a kiss to her cheek and slipped my hand into her bikini bottoms. It surprised me to find she was already wet, her clit swollen after barely doing anything outside of talking.

"You're soaked," I said, my voice deepening. "Does it turn you on when I tell you what to do?"

"No!"

I swiped my finger over her sensitive tissue, and she gasped, then closed her eyes.

"You're lying, Avery. Tell me the truth."

When she didn't respond, I slid my finger over her clit and back again. She clenched her teeth, and her jaw bulged.

"Yes," she choked out, making me forget about wanting her to wait for this.

Keeping my hand where it was pressing against her, I turned her to the mirror and backed us up in the large bathroom so she could see us.

"Open your eyes."

Her eyes popped open, but she looked away from our reflection. With the other hand, I brought her chin up.

"Watch me make you come," I ordered lowly. "I want you to see how beautiful you look."

Her cheeks became tinged pink with embarrassment, but she obediently watched me as my hand began to move in her bikini bottoms. Avery's mouth formed an O, and her lids dropped, but she kept her eyes on what I was doing. She trembled against me, and her hands slipped behind her to grip my swim trunks.

"Tell me what you want," I whispered in her ear.

"To come," she whispered back.

I pressed harder, sliding over her clit in swift motions, and she leaned against me as she let out a low moan and climaxed. She slumped against me, but I kept my finger against her as I kissed the top of her head.

"This was just a preview," I tempted. "There will be plenty more orgasms in your future."

"Gideon," she murmured.

"Yes?"

"Take me upstairs."

I removed my hand, sucking off her sweetness. "You have guests, and what I want to do to you will take hours."

"Hours?" she asked breathlessly.

"Hours," I assured.

I fixed her bikini bottoms, kissed her cheek, and slipped out the door.

CHAPTER 17

Avery

Jesus Christ. What the hell is Gideon doing to me? I looked in the mirror after he stepped out to find my face flaming red. I didn't know if it was from the orgasm or embarrassment or a little of both. A week ago, I hated him, yet now I couldn't get enough of him.

As willing as I was to give him my V card, I was also afraid of what having sex with him meant. I'm infatuated with him now, and I could easily fall in love. My mother would have a heart attack if she learned I was fucking my stepbrother. The scandal to the Berne family would be monumental, but I didn't care, and I didn't think Gideon did either.

I sat on the toilet seat until everything returned to normal: my heart, breathing, and the color in my cheeks. Afterward, I finished my business, and when I came out, the house was quiet. Outside, Gideon had retaken his seat at the table with his friends while I sat back on the lounger.

Duncan also got the message since he was in the pool with Debbie, one of my cheerleading friends. Every so often, I would look up toward Gideon and catch him running the finger he used on me under his nose, leaving me wanting him more than ever. This day was dragging.

"So, birthday girl, how is it going? I saw you talking to Dunc," Clover said, interrupting one of my exchanges with Gideon as she dripped water on my legs.

She sat on the lounger next to mine and used my towel to wipe her hair and body.

"It's going okay."

"And?" she prompted.

"And what?"

"Dunc. Are you two getting together again?"

I scowled. "Hell no. He can try all he wants."

She grinned at me. "He really wants you back."

I wanted to change the subject. When Clover latched onto something, she would keep her jaws shut like a rabid dog. I didn't want her to continue talking about Duncan, especially because he was the jerk who left me just because I was leaving Arlington, even though he knew it wasn't my choice.

As if on cue, he waved to me from the pool. In response, I gave him a tight-lipped smile and jutted my chin out.

"See?" she persisted.

"Clover, let it go. I'm not interested. He dumped me like I didn't matter. I thought if anyone were on my side, it would be you."

She put her hand on my arm. "I'm always on your side. Don't ever forget that. If I weren't, I would've stayed at Arlington."

"I guess."

"No, you don't need to guess, you know," she replied, her tone becoming more serious. "I love you even if your mom hates me."

I segued off to something else. "Thank you. What's going on

with you and Remy?"

"He's delicious, but I'm not sure he's boyfriend material."

I giggled. "Then what type of material is he?'

She got a dreamy look on her face and stared across the pool at Remy. "Good fuck material. These private school boys have interesting sex lives."

"So do you! Anyway, how long are these people staying?"

She rolled her eyes. "They brought you gifts, and they came; you should be happy."

"I would've preferred a quiet day," I said a bit grouchily.

"With asshole and his friends," Clover reminded as she gestured to Gideon.

"Um, newsflash, Remy is one of those friends."

She half shrugged. "He's different."

"He's a rich private schoolboy."

She pointed at him. "And hot as hell. Look at him; he's beautiful."

"Not my type."

"And who is?" she asked, digging back into her earlier hook-up quest for me. "Xavier is on fire. Shit, sizzling Italian with dark hair and eyes? I love his long eyelashes."

I shook my head at her exuberance over Gideon's friends.

"Perhaps you should just have a threesome."

Clover stroked her chin and thought for a moment.

"Oh my God!" I exclaimed. "I was kidding. You're out of control."

She threw her legs over the lounger to face me. "Please tell me you're losing your V card soon."

"To who?" I posed. "I'm the enemy at Bancroft. No guy will come near me."

"Bullshit. Gideon doesn't run the school. I'm sure there are plenty of guys who would want to go for a roll in the hay with you."

I shook my head. "Roll in the hay? You're ridiculous."

There was no one other than Gideon that I was interested in, of course. I somehow wanted the guy who'd threatened me so many times over. Maybe I was stupid or naïve, but I wanted it badly, and I only wanted it from Gideon.

THE PARTY finally ended when everyone left at around 6 pm. I was glad they didn't stay longer because I was bored trying to pretend like I cared. They weren't my friends anymore, and I believed they agreed to come over so they could see the infamous Berne Manor I 'left' them for. It was one of the biggest places in town, only rivaled by Remy's home, which was a few doors down. I went upstairs to take a shower and knowingly let Gideon follow me.

"What are you doing?" Gideon asked, cornering me in the hall before my room.

Unlike my shared bathroom situation at Bancroft, I had a private bath that I wanted to take a long cool shower in.

"Huh?" I asked.

"Don't shower. I want you dirty."

"But Gideon, I swam and got sweaty. I probably stink like chlorine."

"And if you shower, you will ruin your taste and scent." He pressed his body against mine and took my hand, placing it on his semi-erection. I already knew Gideon was big, but now I wondered if he would fit, not only because I was smaller than him but a virgin. I looked up at him as he grew under my hand.

"Don't be afraid, darling Avery. I'll be gentle the first time. You'll remember it for the rest of your life." He looped my hair over my ear and kissed my neck, running his tongue up to my earlobe and sucking. "Eat well tonight because you'll need your energy."

All too soon, Gideon backed away from me and walked

down the hall to his room, where he slipped inside without looking back. I leaned against the wall, weak, and turned on again. Damn him.

"What the hell is wrong with you?" Clover asked a minute later when she emerged from her room freshly showered with Remy right behind her.

"Noth-nothing. I thought you were hanging out with Remy," I said.

She raised a brow. "I am with Remy."

"I meant in his room."

"That's tonight," she said with a wink, Remy staying quiet during the exchange.

I was thankful because Remy's room was at the end of the hall. I didn't want anyone to hear me having sex with Gideon since he'd promised to make me scream. My whole body was reacting to the anticipation of tonight. My heart thumped in my chest, stomach churned with anxiety, and below, my pussy throbbed. I wasn't sure how long I could keep our charade up.

"Are you coming down for dinner and cake?" she asked.

I rolled my eyes. "Why wouldn't I? It is my birthday."

AFTER DINNER WAS FINISHED, which I didn't eat much of because I couldn't think of anything but Gideon's hands on my body, and the cake was served, Remy and Clover disappeared. They were probably getting an early start before we all had to go back to school. Gideon leaned over and placed his hand on my knee, sliding it up to my inner thigh.

"Follow my instructions, darling Avery," he commanded. "I want you to go to my room and sit on the corner of the bed. I'll be up soon."

I frowned. "I thought..."

Gideon cut me off with a raised hand. "No arguments. My

room. Go. Now."

Before I could rise, he slipped his hand between my legs and used his pinkie to stroke the panel of my panties, much like he had in trig class. My stomach was a ball of knots that churned the little food I ate like a washing machine. Taking deep breaths, I slowly walked up the stairs and went to his room.

I'd never been inside, only seeing glimpses whenever I passed by. There was a subtle scent of his citrusy cologne. The room was painted a dark blue and accented by white crown moulding. A smaller version of Payne's mahogany desk sat in the corner, and several drawings were tacked to a bulletin board above it.

Transfixed, I made a beeline over to it as I had no idea Gideon was an artist. Of the pieces tacked up, there was one of me drawn in pencil—a perfect likeness, and I wondered when he did it. I leaned in close to examine my own features.

"I told you to sit on the bed."

"When did you do this?" I asked, ignoring his comment.

"When you first got here. Now sit on the bed."

His voice was harsh, but for some silly reason, I trusted him. I did as I was told, sitting on the corner of the light blue duvet cover. Gideon prowled toward me until he stood directly in front of me.

"Did you shower?" he asked.

I looked up at him. "You said not to."

"Good girl."

He cupped my chin, and I chewed on the inside of my cheek. Gideon removed the clips from my hair, taking it down. My blonde tresses cascaded over my shoulder, and he ran his fingers through them.

"Gideon?" I voiced searchingly.

"Shush, darling Avery. I promise to take care of you. Are you on the pill?"

"I-yes."

He frowned. "Why?" his tone was angry.

"Cramps. They're bad, and the pill makes it better."

"You're a virgin?" he asked as if accusing me.

Now I was angry. I told him I was, and I wouldn't lie. "This is ridiculous. I wouldn't lie to you. I told you I was."

"You've had boyfriends at Arlington."

I glared. "But none I wanted to sleep with."

"Why?"

Done, I pushed myself up, but he bumped me backward and sent me sprawling onto the bed. I sat up and frowned at him.

"What is this, twenty questions?" I shot. "I'm not playing your game. I want to go."

Gideon backed away and put his arms out from his sides. "If you want to go, you can go. I won't force you."

I hesitated. I wanted him—it was the entire reason I was in his room—but his questions gave me pause. I felt like a naughty child whose parents were pumping them for information. This was supposed to be my birthday present, but I didn't want it if Gideon acted this way.

I rose and headed for the door, brushing past him. He grabbed me, spun me around, and slammed his mouth on mine. Cupping my ass, he pulled my body against his, and I fell into the abyss, lost in our kiss, until he broke it and let me go.

"Darling Avery, remember this kiss and come to me when you're ready."

Remembering why I was leaving in the first place, I hurried from the room and ran to my own, where I pushed the door closed and leaned against it. When my lungs stopped burning, and my heart returned to a normal rate, I stripped and took a quick shower. For some reason, I expected Gideon to be standing there once I got out, demanding to take what he thought was his, but there was no one.

Fatigue gripped me, and I crawled into my unmade bed. My room was my only sanctuary in this castle.

CHAPTER 18

Gideon

Stupid idiot! You came on too strong. You pushed her too early.

I paced my room, cursing myself for taking it too far. Avery hadn't lost her free will, and now she was having doubts about us. I promised I wouldn't hurt her, but I offended her. I couldn't let her get away because I was too close to getting her in my bed and under my spell.

I had honed my skills in the bedroom for the last three years —learning how to charm girls into my bed and, when they were there, giving them what would make them come back for more. Most of the girls at Bancroft would kill to be with me. I was Gideon Berne.

But Avery was a totally different animal, and maybe Xavier's words were getting to me. She didn't know me the way those at Bancroft did, but they didn't know the real me either. I wore a façade, one of a successful student-athlete. In her, I could see a kinship—someone who'd lost a parent and whose living parent didn't prioritize us.

My father didn't care what I did as long as the Berne name wasn't dragged into scandal. And if it were, his money would make it go away. It was also obvious from the amount of time we'd been around each other that once her mother was under my father's wing, Avery was also no longer her priority. I felt for her, and I wanted her, but I couldn't bring myself to explain this to her. Tonight was supposed to be our night, so I wouldn't let a misunderstanding chase it away.

Stepping out to make the short trip to her room, I heard the unmistakable sounds of sex all the way down the hall. I had no idea why Remy and Clover were so loud. I paused in front of Avery's door. From underneath, I saw a faint glow and knew the lights were out. The light was from her Arlington Tigers night light.

I quietly turned the knob and opened the door. In the dimness, I could see her sprawled on her stomach, wearing a red lace thong, her glorious ass exposed. The half t-shirt she wore was bunched up under her breasts, exposing her upper back. God, she was magnificent.

"Avery," I whispered.

As I sat on the edge of the bed and rubbed her back, repeating her name, I noticed her anklet and smirked. It was still early, just before 9 pm. She mumbled.

"Darling Avery, wake up."

"Go away, Gideon."

"Don't make me do it," I said.

She didn't turn over. "Do whatever you want. You will anyway."

I smirked and ran my short nails over her skin. Avery shifted as I began to tickle her. She tried to pull away from me but was unsuccessful. Her next tactic was to wiggle and scoot over to the other side of the bed, but I held her in place.

"I-can't-breathe," she panted, emphasizing each word.

I stopped to let her catch her breath. While she did, she turned over to look at me.

"Better?" I asked.

She glared. "I should've locked my door."

"You're beautiful," I said as I rubbed her bare leg.

"And you're a jerk."

"Is your earlier invitation open? It's still your birthday."

Avery sat up. "Do I have to listen to you?"

"Are you still a virgin?" I shot back.

"Unless I screwed Dunc between our fight and now - yes."

A pang of jealousy consumed me for a moment, but I knew she didn't want Duncan. She wanted me. "Then you need to listen." I stood up and yanked off my t-shirt, tossing it on the bed, then added, "Now you."

I crossed my arms and waited for Avery to pull her shirt off. I bit my tongue and counted the seconds until her beautiful breasts were revealed to me. When they were, my dick went into overdrive, immediately growing erect.

She smiled. "Looks like you have a problem."

"It will go away once it's buried inside your pussy or mouth —your choice."

"I thought we were doing this in your room."

I sighed. "We can do it anywhere you like."

"Want me to take care of that first?"

My mouth dropped open in surprise. Even though she'd claimed to have done oral before, I thought I would have to coax and teach her certain things, but now she was offering.

I smirked. "How?"

"With my mouth," she said matter-of-factly.

My dick jumped in my pants, bobbing against my shorts. My balls were aching for the relief that she was willing to give. The thought of my dick in her mouth would make me come like a teenager having his first orgasm, so I stalled.

"Damn, Avery, you have such a dirty little mouth."

She licked her full lips. "And I want to use it on you. You've been teasing me for days and torturing me for months. Payback is a bitch."

"Jesus Christ," I muttered.

Avery was giving me a run for my money. I knew she wasn't totally innocent, but this was unexpected. I wanted to be the one to control the sex, make her beg, but she was turning the tables on me.

"Come on, Berne. Get that big cock out for me."

She moved to the edge of the bed, her gorgeous breasts jiggling. Breasts, I wanted to decorate with my cum. I rolled down the waistband of my shorts and released my dick.

In the dim light, her eyes widened. "Shit."

"I'll be gentle for now."

Her gaze met mine. "What is that supposed to mean?"

I stroked her hair. "It means when I break you in, I won't be."

"Fuck you, Gideon."

"That's later. I'm going to wreck that sweet pussy."

Undeterred, she grabbed my dick, squeezing it in her small fist as she stroked. When a bead of dew bubbled at my head, she licked it, sending spirals of pleasure through me. I was on fire, and she hadn't even taken me into her mouth.

"Maybe you should do it now," she said.

"Noo, darling Avery. Relieve me, and then it's your turn. You'll wake up tomorrow dehydrated by the time I get done with you."

"Promises, promises," she said.

Avery circled my head with her tongue before she swallowed my length. The innocent look on her face as she held me there almost had me coming, but I restrained myself. I moved my hips, pushing another inch in her mouth, then another. She fisted the base of my dick and began to work her mouth over me.

I gritted my teeth. "Darling Avery, suck me hard."

She hollowed her cheeks and took me to the back of her throat as she looked up at me with her large gray eyes. I stroked her cheek with my knuckles, which was tame for what I really wanted to do. If she were anyone else, I would grasp her hair and hold her to me. But I let her take the lead.

Avery slurped at me, running her tongue on the underside of my cock. She moaned and closed her eyes, tasting the endless stream of precum on her tongue. Her hands latched onto my ass, digging into the muscles. I ran my hands through her golden tresses, smoothing them from her face.

I didn't want to miss the moment when I pulled out and coated her white. But in true Avery style, she wouldn't let me back off as I grew close.

"Avery, I'm gonna come. Let me go."

Once again, she gave me a doe-eyed look and shook her head. God, this girl was incredible. Lost in her stare, I grunted out, "Avvverrry." as I came.

She took every drop I gave her as tears rolled down her cheeks. She gagged, but she didn't pull away. When I was done, I wiped the tears from her skin as she cleaned me with her tongue.

When she finished, Avery ran her finger over her lips, sucking off any residual from the tip. "You taste delicious."

My legs were weak. I shucked off my shorts and sat on her bed, falling back on the bundle of sheets and quilt.

"Where did you learn that from?" I asked.

"Practice."

I frowned and sat up. A girl as popular as her probably would have more boyfriends than I had contacted before we left for Bancroft, and I wondered where in the line I was. How many guys had she sucked off before me? It was unfair of me to question her when I had had more than several partners, but I still wanted to know.

"How many?" I repeated.

Avery stroked the ridges on my stomach. "Will you tell me how many you've had?"

"I'm a guy. There's a difference."

"That's a stupid thing to say and misogynistic. You can fuck all the girls you want, but if I do, I'm what, a slut or a whore? Take your pick," she huffed.

I sat up and grabbed her, pulling her against me. "I would never call you a whore."

Avery smirked. "But you have."

I knew she was right. In the beginning, I called her every name in the book to get under her skin—anything I could do to get a rise out of her, and eventually, she just took it. But with renewed vigor, she started to fight back. She'd fast become the only person in my life with the balls to fight me when others wouldn't dare to second guess my dominance.

I played dumb. "When?"

"I'll tell you if you let me sit on your face."

My dick jumped.

"Strip. Let me see that tight little hole."

She rose from the bed and hooked her thumbs in her panties. I scrambled up to her pillow and got in position. Avery did a teasing little dance by shimmying her hips before she pushed down the scrap of cloth which could barely be termed panties. They dropped to the floor, and she stepped out of them.

"I want those," I noted, nodding toward the pair.

"They're my favorite pair."

"I'll get you more, any colors you like."

She climbed onto me, straddling my chest. Her slick pussy left a trail as she moved up my body, and I stroked her taut thighs, anticipating her sweetness. Avery used the headboard to balance; then she lowered herself onto me. She tasted like cotton candy, and I parted her lips with my tongue.

"Fuck!" she moaned.

Just like the past few times I'd gotten a taste of her, I couldn't get enough, and neither could she as I licked her, tickling her clit and tongue fucking her tight hole. She lifted her hips in rhythm with my tongue until she arched her back and howled as she came. I lapped at her, sucking down every sweet drop.

Avery gripped the headboard to anchor her weakened body, but I lifted her like a feather from my face and placed her next to me. Her chest heaved temptingly, so I bent down to suck one of her dusky pink nipples into my mouth. It seemed like everything on Avery was sweet.

"Can you handle more?" I asked, checking the clock. "It's almost ten."

Her eyes were half-lidded, and she looked up at me. "You owe me a birthday present. You said you wanted me naked with just my anklet, and here I am."

I stroked her cheek with my knuckles before I plumped one of her breasts, plucking at the nipple with my fingers. She sucked in her breath and gasped when I slid my thumb over her slick clit.

"I promised," I said.

"You promised," she whispered as her gaze met mine.

"What position, darling Avery?"

She bit her lip, and I took the opportunity to coat it with her juices from my thumb to dislodge it.

"Don't be afraid to tell me," I coaxed.

"How should I know? I've never done it before."

I kissed her full lips, taking the bottom one in my mouth and nipping it.

"Would you like to go to my room?"

She sighed. "I like it here."

I could tell Avery was apprehensive. She started twirling her hair around her fingers over and over again. I kept questioning her in the hopes it would put her at ease.

"What position would you like?" I repeated.

"I want to be in your arms."

I raised an eyebrow. "Come, darling Avery."

I moved her pillows and positioned them behind my back, leaning against her padded headboard. My dick was hard like a steel rod, rising toward the ceiling.

Avery bit the tip of her index finger and gave me another doe-eyed look that nearly broke me.

"What about a condom?" she asked.

"Do you trust me?"

"I'm not sure. Rumor has it that you've been with a lot of girls. How do I know it's safe?"

It was time to tell her the truth.

"I haven't been with anyone since before school ended, and I've been tested. I'm clean, but if you want me to, I'll wear a condom."

"Why?"

I chuckled and rolled my eyes. "Are we having another philosophical discussion? You're good at bringing them up when we're just about to get into it."

She pointed at my hard cock. "It doesn't seem like you're losing any steam. So, tell me why?"

"You. I've lusted after you for months. Imagine my surprise when I found out you were still a virgin. It's been my goal to pop your cherry."

Avery bit her lip again. "You'll hurt me with that," she said as she pointed at my dick.

"I'll be gentle, but it won't always be this way. I need to lead."

"Asshole," she murmured.

My lips curled up in a wicked smile. "Condom?"

"I guess not."

I held my arms out to her. "Climb on, and don't be afraid."

She moved toward me, once again using the headboard to raise herself above me. I took the opportunity to suck at her nipples, and she groaned. Once I was poised at her entrance, I placed my hands on her hips, and she sank, inch by delicious inch, until she fully engulfed me.

"Oh my God, I feel so full," she cried.

"I have a big cock, darling Avery."

In a stupid game of playing big dog, the boys and I measured how big we were after watching porn. I came out on top. I knew I had to be uncomfortable inside her, so I waited, stretching her tight pussy as she acclimated to my size. She fit me like a glove.

I lifted her chin with my fingers and caught her gaze before asking, "Are you okay?"

She sawed her bottom lip with her teeth. "It burns a little."

"It will feel better once we move."

She put her head on my shoulder. "Can't we stay like this?"

I embraced her, holding her against my chest. I could stay like this forever if I didn't have the urge to fill her with my cum. I wanted to mark Avery as my own. She didn't belong to anyone but me. To ease things forward, I played with her breasts, and she shuddered in my arms.

I rocked Avery, and she placed her hands on my shoulders, joining me.

"Oh God, this feels so good," she moaned.

"I'm not God, Avery, but I can be if you like."

"Gideon!" she cried.

I ground my pubic bone against her, grazing her swollen clit with the base of my cock.

"Let's change positions," I said.

"No, please," she begged.

I wanted to be above her, control our union, and drive into her with hard thrusts. But I honored her request because it was her birthday and choice. She latched onto my lip and curled her fingers into my hair, playing with it at the nape of my neck. I swelled inside her as I grew close, but I held back because I wanted her first experience to be memorable.

Avery arched her back, thrusting her breasts in my face. I

took one of her nipples in my mouth, and I felt her shiver against me. Her breath grew rapid, and I could see her pulse thrumming along on the side of her swan-like neck. She moaned my name and squeezed me as she climaxed.

As she went limp in my arms, I thrust upward until I exploded, filling her with my semen. Avery said nothing, just leaned against my chest, and it was perfect. We were perfect together.

CHAPTER 19

Avery

Just as I thought he would, Gideon picked me up and placed me on the bed. Without pause, he got up and walked away, leaving me feeling empty. I pulled the sheet around me and felt tears prick my eyes as I turned toward the wall.

"Avery?"

"What?" I sniffled.

I felt the bed dip, and he stroked my hair. "Did I hurt you?"

"I thought you were leaving."

"No. Turn over so I can clean you up."

Almost hesitating, I turned and let him gently pull the sheet down. In his hand was a washcloth he pressed into my skin as he parted my thighs and used to clean between my legs. He examined the cloth as he pulled it away and loudly sighed.

"No blood."

I stared at him. "Blood?"

"It happens, but there's nothing. You're fine."

He tossed the washcloth into a basket I kept by my dresser with dirty clothing. It made it easy for the maids to take it out for washing. Gideon slipped into bed with me. I turned on my side, and he curled around me.

"Avery?"

"Yeah?"

"If you don't want me here, just say so. This is a lot to process."

I grabbed his hand and kissed it. "It's not. I was prepared, and I wanted it."

He gently sucked at my ear. "Wanting it and doing it are two different things. Sometimes it doesn't match your expectations."

"This beat my expectations. I don't think any other guy could meet them, but you did."

He chuckled. "Even that a-hole, Duncan."

"Duncan could never live up to you. He hurt me, and I would never give him the time of day again."

Gideon's voice turned serious. "Avery, I've hurt you. Don't lie and tell me I didn't."

"You did, but I've forgiven you."

I turned in his arms, pressing my body against his. I got an immediate response from his nether regions as I felt him grow against my leg. I boldly reached for him, wrapped my hand around his dick, and began to stroke.

"Do you want more?" Gideon asked.

"You said I would be dehydrated by tomorrow."

"And you will, that I can promise."

After I woke up, I was aware that every bone in my body was sore and that I'd probably be walking a little funny. I felt like I'd run a marathon. Gideon was sleeping peacefully next to me, and in the morning light, I examined his features. He was so handsome.

"Gideon?" I whispered.

"No more, darling Avery. You wore me out," he said.

His eyes were closed, and I touched my finger to the tip of his nose. Gideon grumbled and turned to his side, but I kept teasing him until he retaliated, flipping over and pinning me to the bed. He squeezed my wrists to the bed and straddled my waist. Despite his protests, his cock is hard.

"I thought I wore you out?" I teased as I gestured to his cock with my chin.

"My balls are killing me. I haven't come so much in a long time."

Wrestling one arm free, I continued my previous stroking until Gideon pushed my hand away, lined himself up, and used his cockhead to stimulate my clit. I gripped his shoulder and latched onto his lips as he slid into me, filling me. He grasped my ass and pulled my leg over his hip.

"You're a dirty girl, Avery. So dirty. Your training is over," he whispers.

"What training?"

"You'll do what I say from now on."

I frowned at him and readied my argument until he thrust his hips hard enough to make me lose my breath. I put all thoughts of protest out of my mind because all I wanted was for Gideon to make me come. I whimpered in his arms as he hammered at me.

"You're mine," he growled. "You won't be dating anyone but me."

"Dating? Are you out of… oh God!" I screeched as I had the hardest orgasm in my life. I scratched at him with my nails, raking them over his skin.

"Mine," Gideon grunted as he spilled into me.

"WOULD YOU HURRY UP!" Clover whined.

It was nearing 6 pm, and I wanted to get back to campus before it got dark. Gideon and Remy planned on leaving after us, and I hoped he was careful. Even more so now, after just one weekend together, I was falling for my stepbrother—and that was a problem. We hadn't thought of the consequences, and though Gideon wanted me for his own, I had no idea how that would work.

"Go to the car. I have to grab something from my room," I commanded.

She walked away, and once I heard her footsteps on the stairs, I knocked on Gideon's door. He opened it and pulled me inside. His hands roamed my body, cupping my breasts and ass.

"Don't forget you're mine," he said.

"And what about you? Are you mine?" I asked.

He grinned. "Darling Avery, I was yours before you knew it. The minute I saw your beautiful face."

"You still didn't answer my question."

He sighed. "You're full of questions. Too many for the time we have."

"But Gideon!" I protested.

He put his finger to my lips. "Shush. We'll talk at school."

I crossed my arms. "Really? When is that? When I'm dodging Clover, and you're hiding from your boys? This won't work."

"Don't say that. We'll make it work, but there's still the question of you doing what I tell you. Last night was a preview of what I can do, but now that you're broken in."

I scowled. "I'm not a piece of machinery."

"I'll explain it all at school."

"Now!" I demanded.

"No. Go. I don't want you driving in the dark."

"Asshole."

Gideon grabbed me once more, pulling me over to the bed. He threw me over his knee and spanked me—hard. I struggled, and after five swift slaps, he let me up.

"What the fuck!" I screamed.

His face was red, and I probably had a shade on my cheeks to match. No one, not even my parents, had ever spanked me. I was too old for it, but what I found odd was that Gideon had a bulge in his shorts that wasn't there when he pulled me on his lap. He was turned on, which shouldn't surprise me since he'd spent the summer insulting me.

"Go!" he shouted.

"Fuck you, Gideon," I said as I stamped out of his room.

"AVERY, did you hear what I said?" Clover asked.

We were fifteen minutes from Bancroft, and I'd been lost in my thoughts most of the trip while Clover napped, played with the radio, or chattered about our weekend.

"Huh?"

I glanced at her and noticed the scowl accompanying her narrowed eyes.

"What's with you? Did something happen this weekend that you're not telling me about? You seem different."

Yeah, I am different. I gave my evil stepbrother my virginity.

I had to make up something because if I told her nothing was wrong, she would badger me until I gave her a crumb. It would only make sense for me to give her something to throw her off the scent.

"Duncan," I blurted out.

"Duncan? Are you thinking about getting back with him?" she asked with surprise.

"He made a convincing argument last night, but I'm not too pro on us long distance."

She grabbed my arm, scaring me. "You could see him on weekends! You don't want to stay at Bancroft all the time, so you can leave on Friday afternoon and come back on Sunday. It would be perfect!"

I frowned at her. "Why are you for me getting back with him?"

"You really want to know?"

"Of course. You're my best friend."

Clover turned toward me as much as she could since her seatbelt restricted her movement.

"I think he was good for you. Yeah, I know, he broke your heart, blah, blah, blah. But you were happy with him."

"I'm not thinking of getting back with him," I told her. "Duncan said something to me yesterday which made me believe he has ulterior motives."

I turned off the highway and onto the main road leading to Bancroft. It was twilight, and I was happy to be at the school before it turned into night. I worried Gideon would be driving in the dark like he had on his trip to the manor, but he was a good driver, and he had Remy with him.

"Ulterior motives? Like what?"

I sighed. "He couldn't stop gushing about the house and how much money Payne had."

"But Dunc's family has money. Not as much as yours, but they have a nice house, and he has a nice car."

"It just struck me as weird. Besides, I'm not interested in him. He doesn't do it for me."

I pulled into a parking space right near the dorm. The lot was only half full, which led me to believe a lot of kids went home for the weekend. I was sure by curfew; the place would be packed since most kids had cars.

"I thought you two would work it out," Clover said as she opened the door. "Maybe you should go for Xavier. He's dark and dangerous."

I laughed. "He's tame compared to Gideon, and I don't think I should go out with any of my stepbrother's friends." *Because I think I'm falling in love with my stepbrother, and the sex we had was incredible.*

"What about Jaxson? He's pretty hot."

I grabbed my duffel from the backseat. "None of Gideon's friends. If he didn't poison all the guys here, I'm sure I can find one."

"Well, if you ask me…."

"Clover, that's just it; I didn't ask you. Stop pushing me to date."

She slammed the door of my Mercedes after she got her bag. "You need to pop your cherry sometime. You're eighteen now; it's time."

I already popped my cherry, and it was fantastic. "What does my age have to do with anything?"

"Because most people your age have lost it already," she argued.

"That doesn't mean shit. Come on, let's get upstairs."

I WAS FINISHING my Spanish homework when my phone chimed with an incoming text. Behind me, Clover listened to music through her earbuds while she tackled her trigonometry homework. I'd finished mine before we left school on Friday.

Have no fear, darling Avery; I'm back. Are you still angry at me?

I SMILED as I read the text, even though I was still upset with Gideon spanking me. I didn't want to be manhandled.

A: I am angry at you. We need to talk.

Come to my room.

A: To talk or something else?

Maybe a little of both.

MY NIPPLES HARDENED at the thought of Gideon touching me. I thought about what we'd done all night, and goosebumps broke out on my skin. I rose from my chair, and the scrape of the legs on the floor alerted Clover. She pulled out an earbud. Her music was so loud I could hear the words to About Damn Time by Lizzo.

"Are you crazy?" I asked. "The music is so loud."

She waved her hand at me. "Where are you going?"

"To get more toilet paper from the supply closet. Why?"

"I thought you were going downstairs for a soda."

I rolled my eyes. "We have soda in the refrigerator."

"Only Pepsi. I want Sprite."

"Well, I'm not going downstairs, so if you want it, you'll have to get it yourself."

Rising from her chair, she took out her other earbud and turned off the music. A bolt of fear gripped me. If Clover was floating around, it would be hard to see Gideon, and I needed to see him. I craved his touch.

"What are you doing?" I questioned.

"Remy has Sprite in his room, and I need a break before curfew. I don't want to sneak down the hall."

I crossed my arms. "You mean you're going to fuck. Be proud; just call it what it is, a dirty booty call."

She grinned. "Shut up. It's a Sprite run with a bit of booty."

We exited our room at the same time. She went down the hall to the boy's side, and I pretended to go to the supply closet. Instead, I stopped in the guest bathroom, washed my hands as I counted to thirty before I came out, and headed to Gideon's, hoping I didn't encounter Clover.

When I knocked, he immediately opened the door, pulled me inside, and hugged me.

"I'm glad you came," he said as he pressed his nose to my hair. "You smell good."

I pushed out of his arms and flopped on his bed, reclining on his pillow. "We need to talk."

He frowned. "You said that. About what?"

I gaped at him. "You hit me, and you enjoyed it! Your dick was hard."

"You were supposed to listen, and you didn't. I had to punish you."

I bit my lip. "Is that what you meant by control? I don't want to be abused. I thought we had something."

"We do have something, but I need other things."

My mouth formed an O. "Other things?"

"I need to take the lead. I let you last night because it was a gift to you, but I warned you it would only be one time."

"Gideon, that's fucked up," I growled.

"Why can't you do it my way?"

I shook my head. "Because this relationship, or whatever it is, has so many obstacles already. We're supposed to be enemies, Clover doesn't know about you, and I don't even want to mention our parents."

"You just did," he said dryly.

"Well, did you think what they would say when they find out we're together?" I posed.

Gideon grabbed for my hand, but I moved it out of his reach.

"They won't. My father doesn't give a crap what I do as long as I don't smear the family name."

I pursed my lips. "I think this is right up there when people find out his son and stepdaughter are fucking. And my mother would have a fit."

"I *need* the control."

I couldn't understand why he was pressing the issue of controlling me. I didn't want a relationship where I was under his thumb. I already had a boyfriend who tried to control me, and I cut it off when he told me I couldn't wear a shirt that showed my upper chest. I didn't need another guy like that.

"So you'll tell me what I can and can't wear and who I can see."

He reached for me and, this time, was successful, pulling me under him. Gideon hovered over me, staring down.

"No. Not like that. I mean in bed. I want to control what we do in bed, and I want you to agree you'll let me."

I reached up to stroke his cheek. "You mean I don't get any say? You get to hurt me, and I get to keep my mouth shut?" I said.

Gideon's lips curled in a subtle smirk. "I wouldn't hurt you, and I highly doubt you'll keep your mouth shut, but *you will learn*," he stated, punctuating his final words.

"What's that supposed to mean?"

I wondered if he meant he would gag me. Would I be one of those girls who had a boyfriend who tied them up, threw a blindfold on, spanked them, and left them begging for a scrap of satisfaction? If it was a possibility, as much as I craved Gideon, I didn't want it. It was abnormal. I wanted a partner, not a tormentor.

"It means if you make noise, everyone will find out about us. And then I'll need to continue treating you like a leper. I have a reputation to uphold."

I slid out from under him and sat against his pillows. "That sounds demented. I'd never be able to kiss you in public or hold your hand."

Again, his smirk formed. "I can get you off in trig or Spanish if that helps for a public display."

"Asshole. If we do this, I have some of my own rules. You will not touch me in public again. I let you because I wanted it."

He shrugged. "Just the fact that you did tells me you wanted people to watch. You allowed me to get you off in front of a group of people."

"I couldn't stop you!" I cried.

"Cut the crap, darling Avery. Admit you loved it."

I slammed my hand into his chest. "I hate you, Gideon. Why do you have to make everything so complicated?"

"Nothing would be complicated if you listened to me."

I jumped up and headed for the door, but Gideon was faster. He pulled me backward and onto his lap as we crashed into his bed. He held me with one hand and pinched my nipples with the other. As he turned me on, I cursed myself.

"I don't want to listen to you," I mumbled.

Gideon suddenly let me go, and I stood up, straightening my shirt. There would be no us, and that saddened me, but I wouldn't be his puppet like the rest of the people at Bancroft. Gideon might be able to control them, but he wouldn't control me. He was nothing but a bully, one I had developed feelings for.

"I expected you wouldn't. It's your choice."

It hurt that he acted so flippantly, like what we shared together didn't matter, even when he acted so caringly the night before. But I didn't show it and instead held my chin high as I walked out of Gideon's room.

CHAPTER 20

Gideon

I fucked up again, but now I wasn't sure I could do this anymore. I had Avery, yet despite my feelings, I needed to move on. There were plenty of girls begging for me to sleep with them, and unlike Avery, they would listen if I asked them to. But they weren't Avery. Part of me loved how she defied me. It was time for a drink, and I knew just where to go. Picking up my phone, I texted:

G: Do you still have some of that mouthwash?

What flavor?

G: Cinnamon.

Be right over.

USING the code Jaxson had set up as our system in case the school's admins ever caught on to us drinking alcohol, they'd at least never find any evidence on our phones. Cinnamon was whiskey, and I needed some. He showed up a couple of minutes later with a small bottle of whiskey colored red in, a bottle marked as mouthwash. No one would be the wiser unless they opened it up and smelled it.

My boy was selling them by the caseload and making a mint —not that he needed the cash. But when he was short because he lost his allowance on poker or spent too much money buying whatever, he had a backup plan without explaining it to his parents.

He stepped into my room and handed me the bottle. "You look like shit," he said.

I screwed off the top of the bottle and took a swig. It burned going down, and I winced. "What is this shit?"

"Old Grand Dad. It's good and cheap."

I took another sip. This time it didn't burn as much, and it would do to take the edge off how I was feeling. Jaxson flipped the chair from my desk around and straddled it.

"I didn't invite you," I snapped.

"What the fuck is your problem? You disappeared last night when we had a good poker game going."

"I had a headache, and you assholes left a mess in the pool house. I told you to keep it clean, or my father will ban us from hanging out there."

He smirked. "Your father is somewhere in Europe getting his rocks off with that hot piece of ass wife of his. He won't be back for weeks."

"Fuck off, Jaxson, and don't talk about Renata that way. Now get the fuck out of here before I decide you're no longer a target on the field."

Jaxson abruptly stood up, and the chair almost tipped. "Screw you, Berne. You know I need the yards, or I'll have to walk on."

"It's fucking Yale," I sneered. "You're not going to the pros."

He pushed my shoulder. I wasn't afraid because even though he had a couple of inches and twenty pounds on me, Jaxson was a pussy when you stood up to him. He knew who ran Bancroft.

"But I want an offer. I don't want to walk on like a loser scrub."

I sat on my bed and took another sip of the whiskey. It was much smoother now that I had a few belts.

"Get the hell out of here," I snarled.

Jaxson pointed at me as he backed away. "You owe me fifty. I'll put it on your tab."

He bolted through the door and slammed it on his way out. *Fucking Avery.* Out of all the guys I was close with, I'd never fought with Jaxson. He was the most easy-going and least confrontational, but I was pissed at the situation I put myself in. I'd made up my mind about not moving on. Avery was mine, and I wouldn't share.

"DON'T TOUCH ME," Avery whispered.

I was exhausted from too little sleep and a whiskey-induced hangover, but I looked forward to trig class because it would be the first time I saw Avery since she left me. My head pounded—

thump, thump, thumping—and the humidity of early September hadn't helped either.

Through everything, she smelled incredible. When I had sat next to her, I put my hand on her knee and ran it up her thigh, which prompted her initial response. She dug her nails into my skin, and I discreetly pulled my hand away. By the time I glanced up, everyone was staring at us.

"Is there a problem?" Mrs. Ordonez asked.

"No," Avery said as she shot me an evil look.

Damn, she was still pissed, meaning I would need to rectify the situation because I needed her in my life and bed. Even though Avery had been a virgin, no girl had ever satisfied me the way she did. I tried to concentrate on what Mrs. Ordonez was saying, but I spent most of the class stealing glances at Avery.

She had once again turned the tables on my expectations, and I felt like a little boy begging for forgiveness. I silently pleaded for her to look at me, but she wouldn't give me the time of day. At the end of class, Clover crowded her, but once we got to Spanish, I would try again.

Jaxson wasn't talking to me either, and he bolted out of class before I could apologize, which I rarely did. But last night, I was out of line. He was one of my best friends, and I would never jeopardize his dreams because that would be a dick move.

Avery hurried from class with Clover, and I followed, only to be cornered by Jillian Cronenberg. I'd slept with her several times last year, and though she could suck the skin off a grape when my dick was in her mouth, she was annoying. She'd also been pushing me to date her exclusively, which I wasn't prepared to do with her or anyone else.

"Giddy, where have you been? You've been ignoring my calls."

I recoiled. Giddy was what my mother and a few other close

relatives used to call me, including my father, when the urge moved him.

"Gideon," I corrected.

"Fine, Gideon."

She flipped her flame-red hair, and it grazed my cheek. She smelled like freesias, which reminded me of Avery. I looked over her shoulder and caught a glimpse of my stepsister weaving her way through the crowd. Her habit was to use the bathroom before Spanish, and I hoped to catch her alone.

I hitched my backpack on my shoulder, turning back to Jillian. "What can I do for you?"

"I've been calling. Daddy wanted to speak to you."

Her father, Miles Cronenberg, owned one of the largest lumber companies on the east coast, and he'd been trying to get a majority supply share of my father's business for years. I guessed he thought if Jillian got close to me, he would have a way in. I was sure he wouldn't have appreciated how his daughter had spent several nights on her knees in front of me.

"I'm busy," I said evasively. "I have school, football, and various other activities."

She leaned in and whispered in my ear, "I'd like to be one of those activities."

"We'll see."

It was my go-to response for the time being to get people off my back. I'd used it on Avery, too. I tried to slip around her, but Jillian stopped me.

"Don't forget our secret," she hissed.

I scowled at her. "What might that be?"

"How you have certain needs in the bedroom. I'm sure it would be scandalous for anyone to learn that Gideon Berne the fifth is a kinky asshole."

"And I'm sure the Cronenberg name couldn't handle the fallout of hearing how you satisfied those needs. Don't threaten me, Jillian. I have more power and money than you."

I stepped around her and walked away, leaving her gaping after me. I wasn't sure if the stream of students around us had heard our conversation, but I couldn't worry about it now. My focus was getting to Avery before class. I practically ran to Spanish class, searching for her. She wasn't there, so I knew my chance was now.

At first, when I entered the bathroom, there wasn't anyone around, and I thought she wasn't there until I saw her pink backpack sitting on the floor. She came out of the far stall half a minute later. I ducked behind the wall in the sitting area, waiting as she washed her hands before I stepped out.

"Avery," I breathed.

"God dammit, Gideon!" she screamed. "You scared me!"

When she fully turned to me, her golden windblown hair fell around her face, making me want to tuck it behind her delicate ears.

"We need to talk," I said.

"We already talked, and it was all about you. It always is," she said, picking up her backpack and lifting it onto her shoulder.

I threw my hands in the air. "Everything with you is an argument. Why can't you see it my way?"

She tried to brush past me, but I grabbed her by her arms and gave her a slight shake. A shot of fear went through her eyes, but it was quickly replaced with anger. The first tone went off, and I knew we only had two minutes to get to class.

"I don't want to see it your way. Thank you for the sex, but I think I'll move on and find someone normal."

"The hell you will!" I yelled.

"Let me go; I don't want to be late for class."

I released her arms and stepped in front of the door, letting my backpack fall to the floor. I didn't care if we were late for class. I needed an answer in the affirmative from her. Her words needed to tickle my ears and tell me she would be mine and do what I asked. But she didn't.

"No."

Avery's defiance was a turn-on that only caused my dick to stir in my pants.

"Get out of my way, asshole," she continued.

She swung her backpack at me, but I caught it, yanked it away, and dropped it to the floor next to mine. Next, Avery came toward me with her fists and tried to hit me. It was almost comical, and I began laughing. Caught off guard by my response, she froze. In the next few seconds, she must have thought the same because she joined me in a laugh, and as the second tone went off, we locked lips.

Avery slipped her hands into my jacket and ran them over my muscles. I was rock hard by then, my dick straining against my zipper. My first thought was being inside her, and my last was Spanish class. I didn't care if they marked me absent. She speared her tongue into my mouth as I inched up her skirt until I got to the promised land.

Her panties were wet, and I knew I'd gotten to her the way she got on me. Craving more, I began to rub the sheer panel, and she moaned in my mouth.

"Fuck me, Gideon," she murmured.

"Here?" I asked.

Avery pulled back from me and caught my gaze. "Are you embarrassed?"

"I'm surprised."

Without hesitating, she worked on opening my belt and zipper, then reached in to extract my cock while I pulled down her panties. Avery kicked off her shoes first before her white lacy panties followed, pooling at her ankles.

"Those are mine," I groaned out.

"You have my red ones."

"Shush," I said as I lifted her against the wall.

I lowered her onto me, and her groan was music to my ears. Avery wrapped her arms around my neck, holding tight; I pounded her until we both came in fast, simultaneous orgasms. As we leaned against each other, she kissed my cheek.

"This doesn't change anything. I'm still pissed at you," she said.

I chuckled as I let her down. "I figured."

~

FIFTEEN SETS of eyes turned to us when we entered the classroom. I nodded at Mrs. Dolan when I sat down, Avery doing the same.

"Mr. Berne and Miss Bedford, care to enlighten me as to why you're late?" Mrs. Dolan asked.

Avery glanced at me, and I gave her a discreet wink.

"We're sorry, Mrs. Dolan. Our parents are on their honeymoon in Europe, and they called us in between classes. The call ran a little late."

She raised her brows in surprise. "I wasn't aware you two were related."

I took my seat next to Avery, fully aware she wasn't wearing any panties because they were in the inner pocket of my jacket.

"Only since this past summer," I clarified.

"Congratulations," Mrs. Dolan replied. "I'll excuse your tardiness but don't make it a habit."

"Yes, Señora."

I took out my tablet and tried to keep my mind off what we'd just done. That bathroom would forever be ours, I thought smugly.

CHAPTER 21

Avery

I let Gideon get to me, and now I was sitting in Spanish class with no panties and full of his creamy semen. It had coated my thighs, and I would need to shower when I got back from class. Every glance from my stepbrother spoke of a seduction where he wanted to consume me whole until I gave in to his every whim. I wouldn't go that far even though I craved sex.

Mrs. Dolan droned on, having us repeat the words she spoke. Four years of Spanish and still stumbled through a conversation in the language. When the bell went off, I stood up, and Gideon brushed his hand across my ass, blocking the view with his body.

I turned to stare him down, but a huge grin crossed his face. Walking to History was a lesson in futility as the wind whipped my skirt around. I held onto it for dear life before I became the embarrassment of the entire school. Gideon was a few steps behind me the whole way, and I was sure he was getting a kick out of my predicament.

"Let it go," Clover called.

She was waiting for me at the front of the building, and as a gust blew up her skirt, she let it happen. She was wearing her favorite purple thong, and anyone around her got an uninterrupted view of her underwear.

"No way!" I hissed as I met her. "Let's get inside."

I WAS SITTING on my bed and reading the third chapter of my history eBook on my school tablet. Clover was changing as she prepared for a dinner date with Remy. In the end, she put on a cute little light blue dress with a short skirt and spaghetti straps.

"Why bother?" I asked.

"I can't eat dinner naked. That's for later."

I shook my head. "You're depraved."

"I'm in lust. Remy is nice."

I put the tablet down. "You think maybe he's more into you than you are to him?"

"Maybe. But you know me, I don't date much." Clover twirled around and looked at herself in the full-length mirror that hung on the inside of the closet door.

"When will you be back?" I asked.

She shrugged. "Figure two hours for dinner and another two hours for other stuff."

"Other stuff?"

"Sex—something you need to have before your pussy dries up and withers away."

I threw a pillow at her, which she caught and threw back.

"It's fine," I replied. "I have a vibrator and my fingers."

Clover put her hands on her hips. "They can't equal a good hard dick, trust me. You will crave having it once you get it."

I've already been craving it.

"All right, enough of this crap," she said, interrupting my thought. "I have to go. Remy promised me raw oysters for an appetizer." She grabbed her purse and breezed out of the room.

A: I know you have nothing going on right now, so why don't you come to my room?

G: How do you know I have nothing going on?

A: Because it's obvious you're waiting for my text.

G: I'm tired. Come down here.

A: I always do... Remy graciously took Clover to dinner.

G: I'll be right there.

A MINUTE LATER, Gideon slipped into my room. His dark hair was damp from a shower and hanging over his forehead rather than in its usual swept-back style. It gave him a dangerous look as he grinned at me, and I sat up, not expecting him so soon.

"It smells nice in here, like you."

I grinned back. "And what smell is that since you seem to be fixated on one scent?"

He sat next to me, his body heat warming me. Everything about Gideon turned me on and not just his looks. My belly clenched, and my heart sped along.

"My favorite smell."

"Are we ever figuring this out?"

Gideon leaned against the wall and pulled me between his legs, wrapping his arm around my waist.

"Do you want to figure this out?" he returned.

"I do. I think we're good together unless you want me to forget you and go out with Duncan."

He swept my hair from my neck and bit me, not hard, but hard enough to make me yelp.

"I'm not sharing you."

"Then I want to know everything. About you and your boys. I knew you had something planned for me."

He sighed, rubbing at the spot he bit. "You'll think I'm sick."

"I want to know all of it," I insisted. "Start with what you thought of me when you met me."

"I'd rather fuck you."

"My pussy is on hiatus until you tell me everything."

Gideon let me go, and I moved away, wanting to see his face when he told me everything. Every dirty perverted detail.

His eyebrows slammed together. "Hiatus? I can't be without it."

"Then tell me the truth, and we'll discuss it."

~

"It started in sophomore year. I had sex for the first time with the hostess at Preppies. She's three years older than me and really knew her stuff. She taught me how to treat a girl in bed."

I narrowed my eyes. "How old were you?"

"Sixteen. I just turned, but she had no idea I was that young and didn't ask. She thought I attended Beane College."

"How long were you with her?"

"On and off for a few months until she found out I was in high school. She said it was better we didn't date. I agreed. I got what I wanted from her."

I hesitated. "Is she the one who taught you to… control?"

"No. That was all me."

"But how?" I asked searchingly.

"I found things in my house—toys, handcuffs."

I gasped. My mother wasn't into that stuff. Why would Payne have it in his home? "Payne?"

He shrugged. "I guess. I found them in one of the guest rooms. Maybe he used them with my mom or a girlfriend and forgot about them. I wanted to ask, but I decided not to."

"How then?"

"I saw some videos that turned me on and thought I could try it with some girls here. Jillian Cronenberg was into it. Until this year, we had a room in the basement of Adwell Hall, where she lived. We all used it. There's a tunnel from here to there. The administration uses the room for storage now."

I couldn't believe what I was hearing. It was outrageous to me. We were so young, and his tastes were already developed into kinky shit.

"Are the other guys doing the same thing?" I asked.

Gideon shook his head. "Not as far as I know. Xavier likes certain things, but he doesn't like the dom stuff."

"And suppose I don't want to do any of it?"

He looked away from me, and right then, I knew the answer. If I didn't bow to what he wanted, there wasn't a future for us.

But I wouldn't be tied down, spanked, degraded, or abused. If Gideon thought I would allow it, he was wrong.

"Can't you just try?" he asked, almost pleading.

"No. I love having sex with you but not if you plan on hurting me," I said.

"That's just it; I wouldn't. You just need to be open to things."

My heart was breaking at him not budging to see my point of view because, as sick as it sounded, I'd fallen for Gideon. He turned me on even though he was mean and abusive. I forgave him for his shitty treatment of me, but I couldn't overlook his need for control. Even so, we still had a few things to discuss before I let him go.

"Why were you so mean to me when I came to Berne Manor?"

"Stupidity and I thought you didn't belong," he answered.

"*Why*? Because I wasn't in the same social circles as you?" I asked.

He chewed on his bottom lip. "That, and I didn't know how I could live with you when I wanted you."

I snorted. "So you acted like an asshole because you are an asshole."

"It was dumb," he said.

"And you owe me an apology."

"I'm sorry. I really like you."

Gideon sounded like a little boy, but I couldn't get past many things that had already indicated this was over before it started. Tears pricked my eyes, and I pushed them back as I got up on my knees, cupped his face with my hands, and kissed his lips.

"I can't do this, and this has to be goodbye," I murmured.

He looked shocked that I was turning him away, but it had to be. I couldn't give him what he wanted, and he couldn't be what I wanted.

"You want me to go?"

"Yes. I need you to go."

"Why can't we be friends?" he asked.

Tears were welling in my eyes, and I couldn't stop them from rolling down my cheeks. "Because I know I can't be or do what you want, and I know if we're friends, that's what you'll try to do until I give in."

He ran a hand through his hair, pushing his bangs from his forehead, but they just flopped back. "Fuck, darling Avery."

I wiped at my tears. "Don't call me that. Please go."

Gideon silently rose from the bed, and I put my face in my hands as more silent tears came. I heard the door lock click closed, and when it did, I let my cries out.

Over the next few days, I tried to keep my distance from Gideon. It wasn't easy having two classes where we sat next to each other, but he honored my request and kept his hands to himself. I also made sure to use the bathroom down the hall when I went in between trig and Spanish. I avoided the other one for two reasons, one - I didn't want Gideon locking me in with him, and two - because it was the last place we had sex.

On Friday, Gideon asked me in Spanish if I would watch his game against Parker Preparatory.

"No. Clover met some guys from Beane College, and we're heading to a party tonight."

"You can't!" he cried.

"Shhh," I said.

Mrs. Dolan came into the room a second later, and there was no more discussion about the party until class was over. Once I shoved my tablet into my backpack, he put his hand on my arm.

"I mean it," he said. "Where is this party?"

"On Apple Street."

He gritted his teeth. "No!"

I ignored him, zipping up my backpack and slinging it onto

my shoulder. Gideon tugged at the straps while everyone filed out of class.

"You're going to the Theta Rho Kappa house? Don't do it."

"Why? Because you don't want me to find another guy?" I challenged.

Gideon's face was bright red. "That's part of it. The other part is that they're a bunch of scumbags. They like to spike drinks."

"I won't drink. I'm underage, remember? Not that it's stopped you," I snapped.

I wrenched my backpack from his grip and hurried out of the classroom. If Gideon thought he would tell me what to do, he was wrong. Two guys Clover and I had met earlier during a break period, who later introduced themselves as James and Frank, had come up to us when we were sitting on the lawn.

They talked to us for a little while before they asked us to the party. They didn't seem like the type who would take advantage, and they knew we were high school girls. After they left, I told Clover that I felt comfortable attending with her because she was street-smart and wouldn't let anything happen to us, even when it concerned college guys.

When I got to history, our class was canceled due to our teacher having a family emergency. Our weekend would start early, I thought excitedly.

"What dress should I wear?" I asked Clover.

"One of mine. Yours are *too, too* tame," she said, emphasizing her words.

"They are not," I protested. "What do you want? My boobs and ass hanging out?"

"No but show something. This could be your chance to find a guy to give up your V card to."

It felt horrible keeping my secret, but what was I supposed to say? My dick of a stepbrother popped my cherry, and we had sex all night? That wasn't happening because Clover would have a fit and tell me to have my head checked.

"Maybe," I offered, "but I'm not giving it up to just anyone."

"Then call Duncan. Lose it and dump him. I'm sure he would be happy to pop your cherry."

"No, thank you."

Shortly after that discussion, we hurried along because we only had a few hours to eat dinner, shower, dress, and get over to the Theta Rho Kappa house. Driving wasn't necessary since their house was four blocks from campus. Despite what I told Gideon if I was offered a drink, I decided I might have a couple.

"Frank is hot, don't you think?" Clover asked.

I wrinkled my nose. His square black glasses, goatee, and brush cut weren't even close to my type. Anyway, there were probably plenty of hot guys at the Theta house. I'd only been to one college party when I was at Arlington, but we'd left early because it turned into a total mosh pit.

"Not my type, but I thought you were messing with Remy?" I questioned.

"He's getting clingy, and I don't want a relationship."

"Sorry."

She tugged me along, and we jumped into the elevator as the doors closed.

THE PARTY WAS in full swing when we arrived, even though it was just before 9 pm. Clover wore the same dress she'd worn when Remy last took her to dinner. I was wearing a little black dress which showed too much cleavage, but Clover assured me it looked fine.

The Theta house was a three-story colonial with a large porch. Several guys were playing soccer on the lawn, red plastic cups in their hands. A few couples sat on the porch in white plastic chairs. Frank was sitting on the stairs when we came up the walk and were met with a few whistles that pierced the air.

"Hey ladies, glad you could make it."

He put his arms around our shoulders as he led us inside. Rock music was playing—Led Zeppelin's Ramble On. I knew the song because my mother used to play it when she cooked. I felt uncomfortable as we entered, surrounded by people older than us. I suddenly had no idea why I agreed to come. We didn't belong here, but we might as well make the best of it, I tried to reason. Frank took us into the kitchen, where a large keg was packed in an aluminum garbage can with ice. Another green plastic garbage can with a black liner filled with red liquid was placed next to it.

"Want some garbage punch?" Frank yelled over the music.

Clover and I looked at each other and nodded at Frank. Using a ladle, he scooped some up into red cups and handed them over, then introduced us to a few guys in the kitchen. I sipped at the punch, tasting alcohol-laced Kool-Aid, and wondered exactly what was in the stuff.

Keeping close, I followed behind them as Frank took Clover over to the living room, whispering in her ear the entire time. She nodded, and he took the cup from her hand. They danced in front of the fireplace in an open space with three other couples. I felt so out of place that I wished I had listened to Gideon. I turned to a tap on my shoulder.

"Hi. Who are you?"

The guy who questioned me was tall with sandy hair and the brightest blue eyes I'd ever seen. He was adorable and wore a Beane College Rugby jersey.

"Avery," I answered, getting lost in his stare.

"I'm Teddy. Where are you from?"

"Bancroft. I'm a senior."

He gave me a crooked smile. "New blood. I guess you won't be coming here for college."

"Why would you say that?" I said as I sipped my punch.

Teddy grabbed a beer from the counter and took me by the hand, leading out to a side porch with a cushioned loveseat.

"It's too loud in there to talk," he said.

"Now, why would you say what you said earlier?" I asked.

"Because Bancroft is a rich girl's school. I bet you have connections at ivy league colleges. Am I right?"

"Maybe. If anything, it would be Yale. My stepfather's family is legacy there."

Teddy drained half his beer. "See, I told you. I'm a junior here, pre-law."

I had no idea what to say. A weird feeling was coming over me, and the hair on the back of my neck stood on end. Acting fast, I accidentally-on-purpose spilled my drink on the porch floor, causing Teddy to pull his sneaker-clad feet up.

"Shit, I'm sorry," I apologized with as much sincerity as I could muster.

"I'll get you another cup; wait here."

Teddy took my cup from me and went inside. Gideon's words echoed in my head about how they spiked drinks. I rose from the sofa and started to head inside when Teddy came out with a fresh cup of punch.

"Where you going, darling?" he asked with a bit of a western drawl.

I shuddered at the word since it was what Gideon called me. Gideon. Why didn't I listen to him?

"I have to use the bathroom," I answered quickly. "Can you tell me where it is?"

"There's one upstairs."

I took my cup from him, intending to dump it into the sink when I got in the bathroom. Something told me not to trust Teddy, but I couldn't avoid him as he led me inside and upstairs. We pushed through a bunch of people leaning against the walls, smoking weed and drinking from liquor bottles.

"Right here. I'll wait for you," Teddy said.

"Thanks."

"No problem, darling."

I winced as I stepped into the bathroom, locking the door behind me. I switched on both lights and tipped my cup to the side. A residue was floating on the surface, and I was pretty sure something had been put in the cup. If I drank this, I had a feeling I would find myself naked and spreadeagled with a massive headache the next morning.

I spilled the punch into the sink. I didn't really need to use the bathroom; I just wanted to get away from Teddy. He began knocking on the door after a few minutes, asking, "Are you okay in there?"

The longer I holed up, the more my stomach churned with anxiety. Suppose Frank was doing the same thing to Clover? She was in danger, and I needed to protect her. I came out, leaving my empty cup in the bathroom.

"Where's your drink?" Teddy asked.

"I sucked it down. It's pretty good."

His lips formed a wide grin.

You fucking dirtbag. You probably think you'll have sex with me while I'm half comatose. Not gonna happen; not on my watch.

"Want another cup?" he asked too encouragingly.

I stumbled a little just to make Teddy think I was getting woozy.

"Steady there," he said and put his hands on my hips.

I wanted to throw up all over him, the bile rising in my throat as my heart began to pound like a jackhammer against my chest. Trying to keep him from touching me too much, I made my way downstairs, where I eventually found Clover sitting on a couch and sipping at her cup of punch. She seemed to be all right.

"Want another cup of punch? I can get it for you," Teddy said.

"I think I'd like a beer, and can you leave the top on? I like to pull them off with my teeth," I replied, sweetening my voice.

His eyes widened. "I'd like to see that."

The second after Teddy headed for the kitchen; I hurried over to Clover. Her eyes looked glassy like she was on something, and her speech was slurred when I asked how she was.

"How ya doing, Avvverrry?"

I grabbed her chin and looked at Frank.

"How much of this crap did you give her?" I growled.

He was flippant. "She's fine. I can take her up to my room to sleep it off."

"Fuck no. We need to go home."

I knew we needed to get out of there, but without a car, there was no way I could get her back to the dorm without help. A glance at my phone told me it was nearing 10 pm. I knew Gideon's game would be over, and hopefully, he would answer his phone. I hid behind a crowd of people so I could watch Clover and keep out of Teddy's view.

My phone rang twice as Teddy reemerged, holding two bottles of beer and craning his neck to look for me, and then Gideon picked up. In the background, I could hear yelling, which probably meant he was in the locker room after they trounced Parker Prep.

"Avery, what's wrong?" he called over the noise.

"The party," I hissed. "We're here, and they put something in Clover's drink."

"Fucking bastards!" he screamed. "Did you drink anything?"

I bit back tears. "No. I'm sorry to call you."

"I'll be there in five minutes."

"Don't hang–" But it was too late. My phone went dead.

"There you are," Teddy said, making me whirl around to him. "Who were you talking to?"

"Wrong number."

He handed me my beer, and I noticed the top was off. I held

it in my hand, running the pads of my fingers over the condensation on the glass.

"Aren't you gonna drink it?" Teddy asked.

"I don't like this type of beer," I made up. "What happened to the Sam Adams?"

"All out. We only have Bud, so drink up. This stuff ain't cheap."

Glancing back to check on Clover, I pretended to drink it, putting the bottle to my closed lips and swallowing. Because of the dark glass and the dim room, Teddy couldn't tell if I drank any. Just as I prayed Gideon would get here and save us, my prayers were answered when he busted in the door, still wearing his dirty uniform. Behind him were Remy, Jaxson, Xavier, and three other guys I recognized from the offensive line.

The second we locked eyes, he pushed his way through the crowd while Remy went to where Clover was slumped and lifted her almost unconscious body into his arms. Gideon walked past Teddy and took my hand.

"Get the fuck off her, rich boy," Teddy growled.

Gideon said nothing as he stepped away from me and slammed his fist into Teddy's face. Blood gushed from Teddy's nose as he crumpled to the floor, screaming in pain.

"Don't you ever put your hands on her again!" Gideon screamed.

No one came to Teddy's aid, and Frank backed away, probably hoping he wouldn't be doled out the same punishment. I barely looked back as Gideon led me out of the house with his football teammates following.

CHAPTER 22

Avery

"Gideon, you're dragging me!" I shouted.

Not missing a step, he turned, scooped me up in his arms, and carried me the remainder to his car.

"You don't listen, darling Avery. What would you do if I couldn't come to get you?" he snarled.

"Put me down."

He carried me to the road where his Bugatti was parked and only put me down by the door to open it and prod me inside. I slumped down in the low leather seat. I'd never been inside Gideon's car, and even when things were bad, I could appreciate how beautiful and sleek it was. Distracting myself, I ran my hand over the leather as he slipped inside, uncaring of the fact that he was dirty.

"You didn't answer my question," he said.

The car came to life with a low purr as he started it, and he gunned the engine before throwing it into gear.

"I don't know. Is that what you want to hear? Where's Clover?"

"Remy is taking care of her. I'm sure she was drugged. Did you…?"

"No. I tipped over the first cup, and when I checked the second, I saw a residue on top of the punch, so I poured it down the bathroom sink."

Four short blocks later, he pulled into the parking lot and whipped into a spot, shutting off the engine.

"You can do whatever you like, but I won't sit by and watch you put yourself in danger," he said into the silence.

Staring hard at him, I felt my breathing pick up. "Shut up, Gideon. Just shut up," I said before I wrapped my hand around his neck and slammed my mouth over his. It had been several days since we had sex, and I wanted him more than ever. I couldn't even bring myself to care about his kinky bullshit. He dug his fingers into my hair, tugging so hard it became painful, but I didn't protest. Gideon pulled away first.

"Darling Avery," he taunted. "You fucked up my game. You fucked up my life. You plain fucked me up."

"I'm not sure what I should say here?"

"Say you'll come home with me."

"I'll go home with you. Let's go upstairs."

Rather than exiting, he turned the car on, backed out of the spot, and pulled out of the parking lot onto the main drag.

"Gideon, where are we going?" I asked.

"Home."

"I have no clothes with me!" I protested.

"You don't need clothes. I want you naked in my bed until we come back on Sunday."

"What about food?" I added, this time more teasingly.

Gideon got onto the highway, heading toward Arlington. We would be home in two hours. The anticipation of being with him again had my nipples hard and belly clenching the entire ride. I couldn't wait.

~

I MUST HAVE FALLEN asleep on the drive home because I woke up abruptly to Gideon removing me from the car. We were in front of the well-lit Berne Manor.

"I can walk," I voiced.

Gideon put me down and took my hand before he closed the door and led me to the entrance to our home. His uniform was stained with dirt and grass stains from the game, but it made me feel good to know that he would drop everything to come to save me from a foolish decision.

Once inside, he let go of me and went to the kitchen, where he grabbed a bottle of water and chugged the entire contents down in one gulp. I was grateful for what he and his friends did for us. If he hadn't come, I hated to think what could've happened.

"Gideon, I want to–"

He held his hand up and cut me off. "I know. You don't have to say it. I need a shower. Will you wait for me in my room?"

I nodded, and he toed off his sneakers, picked them up, and headed for the stairs. When he was out of sight, I tossed the empty water bottle in the recycling bin and pulled two more bottles out to take upstairs.

The shower was running when I entered Gideon's room and placed the bottles on the nightstand before slipping out to head to my room. I quickly changed into a pair of shorts and a t-shirt, removed my makeup, and brushed my teeth before I returned.

By then, Gideon was drying himself and walked out with the towel wrapped around his waist.

"You changed," he said.

"I still have clothes here."

"I said you won't need them."

As if to prove his point, he came to me and grasped the hem of my shirt, tugging at it. I put my arms up, and he pulled it off, gently easing it over my head. I ran my hand over the damp ridges of his stomach and paused at the knot in his towel.

"Lose the shorts and get in bed, Avery," he directed.

Gideon spied the bottles I put on the nightstand and cracked one open, drinking half the water while I undressed.

"Get in bed," he repeated after taking a breath.

I knew he was ordering me, trying to control me, but after what he did for us tonight, I would give him a pass. Maybe we could compromise. I peeled back the covers and slipped in as he tossed the damp towel on his desk chair. Half-naked Gideon made me hot, but fully naked Gideon made me burst into flame.

"Move over, Avery."

"Aren't you shutting off the lights?" I replied.

"Not this time. I want you to see everything I do to you. Every thrust of my cock, every lick of my tongue, every touch on your body. Everything."

I trembled as he slipped into bed with me, parting my legs and climbing in between them. I anticipated his touch, impatiently waiting for his next move. Still, instead of receiving relief, I watched as Gideon stroked his considerable length until a bead of salty dew bubbled at the tip. He used his thumb to slick up the head of his dick, making it glisten.

"Sit up, Avery, and taste me."

I licked my lips as I sat up and stuck my tongue out toward his tip, circling his purple head. He hummed with appreciation, closing his eyes for a moment.

"Enough," he abruptly cut in. "Lie back and prop your head on the pillows."

Gideon waited for me to comply, and once I was propped up, he stroked himself, moving closer. I enjoyed the show as he pleasured himself, but I wanted him to touch me. He panted and bit the tip of his tongue as he fisted his cock, speeding up.

"Darling Avery, I'm going to decorate you."

With those words, he came hard, shooting ropes of creamy semen onto my stomach and mound. He moaned my name, and when he was finished, he knelt back on his heels.

"Look at my dirty, messy girl painted white."

I dipped my finger in the semen pooled on my stomach and sucked it off my finger.

"Fuck, Avery! You're so damn sexy."

Gideon began to stroke himself again as I sat up, pushing his other hand away as semen rolled down my stomach. When he was hard again, he pushed me back, poised his cock at my slick opening, and slammed into me. He stretched out on top of me, not caring about the mess, and latched his mouth onto mine.

I wrapped my legs around his waist and arched my back as he fucked me, moaning into his mouth. And the twisted thing about this whole situation was, as he slammed into me, that I could admit one thing to myself: I was in love with my evil stepbrother. The guy who tormented me for the past few months had redeemed himself with one gesture.

He lifted off me, and I reached up to touch his face, running my thumb over his lips. He sucked it into his mouth and closed his eyes.

"I love how you fuck me," I moaned out.

Gideon let my thumb go. "And I love fucking you. This tight little pussy is like nothing I've had before."

Although I didn't believe it because I knew he had been with several girls before me, something was happening between us that made me think maybe my love wasn't one-sided. He reached back to pull my legs from around his waist, knelt back, and put my legs onto his shoulders, squeezing them together in his arm.

Gideon relentlessly drove into me, and I was panting so hard at the change in position that I could barely breathe.

"Pinch your nipples, play with those beautiful tits, Avery!" he ordered.

I coated my nipples with his semen and circled them with my fingers, bucking my hips in time to the rhythm of his thrusts. I was growing exhausted even though I had napped in the car. I couldn't see how Gideon had the energy to play with me.

"Come, Avery, before I do and leave you to suffer."

I reached for my clit, but he pushed my hand away.

"I know you can come without your fingers. Do it because I'm ready to blow," he growled.

I pinched my nipples harder, and the extra stimulation, coupled with the pounding of his cock had me shattering like shards of glass.

"Gideeeeooonnn!"

He followed immediately, filling me before he let my legs go. When they fell to the side, he collapsed on top of me, raining kisses on my chest. I began to laugh.

"What's funny?" he asked.

"We're a sticky mess."

"How about a shower and a bath?" he asked.

He rose off me and helped me up. Somehow, despite our mess, the sheets remained unsoiled as Gideon led me to the bathroom.

WE LOUNGED in Gideon's deep egg-shaped tub, surrounded by a mound of vanilla-scented bubbles. I sat between his legs while he drew lazy circles around my nipples.

"Gideon, I never thanked you for what you did tonight."

He pushed the curtain of wet hair away from my neck and

kissed me. "Despite what you think, I care for you. You know how angry I was when you wouldn't listen to me?"

"I'm sorry."

"I'm surprised the Theta's chapter hasn't been revoked. Last year two of their members were arrested for assault. They hurt some girls from Bancroft. They have a history of preying on younger women."

He pinched my nipples, and a shock of electricity coursed into my belly.

"I don't know what I would've done if you didn't come," I responded quietly. I stretched my neck, and Gideon bit me, then cleansed the mark with his tongue.

"I should spank you for your behavior. I played like shit because I was so worried about you. Coach screamed at me the whole game."

"You won, though, right?"

"Yeah, by twenty. It would've been higher if I didn't throw a few interceptions."

I sucked in my breath. "But you don't throw interceptions. You're perfect."

"You see what you do to me?" he growled. "Why can't you meet me in the middle? I wouldn't hurt you."

"Because I don't want to be hurt."

"How can you hurt someone you love?"

I had my hands on his thighs, gripping them tightly, digging my nails into his muscles.

I gasped. "What did you say?"

"I love you. I don't want to be separated from you, but I need certain things. Like I said, why do you have to be so damn beautiful?"

I turned toward Gideon, straddling his legs with my knees, so they were planted on the bottom of the tub. The bubbles that surrounded us shifted, and I brushed them away.

"I'm not sure I can give you what you need. You want to dominate me."

I pecked him on his lips, and he gazed into my eyes, reaching his soapy hands up to hold my cheeks.

"Trust me. If you don't like something, we won't do it."

"You mean you want to groom me for some kinky shit?"

He laughed. "What we just did is kinky. You let me come all over you."

I put my head on his shoulder and let him wrap his arms around me in an embrace. I felt safe in Gideon's arms, and we had a day and a half together to discuss things. I yawned.

"Tired?" he asked.

"Yes. I haven't been sleeping very well."

"Because of me?"

"Kinda."

He grinned. "Let's get you into bed—my bed."

I floated away from him as we both stood up in the tub. Gideon climbed out first, then lifted me out, wrapping me in his white terry robe that practically dragged the floor.

I PASSED out almost instantly after my head hit the pillow, with Gideon cuddled up against me and whispering that he loved me. I couldn't say it, but I wanted to. Two hours later, I was wide awake, thinking about what our relationship would be like. Not only would we be hiding from our parents, but I wasn't sure I wanted to tell anyone that we were dating.

"Gideon?"

"Hmm?"

I shifted in his arms. "Are you awake?"

He yawned. "I am now. What's the matter?"

"The control situation is one thing, but what about our parents?"

Gideon sighed. "Avery, it's three in the morning. You want to discuss this now?"

"It's scandalous. We'll be stepsiblings dating and having sex."

"Who said I want to date you?" He cupped my pussy. "I just want this sweet cunt."

For a moment, I thought he was serious. "Has anyone told you you're an idiot?"

"Don't worry about it. I'm sure we can keep it quiet."

"But my mother will have a fit, and I'm sure they'd make me move to one of the bedrooms down the hall or on the lower level."

He kissed my cheek. "You worry too much. It will be fine. Is there anything else you want to discuss?"

I hesitated. The three words were right at the tip of my tongue, yet I was having trouble getting them out of my mouth.

"Avery?"

"I love you," I blurted out.

The sheets rustled as Gideon reached over me to turn on the light. He stared at me.

"When?"

"I think I realized it tonight," I started, staring at the ceiling. "You came for me, and I missed you. It was also hard to sit next to you in class and not talk to you."

I turned over to face him, and he tucked a lock of my hair over my ear.

"That was your choice," he reminded. "You made that decision, not me."

"You hit me," I shot back.

"I spanked you," he corrected.

"Same thing."

My mouth dropped open as a second later, I realized Gideon was growing hard against me. I touched him, and he smirked.

"Avery, don't mess with the snake unless you want the fangs."

I curled a fist around him, slowly sliding my hand over his hot skin. “I want the fangs.”

“This will be nothing compared to what I want to do with you. All you have to do is let go. Just say the word.”

“This is too deep a conversation to have at this hour,” I said, using his point from carlicr. “I think I’d likc you to fuck mc to sleep.”

He moved my hand away and then used the same one to swipe his between my lower lips to check my readiness. In response, Gideon sucked in his breath and pulled my leg over his hip before he poised his dick at my entrance and moved his pelvis. Our union was hard and fast. I came within a minute of him entering me, and he followed two minutes later as I clung to him.

Once we were settled again with my head on his shoulder, I told Gideon I loved him as I faded to sleep. I heard him mumble the same thing to me. If it meant we were now a thing, a couple because I was giving in, compromising, I didn’t know what it meant, but I would probably find out soon.

CHAPTER 23

Gideon

"Hurry up," I said.

Avery smirked at me as she pulled on her shorts. "I thought you wanted me naked all weekend."

I crossed my arms. "You're welcome to walk the halls naked and give the help a show."

"Where are we going anyway?" she asked.

"You have no idea where you live. Have you ever searched the halls of this great abode we live in?" I asked, putting on a haughty air.

Avery smoothed her hair down while she looked in the mirror. I came up behind her and cupped her perky breasts.

"Don't get me started, five."

I frowned. "Five?" I questioned.

She looked up at me. "You're Gideon Berne the fifth. How pretentious of you."

I pinched her nipple. "Pretentious? I didn't choose to be the fifth. It was bestowed on me at birth."

Avery brushed my hand away. "Why isn't Payne the fifth?"

"Because my grandmother wouldn't hear of it. My grandfather was upset, but he let it go and when I was born, guess who got the name."

"So your grandfather is Gideon Berne the fourth?"

"Gideon Andrew Charton Berne the fourth," I clarified.

She giggled. "Your name is Gideon Andrew Charton Berne the fifth?"

I bit her neck and sucked the flesh into my mouth. "Don't kid. It's a regal name."

"It's pretentious," I repeated.

"Enough slander of my name."

I grabbed her hand and opened the door to my bedroom, leading her down the hall. Our footsteps echoed slightly off the twenty-foot ceilings since there was barely any décor.

"Where are we going?" she asked.

"On a tour. I bet you have no idea about this place. I don't even think my father knows about the little nooks and crannies in this place. He's too busy making money, and he's conducting business while he's away."

"My mother wouldn't be happy if he were," she said.

"She'll get used to it. My father is driven by deals and money if you haven't already figured that out, but enough about them."

I led her to a wide door in the middle of the hallway just past the stairs. I opened it to reveal an elevator inside.

Avery's eyes widened in surprise. "I've lived here almost three months and didn't know there was an elevator?"

"It's not used a lot," I told her. "I don't even know why we have it."

I pushed her inside and followed, closing the door behind us. The elevator was big enough for four people. I pressed the L button and bunched Avery's long golden hair in my hand, latching onto her lips. We stayed attached until the elevator dinged and the doors opened to a subterranean pool.

"This is what you want to show me?" she asked, sounding unimpressed. "I know we have an indoor pool down here. I've never swam in it, but I know it's here."

"Shush, there's more to see, and we can skinny dip in this one if you like. It's getting too chilly for the one outside. It will be closed soon."

Avery snorted. "Skinny dip. Don't you mean make it easier for you to fuck me?"

I ignored her and led her to another hallway, stopping at a fuse box to flick several switches. Lights for an enclosed racquetball court, half basketball court, full-size tennis court, and a ten-seat movie theater turned on. Avery tugged at my hand.

"Okay, I *didn't* know this was down here."

"This place is fully equipped just in case we can't get out because of bad weather. We also have a full workout room at the end of the hall."

She let go of my hand and pushed open the door to the movie room. A one hundred twenty-inch screen dominated the wall at one end, and ten double-wide theater seats covered in black microsuede sat in the middle of the room.

On the side were a candy, soda, and popcorn bar, complete with a bunch of jars filled with colorful and wrapped candies, a popcorn machine with red striped cardboard boxes that sat at the ready, and a commercial soda machine with six types of soda. Avery walked over to a jar of jellybeans and pulled the dispenser, letting out a handful before she closed it.

"We could invite half of Bancroft to this place and still have plenty of room," she said as she sucked jellybeans one by one past her sensual lips.

"Come, I'm not finished."

"Not finished?" she questioned.

Another door at the other end of the hall was the most special place because it contained a bar, two pool tables, a poker table with four matching stools, five arcade games from the eighties, and a shuffleboard table.

Top-shelf alcohol graced the glass shelves behind the wooden bar, along with several shelves of crystal glasses in different sizes. Avery pulled away from me and headed to the shuffleboard table.

"I love this!" she squealed.

I laughed. "More than me?" I asked.

"Maybe."

She bent over and pushed a red puck along the table, wiggling her shapely ass as she did. My dick stirred as she grabbed another and did the same. When Avery reached for a third, I came up behind her and put my hands on her hips, grinding my hips against her ass.

She gasped. "You would think you had enough after four times."

"Never. I'd like to bend you over this table and fuck you," I replied huskily.

"Do it," she moaned.

"Dammit, Avery. You could at least offer some resistance."

She stood up and turned to face me. "Tonight is all we have, and then what? How do we see each other at school and spend time together? Have you figured that out?"

I couldn't offer her any answers. "Not yet, but I'll figure something out."

"And in the meantime, what do we do? Have sex in a dirty bathroom?"

"Do you want to waste this time arguing?"

"No."

"Then let me make love to you."

Avery reached down to pull the drawstring on her gray terry

shorts, and I backed away to watch her strip, my dick growing harder by the second.

"No panties?" I asked with surprise.

"Why bother?"

She pulled off her t-shirt to reveal she was braless and stood there, legs spread wide in all her naked glory.

"Well?"

I massaged my swollen prick. "Well, what?"

"Do I need to do all the work?"

"What work?"

"The hell with you, Berne."

She climbed on the bar and laid back on the shiny wooden surface with her legs spread, and closed her eyes. I was intrigued as Avery slid a finger over her clit. Wetness sucked at her finger, and when she inserted one into her soaked channel, I almost came in my shorts.

"Well, Berne? Do I get myself off, or will you do it?"

I stripped, dropped my clothes on the floor, and approached her. The bar was the perfect height for me to eat her out in a comfortable position. I pushed her hand away and took her swollen tissue in my mouth, filling her slick tunnel with my fingers and fucking her with them.

Avery arched her back. "Not your fingers, your dick."

"Your wish is my command."

I climbed on the bar to get on top of her and, poised at her entrance, slicked my tip with her juices.

"Don't tease, Gideon."

I thrust hard, sliding deep inside her as I lowered my body onto hers. Avery Bedford was beautiful and sweet, probably sweeter than I deserved. But my rational thinking was out the window because I was in love with her. When I first saw her, all I could think of was a thousand ways to ruin her, but now all I wanted to do was protect her.

"Harder," she moaned.

If my father knew we were fucking on his prized bar, he would have a fit. Anytime the bar came up in conversations he'd have with business associates he invited to the house, he wouldn't fail to mention how the entire length of the bar top was cut from a single giant maple tree. To guarantee it was protected from damage, he had it encased in many layers of lacquer. But he probably hadn't had our naked bodies sliding back and forth along the surface in mind.

I placed my hands on the thick surface and slammed into her. Avery whimpered, wrapping her legs around me as she pulsed and squeezed my dick.

"Fuck, darling Avery. You're a very naughty girl."

She reached up to cup my face. "I love you."

Though she'd only said it a few times, my heart clenched each time she did. I didn't want to think about the obstacles in our way. Everything faded away while I made love to her. There was nothing but us.

"I love you too. God, how I love you."

It was sappy and so unlike me. I didn't show my emotions to anyone unless it was anger or amusement. I'd controlled everything in my world, and Avery was the only thing I couldn't control. A tiny corner of my brain stored the fear I felt when I lost her after her birthday.

Avery wrapped her hand around my neck and pulled me down to meet her lips. She tugged at my bottom lip with her teeth, then sucked it into her mouth. I felt her ripple against me as she detonated around me. I tried to hold on, hoping to coax another orgasm from her, but I was too far gone and followed with my own explosion.

I gently lowered myself onto her and tucked my hands under her shoulders. Avery ran her hands through my sweaty hair, pushing it back from my forehead.

"What do we do?" she asked, voicing my fears.

I lifted my head to gaze at her. "We keep quiet. Things will work out."

"I don't think they will. I'm afraid they won't, and I can't be without you."

I pressed my lips to hers to shut her up, not because I didn't want to hear what she had to say but because, for once in my life, I had no plan. I. Had. Nothing.

AFTER WE CLEANED up and I wiped down the defiled bar, I restarted the tour by taking Avery to other rooms in the house. First, the library with its floor-to-ceiling bookcases and rolling ladder; next, the wine cellar where I sneaked four-hundred-dollar bottles of wine to drink with my poker buddies; and finally, the tunnel which led from the main house to the pool house.

She swung my hand in hers along the way. "Anything else?" Avery asked.

"A few places—all hidden. I'm not sure my father is even aware."

"Why is there a tunnel from the pool house to the main house?"

"So our guests don't need to walk through bad weather if they're staying."

Avery started to laugh.

"What's funny?" I inquired.

"You have twelve bedrooms in this place," she pointed out. "Why would anyone need to stay in the pool house?"

"Be prepared."

Avery frowned at me. "What do you mean?"

"You've never been here for holidays, especially Christmas and New Year's. You'll see."

After this, I took her to another secret place I liked to go when I was a child—a turret room at the very top of the manor. There were two, one at either end of the house. Because of their height, you could see straight into town from either end of the manor.

A winding stone stairway led up to the turret on the east side of the building. Thick windows formed a wall all around that looked out toward the town. You could see Remy's house from up here over the thick grove of trees which separated the two properties.

"It must be nice up here in the winter," Avery said.

I placed my lips around her ear. "I'd like to fuck you up here, too. In fact, I'd like to fuck you in as many rooms as I can."

She giggled. "Of course, you would."

I cupped her ass, kneading the globes of perfection. "Wouldn't you want me to?"

"I would, but soon we won't be free." Her voice was tinged with sadness, and I had to agree.

"We can enjoy our time together and work on whatever happens in the future."

I took Avery by the hand and led her back down the stairs. I was debating showing her the pass through which connected our bedrooms. She could react in two ways: happy we had a way to be together even when our parents were home or pissed off that I invaded her privacy.

I swallowed hard as we hit the second floor. "I have something to show you. Please keep an open mind."

Avery narrowed her eyes at me. "What's the matter?"

She pulled back on my hand, but I held fast and practically dragged her to my bedroom.

"Gideon?"

I dropped her hand as we reached my bedroom. She hesitated in the doorway, and I prodded her inside.

"You're scaring me," Avery said.

"Don't be. Follow me."

I walked to the closet and stepped inside, then put my hand on the panel, which slid out and popped the latch. It opened, and I stepped into the pass-through before ducking my head out to look at her.

"Are you coming?" I asked.

"Gideon, what is this?" she said as she followed.

Once I pressed the latch to the doorway that held her shoes, and it swung open into her closet, she understood.

"Jesus Christ! You could get into my room even if I had the door locked?" she screeched, staring at me until I averted my gaze. "How many times have you done this?" she asked.

I looked up at her. "Every night you were here. After you went to sleep, I would watch you sleep for a few minutes wishing I could cuddle you in my arms."

She gently pushed me. "That is so creepy. So while you were making me miserable, you were also spying on me?"

I smirked. "I wasn't spying. I was gathering intelligence."

She narrowed her eyes. "What kind of intelligence?"

"I just wanted to see you."

"Gideon, you make no sense. All you had to do was be nice to me. We could've had a nice summer. Instead, you acted like an ass."

"But I'm making it up to you now."

"You got a lot more to make up for," she said.

"And I have so much more to show you."

CHAPTER 24

Avery

The ties on my wrists are loose but not loose enough for me to get away. The only piece of clothing I wore was a light blue lace thong. Gideon was standing over me, surveying my body.

"Darling Avery, are you comfortable?"

I tugged a little at the ties, both silk, one in charcoal and the other dark blue.

"I can't touch you with these on," I whined.

"I'll untie you if you want."

A look of disappointment crossed his face, and even though I thought this was weird, I wanted to please him.

"No."

Gideon crawled onto the bed and between my legs. We hadn't done anything, but his dick was erect and pressing against his gray boxers. I held my breath as he bent down and licked between my legs, grazing my swollen nub. I cried out and glanced at what he was doing, but it was hard to keep my head propped up, so I put it back down.

He rose from the bed, pressed a hard kiss to my lips, then arranged the pillows under my head so I could watch him. His sheets were scented with his cologne, and I turned my head to inhale it deep into my nose.

"Watch me, darling Avery."

I turned my head back as he roughly grasped the waistband of my panties and tugged until the delicate fabric shredded.

"Gideon!" I squealed. "That was unnecessary."

He held up the pieces and pressed his nose to the destroyed panel, closing his eyes. Now I was naked, but as he moved, it was clear Gideon wasn't done immobilizing me. He held up two more ties, one blood red, and the other black.

"What are you doing with those?" I asked, even though I knew exactly what he was going to do with them.

He proved me right when he wound one around my right ankle and secured it to the bed. My left leg pulled as wide as it would go, causing an ache in my inner thigh. Once I was tied, he shucked off his boxers, leaving them on the floor before he climbed my body.

"What are you planning to do with me?" I asked, unafraid because I knew Gideon wouldn't hurt me.

"Prepare for some fun."

His breath feathered my face as he traced my lips with his tongue. When I thrust mine out to meet his, he pulled back.

"Darling Avery, you need to let me lead."

I giggled as Gideon straddled my stomach and teased my nipples, gently tugging at the puckered flesh. I moaned and closed my eyes.

"Eyes open, dear stepsister."

My lids flew open. "Don't," I snapped.

He withdrew his fingers. "Did I do something wrong?"

"The reference. It's creepy to call me your sister."

He snickered. "You know what they say? Incest is best."

I bucked my hips a little. "It's also illegal."

Gideon cupped my chin. "We're not blood."

He slid higher up my body and fed me the tip of his cock, rubbing the head along my lips and coating them with precum. I licked at the salty fluid, causing a rumble to escape from Gideon's chest.

"Jesus Christ, do you know how sexy you are?" he asked.

Before anything else happened, he reached over, pulled, and undid the ties from the slats on the headboard, letting my hands-free.

I was puzzled, so I asked, "I thought you were training me?"

"Fuck that. I need you to touch me."

I inwardly breathed a sigh of relief. Although I trusted Gideon, I was still apprehensive about being tied down. As he released my legs, I rubbed at my wrists. There were indentations from the tiny, raised squares on the ties, but they would disappear.

"You're on top," he said.

I raised my eyebrows. "What happened to Mr. Control? You're giving it to me?"

"I can top from the bottom, darling Avery. I'm not concerned."

All of a sudden, tears pricked my eyes, and I wiped at them, sniffling when I felt my nose starting to drip.

"Avery?" Gideon questioned.

He moved to the edge of the bed and pulled me next to him, cradling my body against his as I began to sob—my cries coming deep inside my chest. I couldn't stop, and I didn't know why now. I had kept my strength when he tormented me during the summer, managing not to cry then. Now, I couldn't help but start to hiccup.

"Fuck it," he said.

Gideon got up and pulled me to stand so he could pull down the covers. He wiped at my tears as I shook.

"Whatever this is, you tell me when you're ready. Get in bed."

I slipped into bed, and he followed, pulling the sheet over us before he curled his body around mine. He gently moved the hair from my neck and kissed my pulse. His lips were soft, and I trembled in his arms.

"I don't want to leave," I mumbled.

"Huh? What are you talking about?"

"Next year," I answered.

Gideon turned my head to look at him. "What are you talking about?"

"College. I love you."

He laughed. "Come to Yale. I already have early admission. I'm sure one more Berne won't hurt admissions."

"But I'm not a Berne," I pointed out, my breathing becoming more even again.

"You are by proxy, and my father can get you in. From what I've seen, you're smart, and you get good grades."

"That's true. I was at the top of my class at Arlington. But we'll still have to hide us."

He coughed. "Not forever."

"Bullshit," I growled. "I know how this blue blood shit works. I also know our parents will blow a gasket once they find out we're together. If my mother caught me having sex with anyone, she would freak out. But you're my stepbrother. Maybe this was stupid of us."

Gideon tightened his hold on me. "I waited for you, and I'm not letting you go. You're mine."

"And what about Clover? Oh, fuck! I forgot to call her. I bet she feels horrible."

"Remy texted me. She's groggy but feeling better. Clover owes you."

"It was stupid for me to let her talk me into that party."

I turned in Gideon's arms to find he was grinning.

"That wasn't funny," I chided.

"What's funny is that Theta Rho Kappa is no more."

"Huh?"

"Remy's father knows the chancellor of Beane College. One phone call and their charter was pulled."

I sucked in my breath. "Just like that?"

"Money and power. Get used to it, Avery, you're part of it now, and I finally have someone to share the misery. You'll understand when our parents get back."

"I've already seen the changes in my mother."

Distracting me, Gideon gave me a bruising kiss and rolled me under him as he palmed my breast.

"AVERY, WAKE UP?" I heard Gideon say.

My eyes fluttered open to see my stepbrother hovering at my side.

"What happened?"

He kissed the tip of my nose. "We fell asleep. I guess I wore you out."

I reached up to stroke the stubble on his face and remembered how it felt on my thighs as he feasted on my pussy. My inner thighs were raw from his scruff brushing against them.

I frowned. "This will be over soon. We have to go back to school tomorrow, but say we don't have to?"

His expression mirrored mine. "We have to. Did you consider applying to Yale?"

"I'm not sure. I had my heart set on Columbia."

Gideon's face flooded with disappointment. "I think you should be with me."

"Giddy," I murmured.

I felt his body tense next to mine. "Why are you calling me that?"

"I think you should have a nickname."

"I do, but only my family uses it. My mother especially. She always called me Giddy."

I pressed my thumb against his bottom lip and brought it down. Gideon sucked it into his mouth, licked the pad, and sent spirals of electricity to my core. Of all the boyfriends I had had since I started dating at fourteen, I'd never had one who turned me on as much as him.

Just my luck; he was my stepbrother. We lived in the same town our entire lives, but because we were from opposite ends, our paths never crossed. I wondered what we might've been if we had met before our parents did. Would we have been drawn to each other like two magnets?

"Can I call you Giddy?" I asked.

"Yes. I'd like that but not at school unless we're in private."

I caught his gaze. "And when will that be? When Remy occupies Clover's time? When I sneak to your room and hope no one sees me going inside? When?" I cried.

I was so frustrated with the situation. Our lives would be sneaking around when we were home or at school. There would be no freedom in our relationship, and it was upsetting.

"Shush, we'll figure it out."

"And what about when we're home? Do we act like we hate each other? Will there ever be a time we can be out in public and hold hands?"

He sighed. "The guys know what my plan is for you. You can come to my room."

"So you need to pretend to be a bastard to me? Say horrible things and control me?"

"I'll make it better."

I sat up and slipped out of bed, searching for anything I could cover myself with. I spied Gideon's t-shirt on the floor and slipped it over my head. It hung on me like a dress, but it covered me.

"Where are you going?" he asked.

"I'm starving, and it's nearly 3 pm. I want to shower and call Clover. I've already been a shitty friend by not taking care of her."

Gideon threw the sheet off and stood up naked in front of me. He was beautiful, tanned, and muscular. Any girl would love to have him as a boyfriend, but there was a darkness about my stepbrother, one which worried me despite my love for him.

He grabbed my wrist. "Are you upset?"

"At you? No."

Gideon didn't let me go. "Then what?"

"The situation. We've both lived in this town for our entire lives, and we never crossed paths. Doesn't that seem strange to you?"

"This is a big town, and I never went to public school," he replied.

"But this town has malls, movie theaters, and restaurants, and you were home during the summers. Why didn't we meet each other then?"

He let me go and scratched his belly. "I don't know."

"My mother had to go to the city to meet your father," I stated. "If she didn't help her friend out, we might have never met."

"But we did."

"And it's like we didn't."

Gideon frowned. "What do you mean?"

"As I said before, we can't be free. I've been thinking about this a lot. Maybe we shouldn't be together at all. We had sex; you got what you want."

He raised his voice, exclaiming, "Fuck that! I'm in fucking love with you. I'm not giving you up. I've loved you from the first time I saw you."

"And you had a shitty way of showing it," I growled, turning my head from him.

"Avery, what is this really about? It's not that we're sort of related. It's something else."

I felt tears prick my eyes, but I forced them back. "It's the situation."

"I told you we'll figure it out. Stop worrying."

My eyes flicked back up to his. "You're not a magician. Sometimes you can't have what you want."

I walked out of the room, his shirt swishing around my bare ass. I didn't care if any of the staff saw me. We would be found out soon enough, and there would be hell to pay.

CHAPTER 25

Gideon

As much as I wanted to, we didn't have sex on Saturday evening. Avery slept in my arms and stayed asleep long after me. My thoughts kept me awake. My entire life, I was always able to manipulate and plan how to get what I wanted, even with my father thought he knew how to handle me. But I had no way to navigate this situation.

Avery was right. If we were caught together, it was over. I couldn't let that happen. Now that she was in my bed, I didn't want to let her go. I knew what my father would do if we were found out. He would send Avery to another school, and our bedrooms would be separated.

My trust fund could also be in jeopardy. My father was its trustee until I turned twenty-one, and I had plans for that money. I wanted to use it to pave my own path once I graduated from Yale. The boys and I had discussed starting a company—one that could rival all our fathers' companies combined.

If I lost that money, I would need to beg my grandfather to help me, but if my father poisoned his mind with my impropriety, it wouldn't happen. I was sure Gideon the Fourth would have a major problem with me fucking my stepsister. The Berne name was not to be smeared at any cost, and something like this might give way to years of scandal.

What were my choices?

~

"GIDEON, ARE YOU ALL RIGHT?" Avery asked.

I had barely said anything during our two-hour trip back to Bancroft. I couldn't even look her in the eye at breakfast, especially after I made my choice for both of us. As much as I wanted her and insisted upon it, I had to let her go. I lied to her; told her it would work out. But right now, I was picking money over love.

Avery wouldn't be far off my radar, though. I would be watching her, and once I was out from under my father's thumb, she would be mine, stepsister or not. I didn't care what our parents or society said. She wasn't my blood.

"I'm tired," I said in excuse.

I pulled into the parking lot, looking for a close spot. A fine drizzle was coming down as I swung into a spot three from Beckley Hall.

"Is that all?" she persisted.

"Avery, just stop," I snapped.

As her face twisted in pain, I felt like shit.

"Are we back to this? The Bancroft mask is back? Big man on campus?" she snapped back.

"It's not like that," I said as I opened my door.

She followed suit, slamming her door as hard as she could. We had no luggage since we left abruptly on Friday night, so

Avery hurried away from me. The door slam alerted a few students who watched us as she cursed back at me.

"Fuck you, Giddy!"

WHEN I GOT out of the elevator on our floor, Avery wasn't anywhere. I figured she was in her room, so I trudged to mine.

"Hey, fucker," Xavier said as he slapped my shoulder after coming out of his room. "You took off so soon on Friday that we didn't get to celebrate our win."

"Avery was screwed up from that shit at the Theta house. I took her home."

He leaned in as I slipped the key into the lock. "Did you finally get to fuck her? When do we get our shot?"

I felt the urge to rip his arms from their sockets. No one was touching her. She was mine, even if she wasn't. If I found out another guy at Bancroft put his hands on her, they would be sucking their meals through a straw.

"No, I did not."

I pushed the door open and stepped into the stale air of my room. He followed me in as I went to the window and threw it open, allowing fresh air to fill the space. Xavier flopped on my bed like he owned the place. I loved the guy, but he could be an annoying fuck when he wanted to be.

"Man, you're taking a long time," he noted. "What gives?"

I reached into my small refrigerator, pulled out a bottle of Gatorade, and popped the top to gulp half the orange contents.

"She's a delicate situation," I eventually said. "I can't just fuck her and leave like the other girls. We live in the same house."

"Then pass her along," he sleazily replied. "Her ass gets me going."

"Don't be a dick. We have a plan, and I'm sticking with it. Don't you have some mafia princess to defile?"

Xavier scratched his balls. "Too easy and been there, done that. The others are too gruesome to fuck with. No thanks."

I slurped the rest of the bottle and tossed it in the trash can near the refrigerator.

"All of a sudden, you're selective?" I spat.

Xavier frowned at me. "What the fuck is with you? First, you take off without a word, then you ignore all our texts except from your precious Remy, and now you come back acting like a total douche."

I rubbed at my temples. A massive headache was on the rise.

"I'm tired, my head hurts, and I have some family shit I'm dealing with."

He rose from the bed. "The only family shit you should be worried about is getting into Avery's panties."

I was so close to hauling off and knocking his perfect, white teeth down his throat. "Do me a favor; go find somebody else to bother. I need a nap."

"Dickhead," he said as he passed through the door and slammed it on his way out.

AVERY WAS SITTING in her seat when I entered our trigonometry class on Monday afternoon. I missed having her in my bed last night. I missed everything about her, and it had only been one day. How would it feel after weeks or months? As I took my seat next to her, I caught her incredible scent in my nose, the familiarity of freesias.

The sheets on my bed at home smelled just like hers, and I felt saddened knowing the maids would change them. Avery wouldn't look at me and even moved her chair a few inches away from me so our legs wouldn't bump into each other. I hated myself for the decision I made without her input, but it was for our own good.

I wasn't paying attention to classwork and instead spent the time doodling in my book. Math wasn't a weak point for me, and because I was good at it, I wasn't worried. Xavier nudged me, and I glanced at him.

"What the fuck are you doing?" he whispered.

I shrugged. This was baby shit. I could pass the tests without taking notes. I'd already done the homework on the syllabus seven chapters into the book. All I could think of was Avery. I could feel her anger; she didn't need to say a word.

Once class was dismissed, she shoved her book and tablet into her backpack and headed to Spanish. Clover stopped me before I could follow.

"Yeah?" I asked uninterestedly.

"I want to thank you for Friday," she said lowly.

I knitted my eyebrows together. "You put Avery's life in danger. Those assholes do that shit all the time."

"It was stupid. But we just wanted to have fun."

"Find another way, and don't include Avery if you want to do something so dumb. I promised I would look after her when she's here," I growled.

"Do a fucking better job," she replied just as firmly. "What did you do to her this weekend? She's not talking to me. If you hurt her, so help me."

The first tone cut us off, and we hurried from the building to get to our classes. *I hurt her, and I hurt me too.*

"Giddy!"

My heart jumped, and I looked for Avery, but it wasn't her.

"I asked you to stop calling me that, Jillian," I snapped.

She put her hand on my shoulder, and I brushed it away. Jillian was a possessive bitch even though she knew I didn't want a relationship. After we had sex last year, it was my fault because I kept going back for more. Jillian liked it kinky. She didn't mind the restraints or the spankings.

"Geez, sorry. I thought we were friends."

I didn't want to upset her, but she was a pest. "We are friends, but I have to get to class."

"Can I stop by tonight? You still have a private room, right?"

I knew exactly what she was implying. After the admins took over our hangout, she came to my room several times. I couldn't keep her quiet, and I had no intention of playing her games.

"Tonight isn't good. I have football and then weight training. I'll be exhausted."

She leaned in close to my ear. "I have a cure for that," she purred.

"I'm sure you do," I said dryly.

"Think about it."

"Yup. Gotta go."

I hightailed it to class just before the second tone, taking the last open seat. Avery was sitting at the end of the table on the other side, and again, she wouldn't look at me. I cursed myself. This wasn't going to be easy on either of us.

"ARE YOU FUCKING KIDDING ME?" Remy said.

He splashed water at me, and I jumped away, tightening my weight belt before I sat down on the bench.

"What's so hard to understand?" I asked as I sat down.

"She practically begged you to fuck her, and you turned her down?"

I lowered my voice. "Jillian is a succubus. She would bite my dick off if she didn't like it so much."

He shook his head, putting his hands a couple of inches under the weight to spot me as I lifted the bar off the cradle.

Don't get me wrong, Jillian had a gorgeous, curvy body and was totally clean-shaven or waxed. Her breasts were large, and her skin almost flawless, but she was overly aggressive, even at sixteen. Now two years later, she was even pushier.

Jillian also couldn't take no for an answer. When she showed up at my room an hour before curfew wearing a raincoat and barged inside. Underneath, she was wearing blood-red lingerie. I remembered the conversation and how I turned her away by explaining I was exhausted.

"I have a cure for that. I'm not asking you to do anything," Jillian had said.

I quirked an eyebrow. "What did you have in mind?"

She cupped my balls, and I stirred but willed myself to stop, thinking of some God-awful documentary on infections they showed us in biology last year. It had worked.

"You just lie back and let me do the work."

"No."

Her perfectly plucked eyebrows had flown up. "Excuse me?" she snapped.

"Not in the mood. Thank you for stopping by."

"You're serious?" she screeched.

"Deadly."

"Giddy, you've changed."

I couldn't control my anger at her use of the nickname.

My hand circled her wrist and squeezed. "I asked you not to call me that. Do you realize each time you say the name, it reminds me of my mother? And I don't need to be reminded.

"Shit, I'm sorry."

Not listening, I yanked the door open and gestured to the hall. If looks could kill, I would be dead by now. Her face was sour as she stepped out and ran into Jaxson, who I was guessing took advantage of the situation and coaxed her into his room. Jillian had been primed and ready to go, and it wouldn't be the first time he got my seconds.

"Yeah, but it's Jillian," Remy repeated, drawing my attention back to the present. "What's with you this semester? Two weeks in, and you haven't fucked anyone yet. Usually, by now, you're leading the pack."

I wouldn't say I haven't fucked anyone, but I would say it was the first girl I've ever loved. Thinking about this, I pushed the bar up and brought it back down, arching my back as I did.

"Maybe I'm over this shit," I voiced. "I'm thinking I should find a girlfriend this year."

Remy took his hands away as he doubled over in laughter. I dropped the bar into the rack.

"What the fuck is your problem?" I asked as I sat up.

"You. A fucking girlfriend? What happened to your little project?"

I fucked my little project, and I fell in love with her long before I slid my dick into her pussy. Of course, I didn't say this as I wiped the sweat from my face.

"You really think it would be wise to ruin her? She's my stepsister, and I still have to answer to my father and stepmother."

"Since when did that matter? It didn't stop you from sleeping with one of your dad's girlfriend's daughters."

"She wouldn't stop bothering me," I corrected. "I just gave her what she asked for."

Remy laughed. "And your father had a fit."

"I gave her a toss. She asked, and I delivered. But you get me? Avery isn't just someone's daughter; she's my stepmother's daughter."

"Well, if you're not going to fuck her, I'm sure Jaxson and Xavier would like to double-team her. They can't seem to stop talking about it."

Bile rose in my throat at the thought of their hands on Avery. No one was getting their hands on her. I would protect her, and no one would fuck her but me. Even though I told myself it wouldn't happen again, she was like gasoline to my match.

"They won't touch her. Avery is off limits."

His mouth dropped open. "Seriously?"

I removed my weight belt and threw it over my shoulder, the buckle jingling as I did.

"Seriously."

~

"WHAT THE FUCK do you mean we can't have a shot?" Jaxson asked.

"Because she's my stepsister. You keep your fucking dick and hands off her. You don't need her. There are plenty of girls you can mess with. I'm not kidding. She's off limits," I warned.

Like the flip of a switch, Jaxson then grinned at me. "Thanks for turning down Jillian last night. Man, that girl is a freak. She stayed over, so Xavier rode the floor in Remy's room.""Fuck off, Jax. You owe me," Xavier growled.

Jaxson chewed on his fingernail. "We'll see."

Xavier launched himself, and they started to wrestle, falling to the floor, where they knocked into my desk. Remy jumped on my bed.

"Knock this shit off!" I yelled.

Xavier slapped Jaxson hard in the face before climbing off him, laughing. They acted like a bunch of little kids. It amazed me that any of them were good students or hadn't been arrested. Xavier's father had plenty of pull with the courts and probably a few judges in the mafia pockets.

Jaxson's father was a high-powered attorney who worked with many celebrity clients, and Remy's family was, like mine, from blue blood money. Generations of well-known Andersons existed before him. Remy was a fourth, his father a third, unlike me after our family skipped a generation.

Jaxson got off the floor, rubbing his cheek. "Who's up for a curfew breaker?"

I wasn't in the mood to prowl around campus or go for an

after-hours burger at Preppies, which usually stayed open until two in the morning to accommodate the study crowd from Beane.

"Where?" I asked.

"Beane. I found out where those fuckers Frank and James are living," he revealed. "They share a room at Adams Hall."

I thought that since the frat house was shut down and the charter pulled, they would have been expelled. I guessed they escaped, but they were the catalyst for what happened to Clover and Avery.

"Idiot," I started. "What are you going to do? Sneak in the dorm and drag them out in their underwear? We can't get in there without IDs."

Jaxson held up his finger and raised his eyebrows. "Oh, ye of little faith. I have someone who can let us in."

"A girl, no doubt," Remy said.

"Darla," Jaxson confirmed. "I met her last year at Preppies. She can let us in."

I wasn't in the mood to go hunting for two idiots who would probably not amount to anything, but I had plans for their future. I had an even bigger plan for Teddy. He put his hands on Avery and tried to drug her so he could take what was mine. They all signed off on their lifetimes of failures that night.

I was disinterested as I asked, "Explain to me what your plan is?"

"We go in, find their room, and fuck them up."

"Sure, makes sense. Fuck them up with dozens of other students on the floor and an RA. Is this a deaf school? Because the last time I fucked someone up, there was plenty of noise."

The three of them stared at me like I had just sprouted a second head.

"We can manage," Xavier said.

"Then go ahead. I don't want any part. We have a game on Friday. Do you want to get benched?" I asked.

Remy snorted. "Like they would."

"Do what you want," I replied.

Jaxson jabbed the front of my shirt. "You've been a total dick that past week. What the fuck is your problem? Are you pissed because you couldn't seal the deal with Avery?" he snarled, his face growing red.

"No. I want a clean record, not something Yale can ferret out. I don't need to waste my time with three jerks who thought they were getting some high school pussy."

"Three?" Remy asked.

"The guy who tried to drug Avery—Teddy. He's the one I hit," I clarified.

"Okay, three guys," Xavier said.

They couldn't understand my argument, and I wasn't about to explain it. If they wanted to jeopardize their spot on the team, Bancroft, and college, let them. I would do what I needed to by protecting Avery my way. Leaving me behind, they headed for the door.

"Let me know if you need bail money," I called as they stepped into the hall.

CHAPTER 26

Avery

"What did you get for number twenty-six?" Clover asked.

I was daydreaming at my desk, staring out the window at the lighted parking lot. My emotions were in turmoil, mostly working between anger and sadness. I had opened my heart, and Gideon stamped on it. He hadn't talked to me in days.

"Avery?"

"Huh?"

"I asked what you got for number twenty-six."

I looked down at the study guide. I hadn't answered but three of the questions. Our history test was tomorrow, and I wasn't prepared. Since returning, I'd spent most of my time feeling sorry for myself and nursing a bruised ego. I already ignored Gideon in the two classes we shared, and if I saw him on campus, I walked the other way.

"I didn't answer it," I replied.

She knocked on her desk. "Hello, the test is tomorrow. Are you planning to fail?"

"Does it matter? With Payne, I could probably get into Yale with a B average."

"But you want to go to Columbia. It's all you talked about since we were in middle school. You wanted an ivy league school in the city. You would get that with Columbia but not if your grades are shit. Why screw up an almost perfect average?"

Clover's chair scraped as she got up and leaned against my desk, looking down at me. The incident at the Theta Rho Kappa house seemed to roll off her like water on a duck. It was also a good cover for me, but mine went deeper. I was heartbroken.

"It will fade. You'll forget what happened."

I supported the lie, stating, "I know. It just shook me up to see you like that, and if I hadn't dumped my drink or poured the other down the sink, I'm not sure what would've happened to us."

"Fucking assholes," she spat. "I hope they suffer."

"Gideon hit Teddy. I think he broke his nose."

"Frank and James wanted us at that party to take advantage of us. Who the fuck does that?"

I didn't look at her, and instead, I scribbled a few lines in pencil over the cover of my study guide. Even if I didn't study tonight, I was caught up on all the readings and was sure I could get a good mark on the exam. Clover wasn't great about reading, so the study guide would help her more than it would me.

"I don't feel well."

Clover narrowed her eyes. "What's wrong?"

"For the past few days, I've just been off."

"I think the shit this past weekend really got to you. I'm sorry. Don't hate me."

I leaned my head against her. "I love you. I mean, you came here for me, and you didn't have to do that."

She smirked. "Well shit, what would I do without my partner in crime?"

I laughed. "Probably find somebody else to get in trouble with."

"I doubt it. You're my favorite troublemaker."

She kissed the top of my head and went back to her desk. Lifted by her comments, I made an effort to answer a few of the harder questions in the study guide. No use being complacent. I wanted to keep my perfect grade point average.

A half-hour later, I stood up to stretch. Some of the girls across the hall and next door had started to make noise, so it was a good time for a study break.

"Are you going downstairs?" Clover asked.

I rolled my eyes. "If you want me to get you something from the machines, just ask."

"We have to get more snacks. Can we go after the history exam? I'm craving cheese curls and Sour Patch Kids."

I dug into my purse, looking for a few dollar bills, but all I had were twenties—the tragedy of being rich. The machine downstairs only took fives or lower.

"Do you have any cash?" I asked Clover.

"I have a few fifties and a hundred. Are you telling me you don't have any dollar bills?"

"I'm not that poor girl anymore. I only have twenties."

"Fuck. Why don't you see if the girls next door can break it?"

I began to chew on my cheek. Since settling in at the school, we learned that the girls next door and across the hall were a bunch of snobs. They would snub us if we were in the bathroom with them and wouldn't bother to acknowledge our presence. I wondered if Gideon had anything with their behavior. Who knew what poison he spread before we arrived.

Clover must've known what I was thinking because she said, "Give me the money. I'll check with the bitches next door."

She got up, plucked a twenty from my purse, and left. I

waited, listening as the voices next door grew louder. A minute later, Clover popped through the door red-faced with deep wrinkles in her forehead.

"Fucking cunts," she spat. "I can't believe these people. I'll see if I can bum some change from Remy."

She was back out the door before I could say anything. I was afraid if she went to visit Remy, I wouldn't see her for a couple of hours. To prepare for that, I dug around my purse, looking for all the coins I could find, and put together four dollars and twenty cents—enough for several snacks. Bancroft had a refillable card you could use on all the snack machines, but neither Clover nor I got one.

Five minutes later, she wasn't back, and I was craving Skittles. I decided not to wait. Once downstairs, I waved to the night security guard as I stepped into the dimly lit and empty snack room. Several machines full of soda, teas, water, lemonade, chips, chocolate, and candy lined the walls.

I stood at one snack machine, counting out a dollar and twenty-five cents to put in, when a familiar scent tickled my nose. I turned to see Gideon behind me, and my stomach churned.

"Get away from me," I hissed.

He ignored my request. His hair was mussed up, exactly the way it looked after we had sex. Gideon's cologne settled in my nostrils, making me dizzy.

"Punch the buttons, I'll pay," were his first words to me in days.

"I don't want anything from you. I hate you, Gideon Berne."

It was like he hadn't heard a word I said because he asked, "Are you going home this weekend? We should talk."

"Fuck off. I don't want to hear what you have to say."

"It's important."

I lowered my voice to almost a whisper so the night security guard wouldn't get suspicious. "We have sex all weekend, and you tell me you love me, then you turn into a glacier. What kind of asshole does that to someone?"

"Come home," he pleaded.

I put my hands on my hips. "I refuse to be your weekend whore."

"Who's a whore?"

We both turned to see Clover waving a few dollar bills in her hand. Gideon backed up a couple of steps to give me room.

"Who's a whore?" she repeated.

"No one," I mumbled as I finished counting my money and popped the coins into the machine before I pressed F9 and watched my bag of Skittles fall into the dispenser.

I bent to reach for them, and since Gideon was close enough, I felt him discreetly brush my ass. I shot him a dirty look as I came upright. I then waited for Clover as she decided what she wanted; all the while, Gideon stared at me. Once she made her selection and we turned to leave, he called out to me.

"I would like a word, Avery."

Clover swung her eyes from me to him and back to me.

"Your word is crap. No, thank you," I hissed.

He looked at Clover. "Remy would like to talk to you."

I silently pleaded with my eyes for her to stay. She tore open her bag of cheese curls with her teeth.

"I just saw him; what about?" she asked.

"Something about an ice cream cone."

She smirked and headed for the elevator. I could've killed her for leaving me with Gideon. I had no intention of talking to him, but once she was gone, he grabbed me by the arm and took me to the corner of the room. I resisted, pulling back against him, but he was far stronger than me.

"I don't want to talk to you," I insisted.

"Tough. You're not in control here; I am."

I prayed someone would walk through the door and save me from this conversation. As Gideon always did, he would speak pretty words and then freeze me out. I wasn't about to get my heart torn to shreds over and over. He'd already made a fool of me once.

"You sure you are?" I challenged.

His forehead wrinkled as he frowned. "*I am*. Now shut up."

I clenched my jaw. "Why should I shut up?"

"So I can do this."

Not wasting a second, he pressed his mouth against mine, and I clawed at him, but he grabbed my hands and pinned them to the wall. Using my next best bet, I bit his lip and tasted blood. He moved his mouth from mine and licked it with his tongue.

"I love when you abuse me," he said, sounding turned on.

"Fuck you," I hissed, trying to get my hands free.

He grinned. "That's later, darling Avery."

"Don't call me that, *Giddy*." I thought using his nickname would anger him, but it had the opposite effect.

"Say it again," he purred. "I love to hear it from your mouth."

"Fucking asshole."

He took my hand and pressed it against his erection, holding me there so I could feel the heat of his dick like hot steel against my skin.

"This is for you. Come home this weekend."

I looked away from him. "I have a date."

It was a lie. I didn't have a date because no one would look at me since they feared Gideon. That much was apparent. Asshole.

"Bullshit," he growled.

I jutted my chin out in defiance. "Why would you say that? Am I so unappealing that no one would go out with me? Or is it that you scared everyone off?"

"You're mine."

"You said you loved me. You don't treat someone you love the way you do. Face it, Giddy, you're fucked in the head. You don't know how to treat people, much less a girlfriend. I'm not coming home just because you want me to. I'm not your toy, and this isn't a game."

It was hard to whisper when I was so angry. I wanted to scream and hit Gideon as hard as I could, mark him the way he'd marked me inside. He'd bruised my soul and tore at my emotions.

He bunched my shirt in his hand and pulled me to him, so we were even more face-to-face. His breath feathered across my lips, and the scent of mint caught my nose. His gray eyes were dark, and it felt like he was looking through me. I trembled.

"Darling Avery, you will come home this weekend, or I will drag you out of your room on Friday night. Be packed and ready to go when my game ends. Better yet, I want you at my game. Support me, and I'll give you a present when we get home."

I pushed him, and he smiled at my defiance.

"I won't be in my room," I challenged. "Imagine you searching the entire campus for me."

Gideon leaned in and, this time, bit my earlobe, sucking the diamond stud I wore into his mouth. My body betrayed me as my core clenched with desire. Maybe I was the sick one. When he released it, he whispered into my ear.

"Make me hunt for you, and you'll regret it. Tomorrow, Avery."

He let me go and walked to the soda machine, pressed the root beer button, and swiped his card. I was too flabbergasted to move. There was nowhere I could go unless I left school after class ahead of him.

Gideon could hunt for me, but I would be home already. It was sneaky and what he deserved, but I also worried he would be exhausted by the time he left for home if he looked for me on top of playing in the game. I didn't want an accident on my conscience.

"Avery?" he called.

I glanced over at him, his erection visible against his shorts. He pulled his shirt out to cover it. I waited as he stepped out of the room, and when I heard the elevator ding, I left. It was sitting open when I exited the room, and he ducked his head out.

"Coming?" he taunted.

"Bastard," I said as I brushed past him.

He pressed the five button and crowded me into the corner.

"I'd love to fuck you tonight."

I pushed at his hard stomach. "I bet you would."

"Come to my room."

I rolled my eyes. "Not happening."

"I know you want it. Your nipples are hard. You're as turned on as I am."

The elevator dinged as it reached our floor, and I slipped around him.

"Dream on, Giddy."

I WAS SO nauseous when I went to sleep that the Skittles I bought sat on my desk unopened. After Clover disappeared, she eventually dragged herself back to our room at 4 am, way past curfew. I was awake but pretended I wasn't. If she knew I was up, she would start telling me about her night, and I wasn't in the mood.

"Get up, Clover," I said when my alarm went off.

She grumbled and turned over. "I'm sick."

I threw the covers off me. "You're so not sick. Stop spending all night with Remy."

Clover turned toward me. "He's so good in bed. It's hard to leave. You really need to get with the program and give up your V card. I have no one to talk to about orgasms."

I rolled my eyes. "I have orgasms."

"By your own hand. You need someone else to give them."

"I did, and he broke up with me."

She clucked her tongue. "Dunc?"

"Of course. He dumped me, or I would've given him my V card."

"Seriously? Are you going home this weekend?"

Either way, I looked at it, I had no choice. I was afraid of what Gideon would do if I said no. I thought about so many potential solutions down to staying at a hotel in town. They had several, but I knew he would find me. It just made sense for me to go home and face whatever he planned.

"Yeah," I sighed. "I need a break from this place and some good food."

I rose from my bed and headed to the bathroom. It would be a long day and probably a longer night. Still sick, I dry heaved in the shower, but when nothing came out, I brushed my teeth.

Clover was asleep when I came out and yanked at her pillow. "Get up before you miss class."

"It's Friday."

"I'm not sure what that's supposed to mean."

She mumbled something incomprehensible before she sat up, pushing the sheets off her. I was dressed and counting coins for a ginger ale before she got out of the shower. I needed something to settle my stomach. Leaving our room, I jammed my finger on the up button of the elevator, and when it arrived, Gideon stepped out, soaked with sweat from what was probably an early morning run.

"Darling Avery, don't you look good enough to eat this morning."

"Do you always have to be so crude?" I hissed.

Gideon ran his knuckles over my cheek. "Remember what I said last night, be ready."

"Asshole," I mumbled as I stepped into the elevator.

I heard his laughter as the doors closed.

My nausea persisted throughout the day, and I barely ate anything at lunch while Clover chattered about Remy. I only listened with half an ear. Across the cafeteria, Gideon stared at me. His eyes never left me, and if I moved, so did they. It was creepy. He was controlling me even when he wasn't near.

I couldn't escape him in trigonometry since we had assigned seats, so when I arrived early, I steeled myself while Clover joked around with Jaxson. With the way she fitted right in with the biggest bullies in the school, it seemed like they were old friends. Gideon breezed in just before the second bell sounded, taking his seat next to me.

As Mrs. Ordonez began to teach, Gideon's hand covered my knee and began a familiar upward trek toward my thigh. I put my hands in my lap to stop him, but he was stronger than me, and as he had done our first class, he kneaded my thigh. I gave up fighting. My mind raced in a million directions. How would I cover up my orgasm this time?

I bit my tongue and waited, but he stopped touching me and removed his hand from my thigh. I breathed a sigh of relief as my heart thudded in my chest. Gideon didn't touch me for the rest of the class, but he followed me to Spanish. I had to pee as I entered the building and glanced at the bathroom we'd fooled around in before going to the other one down the hall.

He ignored me in Spanish, turning into his glacial self. I tried to pay attention, but I kept glancing at him. I couldn't help but wonder what Gideon had in store for me tonight.

CHAPTER 27

Gideon

She was up in the stands, cheering me on. I saw Avery as soon as I walked to the bench after I threw a touchdown. I appreciated her following my instructions. I also couldn't wait for the game to be over so I could have her to myself. Despite what I decided, it was too hard to stay away from her. I didn't care about the consequences.

The Doyle Academy guys were a bunch of pushovers. By the third quarter, we were beating them sixty-three to three. It was so pathetic that Coach took me out and put the second-string QB, Riley Marsden, to do mop-up duty. Knowing where she sat, I removed my helmet and kept looking up into the stands, meeting Avery's eyes each time. I couldn't wait to touch her tonight, use my mouth on her and slide my dick inside her tight pussy.

"Beers tonight?" Remy asked as he slurped a cup of blue Gatorade.

"I'm going home."

"Again? Why?"

"Anderson, if you have to ask, then you're stupid. Our parents are in Europe until October. I want to take advantage."

Remy pointed with his thumb into the stands. "Are you taking her with you?"

I grinned. "She has orders."

He laughed. "So this weekend?"

I knew what he was referring to. Remy was a nosy asshole, always in competition with me. It bothered the shit out of him that I was top dog at Bancroft. He was just waiting for me to fail, but he didn't know I'd already succeeded.

"Possibly. If everything goes to plan."

I wiped my sweat-soaked hair from my face and focused on Avery in the crowd. She caught my eye and gave me a sour look which I knew was bullshit. A couple of minutes ago, she was cheering for me. By the end of the game, the second stringers had it well in hand, and we won seventy-three to ten.

"You showering?" Jaxson asked as I stripped out of my uniform in the locker room.

"Yeah, a quick one. Avery is waiting for me. We're heading home this weekend."

He nudged me. "I get her next."

The fuck you do. No one is touching her but me. She's mine.

"When I'm done with her," I replied evasively.

I would never be done with Avery; that was a promise. We were bonded for the rest of our lives.

AVERY WAS WAITING for me by my car, her bag sitting by the passenger side door.

"I'm here; let's get this over with."

I smirked as I popped open the trunk to toss her bag in next to mine, which I'd placed before the game.

"Why can't we just discuss this here?" she asked.

"Because I want privacy. Now get in."

I pulled open her door and waited until she was inside to gently shut it. As soon as our belts were secured, I started the Bugatti, revving the engine a few times before I backed out of the space. Avery said nothing to me as I navigated to the highway.

"How was your day?" I asked.

"Fuck off, Giddy. I'm only going home with you because I wanted a break from school."

I slapped my hand to my chest. "I'm wounded."

"Asshole."

She looked out the window as she hummed along with the songs coming from Sirius Radio's classic rock station. Forty-five minutes into the trip, Avery cupped her mouth with her hand and grabbed my sleeve.

"I have to throw up; pull over," she demanded.

"Fuck."

I slowed the car so quickly that I almost skidded on the gravel shoulder. She threw her door open and leaned out. Her body was wracked with movement, but from where I sat, I couldn't see anything come out of her mouth. While she heaved, I bunched her hair in my fist. When she was done, she wiped her lips with the sleeve of her jacket.

"Are you sick?" I questioned.

Her lip began to quiver, then fat tears escaped over her lids, rolling down her cheeks.

"I'm fucking stressed, and it's your fault," she cried.

At that moment, I felt like the biggest piece of shit. How long had she been feeling this way? I stroked her golden hair, pushing it over her shoulder, and then wiped her tears with my thumbs.

I softened my tone. "Don't cry. I'm sorry."

"Giddy, why are you such a bastard to me?"

"I don't mean to be."

Seconds later, blue and red lights flashed behind us, and I rolled down my window as an officer approached the car. He blinded us with his flashlight.

"Do you need assistance? You can't park here."

I flashed him a million-dollar smile. "My sister wasn't feeling well. We pulled over for a few minutes."

The officer flashed his light at Avery, who was still looking a bit green.

"Do you need to go to the hospital?" he asked.

"No," I said. "She's fine."

He looked at Avery. "Miss?"

She answered. "I'm fine. I haven't been feeling well the past few days. It's stress, new school, tests, and all that fun stuff."

He gave us a tight smile. "I understand. Please move along."

"Yes, officer."

I waited until he was inside his patrol car to signal and pull back onto the highway. Avery leaned her head against the door, and I reached out to take her hand in mine. She offered no resistance, so I stroked the back with my thumb.

"You sleep with me tonight," I finally said.

"I don't want to have sex with you anymore."

"We're not having sex. I want to take care of you," I said softly.

If she were feeling better, I would ravage her—tear her in two as I fucked her as hard as I could. It had been almost a week since we did anything, and I was dying to be inside Avery, taste her pussy and press my nose against her sweet, scented skin. But I would settle for her in my arms.

The house was dark when we arrived home. I hadn't called any staff to tell them we would be there this weekend. They were probably happy no one was at the house, especially since my father graciously offered to pay everyone's salaries even though they would be doing minimal work.

"Can you walk?" I asked Avery.

"I'm fine. I just want to sleep."

"ARE YOU COMFORTABLE," I asked.

Avery was cuddled up against me, her arm around my stomach. The acidic words she'd spoken earlier came across as the polar opposite of her actions.

"Giddy, why are you being so nice to me?" she muttered.

I stroked her hair. "Because I love you."

"Love me or want to fuck me? There's a difference."

I pressed a soft kiss to her head. "Darling Avery, I know the difference. I love you."

"Then why?"

"It's late, and this conversation will take time. Go to sleep."

She sighed. "You love to tell me what to do."

"Avery, if you keep it up, I'll show you what I would love to do to you."

She nuzzled my chin with the top of her head and, reaching backward, moved her hand from my stomach southward until she cupped my balls. There was an immediate response as my dick began to harden under her touch.

"Don't start something," I growled.

"I want to. We can always sleep in."

I pushed her hand off me and turned her, so we were facing each other. In the dim illumination of the nightlight, I saw her beautiful face, scrubbed clean of the makeup she didn't need.

"And you will if you get me started," I warned.

"Why, Giddy?"

Fuck. She pressed this conversation, and it would probably torpedo anything physical between us.

"I would ruin you, and that wouldn't go over well with the family."

"That's a lie."

It was a lie, and she saw right through it because no matter how many times I told her I didn't care, I did. It came down to dollars and cents, but she would always be in the background, and when I reemerged, I wanted her by my side.

"Money."

"What money?" Her tone grew harsh.

"My trust fund. Without it, my plans for the future won't come true. I don't want to be my father's puppet. I want to make it on my own."

"That's stupid. Why put in all the work when you can have it built in?"

I laughed sarcastically. "You don't know my father. You haven't been here long enough. I feel sorry for your mother because she will eventually take a back seat to his company."

"We're getting off subject. You're telling me you became an iceberg because of money—a shitty trust fund? It says you care about money more than me," she growled.

"I'm protecting you."

Avery placed her palm against my cheek and slapped me. It was basically a tap, but it illustrated her point.

"You're protecting yourself," she argued. "You hurt me."

"It's not for just me," I stressed. "I'm setting us up for the future. I want to take care of you. I want you in my life."

"Giddy, you're being ridiculous. We're kids. Do you think our relationship or whatever this fucked up thing we're involved in will last? I'm not keeping us a secret until you're ready to reveal what we have."

I pressed my mouth to hers, prying her lips open with my tongue. Avery didn't fight me as I searched for her tongue. She curled her fingers into my hair and lifted her leg over my hip. Her fingers stroked me through my shorts, and it didn't take long for my cock to become rock-hard.

"Fuck me," she mumbled against my lips.

I brushed her hand away, fumbling with my shorts to get my

dick out. In her own haste, she struggled with her panties, so I wrenched the panel to the side and thrust inside her plush wetness. She tore her mouth from mine and cried out as I penetrated her. I thought I'd died and gone to heaven. A week without this was too long.

Her panties scraped against my cock as I fucked her, providing friction that her soaked pussy could not despite her tightness. She moaned into my mouth and clawed at my back with her nails. Our position wasn't the easiest to navigate, but I managed.

On the next thrust, she threw her head back. "Make me come all over your dick!"

I fucked her harder, slapping my hips against hers. Her channel tightened around me, and her nails dug deeper into my flesh.

"Come, darling Avery," I coaxed.

She detonated, her head still thrown back, and she arched her back. She moaned my name as she went limp in my arms, but I kept on, holding back with all my might.

"Again."

She looked up at me. "Wh–what?"

"I want you to come again before I do. It's a simple request," I said through gritted teeth.

"I don't have another in me," she said breathlessly.

"What about last weekend? You had so many in you."

"But…"

Her voice trailed off as I rolled her onto her back, keeping us joined. I propped myself up on my hands and pounded her for all I was worth. I was hasty, fucking her with all my clothes on, but I wanted to feel her naked body against mine. I withdrew, my dick glistening with her arousal, and I slid off the bed to shove my shorts down.

"Get naked, now!"

She gave me a lazy smile as she stripped off her t-shirt and shucked off her panties. I climbed on the bed next to her, stretched out, and waited.

"What are you doing?" she asked.

"Fuck me. You bitch about me controlling you. Now it's your turn," I said seductively.

I shoved my hands under the pillow and waited. Avery chewed on the tip of her fingernail before she moved, looking as shy as a little girl on her first day of school.

When she sank on me, I thought I would come right then, but I held back.

"I'm so full," she groaned.

I smiled. "It's not the first time. Move, darling Avery. I want to fill your tight, little cunt with my cum."

"It's my show."

I loved her defiance.

She began to move, putting her knees on either side of my hips and leaning forward. She placed her hands on my stomach for balance and bounced up and down. Her tits jiggled, and her beaded nipples begged to be sucked. I couldn't be a passive participant.

"Faster, darling Avery. Ride me."

She closed her eyes, and I sat up, taking one nipple in my mouth to suck on while pinching the other.

"Giddy," she moaned.

I buried my face between her breasts, inhaling her scent into my nostrils. I clenched my jaw as I tried to hold on, make it last and give her another orgasm, but I was too far gone. I gripped her hips, holding her to me as I exploded inside her while grunting her name.

When I was finished, I embraced her and kept moving. She tightened over me and had her second detonation, squeezing and relaxing, squeezing and relaxing until her body went lax, and I leaned back with her in my arms.

"Giddy, I love you. I can't help it."

"There's nothing to help," I said.

"But it's one-sided. You love money, not me."

I hooked her hair around her ear. "What can I do to make you believe me?"

"Out us."

I couldn't. I knew what the result would be, and it had nothing to do with my trust fund. My father would separate us. Avery would either go to some all-girls school or back to Arlington. Our bedrooms would also be set up at the opposite ends of the hall, if not on different floors.

"No. It's not an option. It won't prove anything, and we'll be apart. Do you want that?"

Avery circled my nipple with her fingertip. "Not really."

"Then figure out another way for me to prove it. Trust me, you haven't been part of the Berne family long enough to see what goes on, but you will."

I was afraid for her because once the newness wore off, Avery would need to toe the line with everything: grades, achievements, honors, and awards. She would have to become a Berne even if she wasn't blood. My father had expectations for his children, and as long as they met them, he would allow us to do what we wanted.

CHAPTER 28

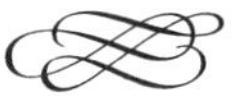

Avery

Life loving Gideon was complicated. Our schedules for free time didn't mesh, and sharing a bed at school wasn't easy. As it got closer to November, we managed to have a few stolen moments during the week and through escape home. But soon, our parents would be back from their honeymoon, and we would need to be careful or lose each other.

He was still bullying me in public and controlling me in private, but I was getting used to his behavior because I knew it was all an act despite him getting his way when we were alone.

"Last weekend," he whispered as I sat down in Spanish.

"I know," I whispered back before our teacher began.

He slid his hand under my skirt and rubbed my leg, kneading the taut flesh. His touch was all I needed to cause my clit to throb. After this weekend, we would have to hide all the time: here, home, wherever. Despite keeping things on the downlow, I still wanted the freedom to hold his hand and kiss him in public.

"I'm planning a project which will be presented at the end of the semester in Spanish," Mrs. Dolan said over us.

Yet another project. The only class I didn't have a year-end project was trig.

She continued, saying, "You will work in pairs, select a speech, and translate it. I've put you together in alphabetical order. Berne and Bedford, you'll work with each other."

I heard nothing else as she called out the other names. Turning to Gideon, I said, "I guess you're my partner."

He grinned and squeezed my thigh. "We'll need to figure out a schedule for working together."

"I'm sure that won't be a problem."

As Mrs. Dolan talked about the project, it kept echoing in my head that Gideon and I would be together. I could *actually* go to his room, and we could fool around. The project wasn't one that would take a lot of time to do, however. We didn't need two months to figure out a midterm project.

Once class was over, he leaned over to me. "Tonight, my room."

My belly clenched so hard it hurt. I wanted him now and wished we didn't have an eighth period or activities. After class, Clover was waiting for me so we could walk to history together. As we did, I broke the news to her.

"I have to work on a project with asshole," I said, mustering all my frustration to pass off what I hoped she thought I'd felt.

She sucked in her breath. "Seriously? For Spanish?"

"Yeah. We decided to work on it tonight."

Our walk to class was interrupted by a fine drizzle. I hated the gloomy weather fall brought. I preferred the summer. I shivered and pulled Clover along to get inside before a heavier rain came.

~

GIDEON WAS FINISHED with weight training and a shower by 8 pm. I couldn't wait to see him since it had been four days of no sex. I craved every inch of him, and I was getting used to his dirty requests.

He must've been waiting for me because he opened the door the second I knocked, tugging my notebook from my arms and tossing it on the desk. He slammed the door shut and pushed me against it, leaning his body against mine. Gideon tangled his fingers in my hair as he kissed me senseless.

"I need to fuck you now."

I pushed him away and walked further into the room. "Mr. Berne, this is strictly a homework visit. We have to work on our project. Hands off."

His mouth dropped open. "You're kidding?" Gideon flipped the lock on his door and stalked me like prey. "Darling Avery, I call the shots here. I want that dirty, little pussy."

"Work first."

"Fuck first," he insisted. "Or you can suck me off. I've been thinking about you all day."

I frowned and flipped my hair. "Just all day?"

"Stop teasing."

He moved me to the wall, wrapped his hand around my throat, and wrenched my yoga pants down. I'd chosen not to wear panties.

"Fucking sneaky bitch," he growled. "Why didn't you wear panties?"

"My pants look better without them."

Gideon pressed his lips to my ear. "Or was it for easy access? Please, Avery? I'm dying here," he whined.

I giggled. "What? No demands."

"Please, darling Avery. I need to fuck your pretty pussy."

He began to plant butterfly kisses all over my face and the

back of my neck while keeping his hand firmly around my throat. Gideon needed control, something I understood and was learning to accept.

"Do it," I breathed.

"Quick and hard, baby."

He tugged my pants to my ankles and dropped his to the floor, thrusting his cock inside me. I was dripping wet before I got here. I hated to admit it, but I was addicted to the sex Gideon provided, and what's more, I was addicted to him.

He reached between us and circled my clit with the tip of his finger, teasing, bringing me to a faster orgasm which happened less than a minute after he entered me.

"Fuck me, Giddy!"

His hot breath warmed my skin as he asked, "You want it harder? You want to come again? Catch up to me, darling Avery because once I come, I'm leaving you."

"Asshole."

"You better believe it, and speaking of which," he panted in my ear.

"Maybe."

The past couple of weeks, Gideon talked about having my ass. I wasn't sure.

"We'll build up to it, and I'll make sure you're good and wet. Hurry, Avery, I'm going to fill you with my hot cum in about ten seconds. Come or get left behind."

He continued to pump, his pelvis slapping against my ass. Hoping to beat him, I rubbed my swollen nub.

"Now," he demanded.

I rubbed harder as I felt him release, and I found my orgasm as he finished his. We stayed together for a couple of minutes, with him pressing his body against me.

"Come to Yale," he said.

"Come to Columbia," I replied.

"Three generations of Berne," he noted breathlessly.

"Then change."

Gideon turned my face to his, and I could see his look of torture. Inside, I felt the same way. I didn't want to be separated from him by less than a hundred miles, but it was inevitable. And it was almost a year away. We might even despise each other by that time and go back to what we were in the beginning.

"I can't," he said tonelessly. "I'm already in."

He pulled out and toed off his sweatpants in preparation for a quick shower.

"Are you joining me?" he asked.

"We've been through this," I said. "How would I explain my wet hair to Clover?"

"Please," he begged.

Sometimes our control switched positions. As much as Gideon needed it, he sometimes handed it to me. It was out of character for him, but he was in love.

Following his lead, I pushed my yoga pants off, and he helped me take off my sweatshirt. Underneath, I wore a gold chain with his football number, seventeen. It was our secret. When I wasn't wearing it, it was somewhere close to me, like my pocket or my purse. I wound my hair in a tight bun and followed Gideon into the shower.

We'd spent plenty of time in the shower built for twenty people in our parent's master bathroom, making love until our hands pruned. But this time, our shower was quick, and we were dressed in a few minutes.

"You know what I'd like to do?" he asked as we settled back to work.

I rolled my eyes. "If we did that, nothing would get done."

"Not sex."

Our conversation was interrupted by a knock on the door. Gideon pulled my notebook from the desk and shoved it into my hands before he went to the door and yanked it open. The boys were standing there with stupid grins, one of them holding a flyer.

Remy stepped in and raised his eyebrows. "Hello, Avery."

His eyes swung from me to Gideon, waiting for an explanation. I was about to speak up when Gideon mumbled, "Spanish project. We're working on the particulars."

Jaxson sat next to me and put his arm around my shoulders, all the while showing me the flyer. I plucked it from his hand.

"Sadie Hawkins dance? What the fuck is this?" I asked.

I glanced at Gideon, who was practically gnawing on his fingers in anger when Jaxson put his hands on me.

"It's a thing where girls ask guys out to a dance," Jaxson explained. "I could use a date."

I bit my lip. "I probably won't go."

Jaxson pulled me against him, and Xavier laughed. I once again glanced at Gideon, whose nostrils were flaring.

"Come on. Don't let stepbrother dearest get to you," Jaxson said. "I promise we'll have a great time."

"Fuck off, Jax. She said she doesn't want to go," Gideon said.

"Then go with me," Xavier said.

Gideon clenched his fists. He was agitated, and if our relationship weren't a secret, there would be carnage. Remy looked amused.

"I'm probably going home this weekend," I said, pushing Jaxson's arm off my shoulders.

Xavier pushed Gideon's shoulder. "I heard Jillian is going to ask you."

My head shot up. I knew who Jillian was since I had history and chemistry with her. I didn't like her. She was one of the snobs who turned her nose up at Clover and me. I looked at Gideon to see his reaction, but his face was stoic.

"I'm going home," he responded. "This is our last weekend without our parents. They come home from Europe on Tuesday."

"You're fucking stupid. She talks about you all the time. Go with her, and I'm sure you'll score," Xavier said before turning to me and adding, "No offense."

"Why would I be offended?" I asked.

Xavier shrugged.

"Can you guys get the hell out of here so we can finish what we're working on? Little Avery doesn't want to miss her bedtime," Gideon said snidely.

I knew Gideon was playing a role. If he eased up on me, they would know something was up.

"Think about it," Jaxson said.

"Get out," Gideon growled.

He held the door for them, and they filed out. After they were gone, I questioned him.

"You had sex with Jillian?"

Gideon rubbed the back of his neck. "She's old news. It was last year, and she wouldn't leave me alone."

A pang of jealousy gripped me, tightening my chest. "Does she like the kinky shit?"

"Avery, why does it matter?"

"Giddy, tell me the truth. Does she let you tie her up and spank her or fuck her ass when I won't let you?"

"It's irrelevant."

"I'm sure she does. She can give you what I can't."

He sat next to me, and when he put his arm around my shoulders, I shrugged it off.

Gideon frowned. "She doesn't mean anything to me. If I wanted her, I would have slept with her. I'm not interested."

"Go with her," I bit out.

"Are you mad? Why the fuck would I do that?" he yelled.

I put two fingers over his lips. "Shush. You want everyone to hear you?"

"Why would I?" he repeated.

I sighed. I'd heard the talk around campus. Girls my stepbrother must have previously slept with and were used to coming back for more were wondering why he wasn't sniffing around.

"Because people are talking," I pointed out. "You need to throw them off."

He shook his head. "She's a fucking viper. She'll claw at my dick a minute after we arrive, or she'll try to talk me into not going. You want that?"

I put my hand on his cheek and met his gaze. "I trust you."

He leaned into my hand. "You don't know what you're asking."

"Giddy, just do it. Stay for a couple of hours, and then we'll go home. You don't have football on Friday."

He opened his eyes. "And who will you go with?"

"Jaxson or Xavier."

He wrinkled his nose. "Absolutely not. They'll have you in the front and out the back. They both want to fuck you. Hell, even Remy wants to fuck you, and he's getting it regular from Clover."

I frowned. "You think I can't handle them?"

"You don't know them the way I do. I've seen them in action, their seduction, their pretty words, and what they do after. No."

Rather than paying attention to his words, I started thinking to myself, planning, but before I could think further, he grabbed my chin.

"I said no!" he growled.

"Asshole," I murmured.

He pressed his lips to mine, his mouth full of hunger before he pulled me under him. I broke from him.

"No. If you start, I'll never leave."

My body was already reacting to his kiss as my nipples tightened and belly clenched. It was also late, and I had to get back to my room.

"Good. Clover already sleeps over at Remy's."

"I'm not Clover, and we can't get tongues wagging. You don't want them to know."

He sighed. "Sometimes I do."

"Then think of the consequences."

Gideon backed off me and sat against the wall. "I hope you're ready for this weekend because I'm not letting you leave the bed."

I chuckled. "Like every other weekend? Who do I go with?"

"I'll find someone."

"You mean appoint someone scared as shit to cross you?"

"Probably. I'll let you know tomorrow morning. You ask them. We can go to the dance and leave at 10 pm."

"Deal. One last weekend together."

CHAPTER 29

Gideon

I was right. Jillian was all over me the minute I picked her up from her dorm.

"Giddy!" she said excitedly.

"Jillian," I cautioned.

"Sorry, Gideon. Maybe you can let me say it when you fuck me," she whispered.

My stomach churned, and bile rose in my throat. I forced it down. There would be no fucking. I didn't desire her like I did last year anyway. Avery was my turn-on, my guilty pleasure. Jillian pressed a kiss to my cheek and grabbed my hand. When we walked into the dance, I searched the room, finding my stepsister in the arms of Xavier.

"Goddammit," I cursed.

I had set her up with Timmy Williams, a shy senior who would probably have been sitting home all night if Avery didn't ask him.

He was looking forward to escorting my stepsister and was surprised when I told him she was interested in him. He was safe, and I knew he wouldn't touch her the way Xavier or Jaxson would.

Through my frustration, I looked Avery over, taking in her little black dress with thin straps. It accentuated all her curves in a tasteful manner with a hint of cleavage. The four-inch heels she wore gave her height, bringing her forehead to Xavier's nose. Maybe I would ask her to keep them on while I fucked her. I wondered where my chain was, in her purse or somewhere else?

Jillian frowned as she handed me her coat, and seeing her dress made me want to groan out loud.

"What's wrong?" she asked.

"Nothing."

She gave me a wicked grin. "How do you like my dress?"

It was barely acceptable for Bancroft events. The skirt was so short that if she bent down, her underwear would be displayed. Her neckline showed more breast than appropriate, and it hugged her like a glove, revealing every seductive curve on her body. And the color, blood red, as if Satan created the dress in the pits of hell.

Several guys looked her way, their eyes traveling her body and settling on her cleavage. *Boys, you can have her.*

I checked her coat, and Jillian possessively put her arm around my waist. She knew I didn't go for that shit, so I leaned into her ear to remind her.

"Knock it off," I growled.

She giggled. "Save some of that anger for later. Play your cards right, and we can have some fun."

I swore I wouldn't entertain sex with her again, even before I met Avery. Jillian never wanted just sex from me—she wanted a relationship, and a girl like her was trouble. Before you knew it, she would have me joining her for family dinners. It was no secret her father was courting mine to get some business. I wouldn't be a pawn.

I glared over in Xavier and Avery's direction again to watch his every move. When he stroked her bare back, I almost lost it. I knew Xavier's moves, and he was putting them on Avery.

"Excuse me, Jillian. I need to talk to my stepsister for a moment."

Her face turned sour. "I thought you hated her."

"I am trying to be civil for our parents' sake."

A friend of Jillian's, Julie—another rich brat with an attitude —came over to speak to her, which gave me the opportunity to talk to Avery. By the time I reached them, she was leaning against Xavier who had his hand dangerously close to her ass.

"What the fuck is this?" I hissed.

Xavier smirked and tilted his toward where I'd just come from. "Jillian? Someone is getting fucked tonight. Why did you even bother coming to the dance?"

I grabbed Avery's arm. "We need to talk." But before I walked away with her, I pointed at Xavier. "Keep your damn hands to yourself."

He gave me the finger and removed a silver flask from the inside of his jacket. Avery still hadn't said anything, and I couldn't wait to hear her excuse for asking Xavier.

"What the hell are you doing with him? What happened to Timmy?" I demanded.

"He... he chickened out," she stuttered. "What did you tell him?"

I ground my teeth and squeezed her arm tightly in my grip. "I told him to keep his hands off you. He was merely a placeholder for the dance. I warned you about Xavier. He wants to get you into bed."

"I ran into him in the hall, and he asked who I was going with. I told him what happened, and he just pulled me into the elevator."

"He's a fucking predator." I frowned as the scent of alcohol on her breath hit my nose. "Did you drink something?"

"Just a few shots from his flask. Peach vodka, delicious."

This was also typical for Xavier. He would ply the girls with alcohol, treat them like queens, and then move in for the kill the next time he took them out. Based on the long list of girls who wanted another shot at Xavier Toscano, it usually worked. Avery, however, would not be another notch in his belt.

"Stop fucking drinking, or we're leaving right now. I'm not babysitting you all night."

Thankfully we were out of anyone's view because she cupped my crotch. "Take me home. I don't want to be here with anyone but you."

One little touch of her hand and I was already semi-erect. The look in her eyes said desire. *Crap*. I had to get her home and into my bed if we could last that long.

"Darling Avery," I breathed. "Here's how it's going to go. I'm taking a phone call with an emergency at home."

Her eyes grew wide. "What kind of emergency?"

I had no idea but taking her home was a much better prospect than fighting off Jillian Cronenberg.

"I'll think of something. Don't drink anymore, and I don't want Xavier touching you, either. Stay away from him."

"He's my date. How do you expect me to do that?" she asked.

"Do what I say, or I'll punish you when we get home."

Avery bit her lip. "How?"

"Don't test me, darling Avery. Just do what I said."

To illustrate my dominance over her, I gave her a little push as she walked by me. Now to figure out what emergency would get us out of here. I sauntered over to Jillian who was drinking punch and talking to her friends.

"What was that all about?" she asked.

"Family business."

She scowled. "What could you possibly need to discuss with

her? She's beneath you. I heard her mother was a waitress. How could your father stoop so low to marry someone like her?"

Anger bubbled in my chest. Renata wasn't a waitress; she worked as an assistant for a real estate company. It also hadn't surprised me that he asked her out. My stepmother was stunning, and Avery was a younger version of her.

"Don't talk about my father or stepmother for that matter. I'm sure your father wouldn't like to hear you speaking poorly of someone he wants to do business with."

Jillian's face went stark white. "I didn't mean anything. I was talking about her," she said as she pointed at Avery.

I wanted to slap her. She couldn't hold a candle to my stepsister.

"We need to get back home early," I said in my most restrained voice. "I'm sorry to tell you we need to cut our date short. I'll make it up to you."

I had zero intention of making anything up to Jillian. She was a vapid bitch who thought she was better than everyone. If her father only knew the depraved things she enjoyed in the bedroom. How she got on her knees and sucked me dry as I called her names.

"But Giddy," she protested.

"I have to get the house in order before my father gets home. You know how servants can be."

It was a poor excuse since I didn't feel that way. Our staff was well trained and didn't take advantage. The entire manor and pool house were probably neat and clean. But I was playing to Jillian's disdain for those less fortunate than her. The only motivating factor for me to sleep with her was her freakiness in bed. Period.

Her face turned sour. "I do. You better check to make sure they haven't stolen anything."

"We have cameras."

"Still. Will you take me to dinner and bring flowers? I like pink roses, the long-stemmed kind."

I nodded, watching Avery from across the room. She was keeping a couple of feet from Xavier, but I didn't trust him.

"Yeah, dinner and roses."

She stroked my face, letting her blood-red talons scrape across my skin before she pressed her lips against mine. I didn't move mine, and as much as she tried, I kept my mouth closed so she couldn't invade it with her tongue. Jillian pulled back with a look of disappointment on her face.

"You owe me," she snapped.

"Payment in full when I get back."

"Promise?"

I wouldn't say I promised, so I nodded. She was another problem I would need to work out. Maybe I could toss her off to Xavier. I walked over to Avery.

"We have to go."

"Go? What the fuck!" Xavier said.

"We have to get home," I said.

He looked at Avery. "Do you want to go with him? You can stay."

"I should go," she said.

I looked at Xavier. "Jillian is primed and ready to go."

Xavier's face brightened. "Yeah?"

I slapped him on the back. "Go for it."

AVERY DIDN'T SAY much to me as we walked to the car, my hand firmly on her back. Once inside, I turned the radio on, settling on a rock station before I gunned the Bugatti and pulled out of the space. Once we hit the highway, Avery shut the radio off.

"Giddy, you kissed her."

Fuck.

"Correction," I returned. "Jillian kissed me."

"I wanted to scratch her eyes out."

I smirked at Avery's admission of jealousy. It warmed me inside.

"Not more than I wanted to punch Xavier in the mouth. He's dying to fuck you."

She grasped my hand and laced her fingers with mine. "He asked if I really wanted to be at the dance or if I'd rather have our own private party in his room."

"Fucker."

"This school is screwed up. I've never met so many self-righteous, arrogant assholes in my entire life. They think the sun revolves around them."

"It's only for a few more months."

Avery took my thumb in her mouth and sucked, licking the pad with her tongue. Instant erection.

"Jesus Christ. Don't do that; I'm driving."

She popped my thumb out of her mouth. "You have something else I'd like to suck more."

My dick went into overdrive, and my slacks became incredibly uncomfortable. The prospect of a blowjob while driving was something I'd done before, but not with Avery. I didn't think I could control the Bugatti while she sucked me off.

"No."

"Why not?" she whined.

I reached over to cup her chin. "Darling Avery, I don't want to end up wrapped around a guardrail."

She pouted, and I stroked her cheek with my knuckles.

"I promise to make it up to you when we get home."

Promise was a word I would use with her.

"STRIP. LEAVE THE SHOES ON."

Avery put her hand on her hip. "How can I strip if I'm wearing my shoes?"

I loosened my gray tie and slid it over my head. "Let me amend my request. Take off your shoes, remove your panties, and put your shoes back on."

She giggled as she backed toward me. "Unzip my dress."

I shucked out of my jacket before I grasped her zipper, slowly pulling it down. Once her creamy skin came into view, I couldn't resist kissing it until I got to the top of her ass. She shivered as my lips touched her skin.

I stepped away and continued divesting myself of clothing. When Avery took off her dress, I saw the necklace I had given her was wound around the waistband of her thong.

"I was wondering about that. You can put it back on."

She removed the necklace from her thong and clipped it at the back of her neck. It settled between her ample tits. Avery kicked off her shoes and removed her thong before slipping them back on again. She was a picture, standing there with her legs slightly parted, golden hair hanging down her back, and looking at me with those big gray doe eyes.

"Come here," I commanded.

She approached, and I pulled her into my arms, cradled her head, and kissed her. Just like every time I touched her, my heart pounded, and every nerve ending in my body came alive. I cupped her breast, rubbing my thumb over her puckered nipple. She stroked my back with her fingertips, sending shivers down my spine.

"Enough," I whispered.

I lifted her in my arms and carried her to the closet door, pressing her back against it and using it to steady her as I positioned my cock at her slick entrance. She cried out when I entered her, a loud guttural howl.

Her heels dug into my ass as I fucked her. Each thrust drove her up the door, scraping her back against the framing around the panels, but she didn't complain as a minute later, she was screaming through her orgasm.

"Avery," I breathed.

I continued hammering at her even though her limp body made my arms burn and ache.

"Another," I demanded.

Her eyes widened. "I can't."

"You will. You can," I coaxed.

I buried my face between her tits, kissing her sweat-misted skin. She was still pulsing around me, but my action caused her walls to tighten against my girth.

"Let go, baby. Let me have it."

She scratched me, raking my shoulders as she exploded once again. This time, I met her orgasm with my own, pumping endless amounts of semen inside her. When I finished, I carried her to the bathroom.

CHAPTER 30

Avery

We were sitting in Gideon's large oval tub in a mountain of vanilla-scented bubbles. I was leaning against his back.

"Giddy?"

"Yes?"

"If I go to Yale, would we live together?"

He alternated between playing with my necklace and my breasts, circling my nipples with his fingers, which sent shocks of electricity right to my core.

"We could but in the same dorm. Yale doesn't allow freshmen to live off campus. Of course, I would love it because I could have my way with you anytime I want without worry."

"Worry about what?"

"People barging in and bothering us. You could walk around the apartment naked for easy access."

I turned to look at him. "You're ridiculous. I would never do that."

I gasped when he pinched my right nipple.

"Naked *and* in sexy heels."

"What about my necklace?"

"That too. Jewelry and heels."

I giggled. "We would have classes to go to and homework to do."

"We could work around our schedules."

I hadn't decided to go to Yale, but I was planning on applying. I had no doubt I would get in. I would also still apply to Columbia and Stanford. I wouldn't mind living in California, but it was so far from Gideon.

"Are we sleeping in my room or yours tonight?" I asked.

He ran his hand over my stomach. "We're already in my room. I vote my bed, but I don't think sleeping is on the table."

I yawned. I'd been up since 6 am this morning, and it was nearing midnight.

"I'm not sure I have energy for all night."

He moved my wet hair from my neck and gently bit into the flesh on my shoulder.

"I think it's time for you to give me something I've been asking for."

My stomach churned. He'd been begging for my ass, but I wasn't sure I could give it to him or if I wanted to, for that matter.

"I'm not ready."

"I'll be gentle," he pleaded.

"Please, Giddy. No."

He sighed. "I want to spank you and fuck you from behind."

"Will you be gentle when you do it?"

Gideon's dick was growing hard against my back.

"I promise."

I snorted. "You like to say that a lot."

"Only to you."

~

OUR NIGHT of sex turned into a night of sleep. Neither one of us had the energy, and I fell asleep in Gideon's arms. Sometime later, voices in the hall woke me, and I knew it couldn't be the staff. They usually didn't get started upstairs until after 10 am.

"Gideon," I whispered.

He grumbled and opened one eye. "What's the matter?"

"I hear voices."

He frowned and listened. "Fuck, I think that's my father."

I tried to pull out of his grasp, but he held me tightly in his arms.

"Let me go, or this is over."

"We won't be caught. My father respects my privacy."

I again tried to pull away. "But my mother doesn't, and I haven't seen her in weeks. She'll want to wake me up."

Gideon let me slide away so I could grab my clothing before I headed into his closet. This is the way it will be from now on. We had to be careful because I didn't like the potential consequences if we were caught. After I stashed my stuff in the closet, I slipped under the covers of my bed. Two minutes later, my door opened.

Pretending I was asleep, I waited until the bed dipped and my mother smoothed my hair from my face. I opened my eyes.

"Mom, you're home!" I yelled.

She hugged me and pressed a flurry of kisses to my cheek.

"I'm so happy to see you," she returned. "I didn't know you were home this weekend."

"I needed a break from Bancroft. Gideon came home too."

My mother kissed me again. "Are you getting along with him?"

"Yes. We're working on a Spanish project together. Our teacher put us in pairs."

She raised her eyebrows. "I'm glad. I got you some nice things."

"Mom, you weren't supposed to be home until Tuesday."

"I haven't been feeling well," she said. "We got home yesterday afternoon."

I swallowed hard. I'd lost my father four short years ago, and the potential to lose my mother frightened me.

"Are you okay?"

"Don't tell Payne I told you; we wanted it to be a surprise, but I'm pregnant—about seven weeks."

"Mom! That means you got pregnant your first week in Europe."

She nodded, and her smile lit up her face. I was happy for her and Payne, but I hoped her pregnancy would go all right. I'd heard stories about when she was pregnant with me. My father had to take her to the hospital twice for dehydration.

"Well, it was our honeymoon. What time did you get home last night?"

"Late."

She rose from my bed. "I'll let you sleep. Let's have lunch when you wake up."

"Thanks, mom. I'm happy you're home."

She walked across the room, blew me a kiss, and left. I glanced at the clock and saw it was 7 am. I was still tired as I got up to click the lock on my door. I put on a t-shirt and slipped through the passage in the closet. Gideon was lying in bed with his hands shoved under his pillow.

"Gideon?"

He smiled with his eyes closed. "I was hoping you would come back."

"Is your door locked?"

"My father already stopped by. He won't bother me again."

I looked over at the door. "Can I lock it?"

"Are you expecting something?"

"No, but my mother is."

"Your mom told you?"

I went over to the door and popped the lock before I slipped into bed with him.

"By next year, we'll have a sibling," I noted.

Gideon pulled me on top of him, and I tucked my head under his chin.

"Maybe my mother will stop nagging me so much if she has a baby," I said.

"But you'll still be a baby, my baby."

"I love you, Giddy."

He kissed the top of my head and embraced me tighter. "So, do you want to?"

"I do, but we have to be quiet."

"They're down the hall."

I grinned and looked up at him. "I thought you were going to spank me? You said I needed to be punished."

"I'd prefer to have sex like this with my dick buried inside your pussy and you lying on my chest."

"It's a deal."

THREE HOURS LATER, I woke up with Gideon curled around me. Our lives would become more complicated now that our parents were home.

"Giddy, we have to get up."

"Why? Can't we stay like this all weekend?"

"Those days are over."

He yawned. "Don't remind me. We're entering the fun season."

I turned in his arms to look at him. "Fun season?"

Gideon kissed the tip of my nose. "The dog and pony show. The holidays. My father likes to invite a bunch of people over on business, especially New Year's Eve. Jillian will be here."

I sucked in my breath. I hated her, and now we would see her for at least one holiday. It made me sick. I was undoubtedly jealous of any girl who'd once gained Gideon's attention.

"Why can't it just be family?" I asked.

"Because it's how my father does things. It will be a grand show when they announce Renata's pregnancy."

I played with Gideon's fingers, kissing the tips before I took one in my mouth.

"Don't do that," he growled as he tried to take his hand away.

I felt him stir against my belly and knew if I continued, we would be having sex before we got ready for the day.

"I don't like when Jillian puts her hands on you."

He smirked. "You don't need to worry about it. She won't do it again."

I didn't know Jillian well, but I felt that wasn't true. She wanted Gideon and would probably try her best to get him in bed. I trusted him to resist, but that didn't mean she wouldn't pursue him for the rest of the year.

My mother was sitting in the sunroom when I came downstairs. The manor had everything you could possibly want, and if it didn't, Payne would bring it in, especially if my mother made a request.

"Wow, you slept late," she commented.

"I was tired."

And I had to take some time this morning to fuck Gideon after sucking his fingers.

She patted the floral cushion on the wicker loveseat she was sitting on. Once I sat beside her, she pulled me into her embrace, kissing my forehead.

"I missed you."

"I missed you, too."

"How do you feel about the baby?" Her voice took on a tone of seriousness.

It had been a running joke between us that she'd find a way to have another baby since before my father passed away. Since I wanted a sibling, I was happy when I found out she was marrying someone with a child until I first met Gideon. My dream became a nightmare that circled back again.

"I would love a sister or brother. I've always wanted a sibling."

"Well, you got one in Gideon."

And I'm in love with him. "But he's a stepbrother, not blood."

She kissed my forehead again. "I hope you're not lying to me about getting along with him. I want you to be happy. It was a bit rocky between you two when we moved in."

Oh, mother, if you only knew how well I'm getting along with him, you would be shocked.

"It's fine. He watches over me at Bancroft."

"I'm glad. I moved you to Bancroft so you would get a good education. It can help you get into Columbia. Bancroft is a top preparatory school."

I broke from her embrace to catch her gaze. "I was thinking of applying to Yale too. Gideon told me it's a family tradition."

She raised her eyebrows in surprise. "Really? I thought you had your heart set on Columbia."

That was before I gave Gideon my virginity and fell in love. "I did, but it always makes sense to have a safety school. Gideon said I would be a legacy."

"Are you worried about getting into Columbia? You have great grades and a lot of extracurricular activities. Though I wish you would take something on this year."

I shook my head. "Bancroft is harder than Arlington. It's better I just take care of my classes."

"Gideon has football and a few other things; he does fine."

"What do I do fine at?"

We looked up to see Gideon entering the sunroom, freshly showered and dressed in a pair of ripped blue jeans and a Bancroft football sweatshirt.

"Extracurriculars," I said.

He gave me a knowing glance before he paid attention to my mother.

Gideon approached my mother and hugged her. "I heard congratulations are in order," he said.

My mother smiled. "You'll be a big brother by this time next year."

"I'm already a big brother," he said, winking.

With big being the operative word. "Only by a week," I said.

"Still older than you," he said as he stuck his tongue out.

We all laughed, and Marta, the chef's assistant, called us to lunch. Payne was sitting at the slate table in the kitchen when we arrived, and I went to hug him. He was an older version of Gideon except for his eyes. Payne had blue eyes, whereas Gideon had gray.

I hugged my stepfather, who was looking fit and tan. He kissed me on the cheek.

"Did you two come home while we were gone?" Payne asked.

"A few times," I said as I let him go and shot Gideon a look.

Gideon cleared his throat. "We needed a break."

His father smiled. "Then you took my request into consideration?"

"Yes, I did."

I frowned, wondering what they were talking about. I decided to ask Gideon later. Our parents chattered on about

Europe and all the sights they saw, restaurants they ate in, and items purchased.

"I got you some nice gifts," my mother said.

"Thank you, but that wasn't necessary."

I almost choked on a piece of cantaloupe when I felt Gideon slip his hand around my inner thigh. I looked at him and slightly shook my head. He removed his hand but pressed his knee against mine.

"Are you okay?" my mother asked.

I cleared my throat. "I'm fine. It just went down the wrong way."

"What are you planning to do today?" Payne asked us.

Gideon looked at me. "We have to decide on a speech to translate for our Spanish project. We'll probably work on that unless you have other plans."

I knew he had no intention of looking for a speech.

CHAPTER 31

Gideon

Avery slapped at my hands. "You said we would study."

I grinned wickedly. "I said that to them, but you knew different. I saw it on your face."

"We need to find a speech. We have six weeks to get this down."

I pulled her between my legs, and she leaned against my back as I cupped her breasts, making tight circles around her areolas.

"You're not wearing a bra, are you?" I asked.

She tried to brush my hands away, but it was half-hearted. I knew she liked what I was doing.

"No. Do you think I need one?"

"Not at all. I'm craving something."

Avery turned and looked at me. "What?"

I kissed her neck. "I want you to sit on my face. I need some of that delicious pussy."

"No way," she protested. "Anyone can walk in on us."

"Don't be ridiculous, darling Avery. No one will walk in on us."

"Gideon, our freedom is over. You can't fuck me over the kitchen counter or on the bar downstairs or make me scream."

I stroked her face with my knuckles. "I'll do all those things. Let's take some risks."

Avery shook her head. "Those are risks I'm not willing to take. Do you want to be separated?"

I didn't want to believe we would be separated, but there was a possibility. My father and Renata might go as far as sending Avery back to Arlington, where they could watch and encourage her to find a boyfriend. And I wondered when my father would "introduce" me to one of the daughters of his business partners. He'd done it before.

"Gideon?"

She tore me from my thoughts.

"No. But I was hoping you could sit on my face. I want you all the time, every delicious inch of you."

Avery got up and clicked the lock on the door before she opened her jeans. A hint of her lavender underwear got me going. My mouth watered as I remembered her taste, like cotton candy. She was pushing her jeans down her hips when we were interrupted by a knock on the door.

Her face went stark white as she fumbled with the zipper of her jeans. I scrambled off the bed as she ran to my desk, where she sat down before I opened the door. My father was standing there, and he peered inside.

"What's up?" he asked, looking suspicious.

"We're still working on our speech," I said.

"Do you want to play some racquetball? I booked a court at the club for tomorrow."

I didn't want to play racquetball. It wasn't my favorite sport, and my father would get pissed if I beat him. Sometimes, with how he could act, I thought our roles had been switched, and I was the parent. Knowing him, I bet the court was booked for some ungodly hour on a Sunday, like 8 am. He liked to conduct business with Asia early, then spend an hour beating the shit out of a little blue ball.

I glanced at Avery. "I shouldn't. My calf muscle is tight. I don't want to aggravate it. I have a game next week against Chisholm Prep."

He frowned. "You should talk to the trainer. Get some therapy for the muscle. You want to up your stats on Friday."

Here we go.

"Does it matter? I'm not going any further than high school."

My father's face clouded. "The coach at Yale said you would be a lock if you wanted the position."

I chewed on my thumbnail. "Not interested. I want to concentrate on my studies."

"I think you're making a mistake." My father turned to Avery. "Your mother tells me you're interested in attending Yale. Did you apply yet?"

"No, not yet," she responded.

"Let me know when you do because I'll contact administration. You're a legacy."

"Not really, dad," I said.

"Avery is my stepdaughter and a Berne."

I sighed. "Can we get back to work?"

"Yeah. Aside from racquetball, I wanted to let you know Renata, and I have dinner reservations with the Cronenbergs. We should be home around eleven," he noted.

"Fine. We can scrounge around the kitchen for dinner."

"Just ask the chef for whatever you want."

"Yep."

Once he left, I turned to Avery. "Get naked."

She rose from the chair and stripped off her sweatshirt, revealing her perky tits. I stood there watching as she undressed before I locked the door. I tore off my clothes, throwing them in a pile on the floor.

"I'm naked. What do you plan on doing with me?" she asked shyly.

I thought for a moment because I had changed my mind about her sitting on my face. Her innocent demeanor always got me hard when she looked up at me with her big gray eyes.

"Put your hands on the bed, bend over, and spread your legs," I commanded.

Avery complied, and I stood behind her, resisting the urge to plunge into her glistening pussy. I knelt behind her and spread her lips, then proceeded to taste the sweetest ambrosia. Her legs began to quiver, slightly shaking as she whispered my name.

"Darling Avery, you can say my name out loud."

Her reply was stifled as I thrust my tongue inside her and used my fingers to tickle her clit. I lapped at her, savoring her juices in my mouth. I felt her body tense, and Avery's legs trembled faster.

"Giddy," she moaned before she came.

As she cycled through her orgasm, she climbed on the bed.

"No! You stay there," I growled.

Avery whimpered but obeyed me. I rose, positioned myself at her entrance, and plunged inside. She was plush and wet, just the way I liked her. I was fucking her so hard I thought she would rip in two. Her moans and my groans filled the air, and at that moment, I didn't care if anyone heard us.

I sank into her pussy twice more before she tightened around me and detonated for the second time. Avery's arms and legs shook, and I wrapped my arm around her chest to hold her up, coming at the tail end of her orgasm.

"Fucking hell. I can't get enough of this sweet pussy," I panted.

"Let me down," she begged.

I pulled out and lowered her to the bed. She crawled to the

top of the bed and put her head on my pillow. Avery's hair partially covered her face, and the picture was beautiful. My chain hung around her left breast, and the number seventeen dangled from her nipple.

I sat next to her, stroking her golden hair from her face. Her cheeks were pink from the afterglow of sex.

"You're gorgeous. Come to Yale with me."

She bit her lip. "I don't know. I've always wanted Columbia."

"Apply and think about it," I said.

"I'll apply, and if I get in, I'll think about it."

"Quick shower and back to work?"

Avery snorted. "Work? We weren't working. You were priming me for sex, and you know it, Gideon Andrew Charton Berne the fifth."

"Mmm, I love how you say my name."

"You're silly."

"And you're hot."

I brushed her breast as I plucked the necklace up and centered it between her cleavage.

She smiled at me. "I'm not sure if I should believe you since you're in love with me."

I pointed at her. "You–up–shower–now."

DINNER WAS SANDWICHES, and our chef seemed happy with the choice. We gathered our plates and went downstairs to watch a movie.

"This place is crazy," Avery said.

I sat down in the front row, pulling up the side tray. "You don't have to wait for me. This is for everyone. If you want to come down by yourself, it's okay."

She put her sandwich on my tray and pressed a kiss to my lips, running her fingers through my hair.

"I don't want to be here with anyone but you. I love you, Giddy. I love you so much. Is that fucked up?"

I scowled. "Why would it be fucked up?"

"Because you were a bully. You were mean to me. I should hate you."

I hung my head. "You should. You won't get an argument from me."

"I hate that we're a secret."

"It's better this way."

Leaning further toward her, I ran my lips over her creamy neck. My appetite was quickly disappearing, and I wondered if there would be a time I wouldn't want Avery.

"What about Yale?" she asked.

"I don't know. We can live together, but if Remy, Xavier, and Jaxson go there, it would be complicated."

Avery pouted. "Then I'm attending Columbia. What's the point?"

She stamped off to the soda bar and grabbed a cup, filling it with ice before mixing Mountain Dew and orange soda together. She ignored me, moving on to the candy bar. Avery filled a popcorn cup half full of Skittles.

"Avery?"

"Just put the movie on," she grumbled.

I copied her and filled a large cup with ice and root beer. Once she had her tray up, and everything was set out, I grabbed her before she sat down, pulling her into my arms.

"You're misbehaving. You know what naughty girls get?"

She struggled to get away from me, but I was stronger. "Blah, blah, blah. It's always the same with you."

I cupped her ass, kneading her cheeks, and noticed her yoga pants were smooth, no lines. "You're not wearing panties."

"Big deal. It's more comfortable. Is there a point to this? I want to eat my sandwich and watch a movie without you trying to seduce me." Avery's tone was dull, and I knew she meant what she said.

I let her go and grabbed the remote, hitting the search key. A list of movies in alphabetical order came up.

"What do you want to watch?" I asked.

She took a petite bite of her turkey sandwich and chewed before she answered. "Heathers."

I wrinkled my nose. "You're pissed that I'm a bully, and you want to watch a movie about bullies?"

"Put it on."

I scrolled to H, found the movie, put it on, then used the other remote to dim the lights. Every so often, I glanced at Avery. She wouldn't look at me, and I didn't know how to make it better.

"Can you stop the movie? I have to pee."

I laughed. "I would too if I finished a big cup of soda."

"Just put it on pause and stop being a dick."

I stopped the movie and raised the lights. She took her paper plate, tossed it into the garbage by the candy bar, then exited the room. I finished my food and waited, checking my phone for messages. My mood soured further when I found a text from Jillian.

> At the dinner with my parents and yours. Where are you?

WHEN THE HELL did she get back? I thought she was staying at school this weekend. I was glad I wasn't asked to go because Jillian would annoy me. It was bad enough I would have to dodge her at school.

Fifteen minutes later and Avery hadn't come back. I went to the bathroom nearest the bar and knocked.

"Avery, are you okay?"

She didn't answer, but I heard her crying, so I turned the doorknob to find it was open. She was sitting on the toilet with her face streaked by mascara from her tears. My heart was heavy as I went to her.

"Oh, baby. What's the matter?"

Avery hiccupped. "Just leave me. Go back to your fucked up life. You achieved your goal."

I put my hand on her shoulder, but she shrugged it off. "What goal?" I cried.

"You broke me! I'm ruined. That's what you wanted. We need to end this. As much as I don't want to, it's not going to work between us."

A lump formed in my throat. "You can't decide this without me."

She wiped at her tears, smearing her mascara. "Breakups are ugly. Someone always gets hurt, and if you think this isn't hurting me, you're wrong. I don't want to hide."

I knelt next to her and pulled some toilet paper from the dispenser to wipe her cheeks. "It doesn't have to end."

She took more toilet paper to wipe her nose. I hated to see her in such distress.

"It does. This isn't a normal relationship. It's fucked up. We're fucked up."

"It's not," I insisted.

"It is. I want to go to prom and dance with the one I love. I want to hold hands and kiss in public."

Avery was tearing me apart. A few months ago, I pledged to ruin her, break her, but it was me who was broken at the prospect of losing her.

"Please," I begged.

"I can't do this anymore. Let me find someone else."

I grabbed her by the shoulders and shook her. “Can you live without me? Can you look at me and not want me?”

She wiped her nose. “I’ll always want you. But that doesn’t mean I can live with what we have.”

She rose from the toilet, threw the tissues in the garbage can, and brushed by me. A fresh round of sobs escaped as she ran down the hall.

CHAPTER 32

Avery

Gideon didn't come after me, and that night I slept alone, soaking my pillow with tears. I woke with a horrible headache. Later, I paused at his door, ready to knock, but I decided against it. Leaving him, I trekked downstairs to find my mother sitting at the table in the kitchen, sipping tea and munching on a bagel.

"Avery, you're up."

"Yeah, back to school today."

She frowned. "Did you have a fight with Gideon last night?"

I shook my head, afraid my voice would crack if I said anything that would give away something was wrong.

"He left early this morning," she explained. "He said he had to do something for football."

I chewed on the inside of my cheek. "Can you take me back to school?"

"Sweetheart, I'm not feeling well. I could have Watkins take you back in the limo. Are you sure nothing happened with Gideon? He didn't seem happy this morning."

"No. I should get ready to go. I have some homework to finish."

"Are you sure?" she pressed.

"Yes. Clover is…" My voice trailed off because she didn't know about my best friend attending Bancroft.

She frowned. "Clover? Did you see her while you were home?"

"No. She's busy with cheerleading."

"Good. You should make as many friends at Bancroft as you can. *Those* are your friends for the future."

My mother was such a snob.

"They're assholes. It's like having money allows you to treat people like crap. I can never be that way."

"It comes with privilege."

"If that's the case, I don't want it."

I turned to go upstairs. I knew Gideon was hurt, but so was I. Why couldn't he have found me before our parents met?

"THANKS, WATKINS."

He smiled at me. Watkins had kind blue eyes and salt-and-pepper hair. I heard he'd worked for the Berne family for over thirty years. First Payne's father and now Payne. He handed me my duffel bag from the trunk. It was a gloomy day, so I hurried into the dorm.

As I waited for the elevator, I noticed Gideon approaching me. He was wearing gray Bancroft football sweats and was soaked to the bone. He didn't say anything to me and instead coughed loudly. We stepped into the elevator, and it was an awkward ride to the fifth floor. He stepped out first. I wanted to comfort him, soothe the wound I created.

"Giddy?" I asked quietly.

"No."

I looked after him as he walked to the boy's hall. Clover was blasting music and dancing around like a fool when I stepped inside our room. I flicked the button on our Alexa to shut the music off. She wheeled around.

"Hey, why did you shut that off?"

"It's too loud."

Clover plopped on her bed and played with one of her red curls. "Thanks for abandoning me this weekend."

I opened my duffel bag and removed my clothing to stuff them into a drawer.

"Me? You were holed up in Remy's room when I went to the dance."

"And Xavier told me you bailed early. Some shit about an emergency. I know that's nonsense. You've been acting so strange lately. What's going on?"

I sighed and threw my duffel in the closet, then sat on my bed. I'd been keeping this secret from her, and I couldn't do it any longer, especially after our breakup. My heart was heavy, and I needed someone to talk to.

"You have to promise not to tell anyone."

She knitted her eyebrows together. "You can trust me. You shouldn't need to ask."

"Clover, promise me. Not a word."

She held her hand up. "I promise."

I swallowed the lump in my throat. I needed to get this out because I was miserable. I wanted to reveal everything.

"I'm sleeping with Gideon," I stated.

I let it sink in as I watched her mouth drop open. It hung there, and her eyes grew wide.

"You're shitting me? Gideon?"

"Yes, Gideon. I'm in love with him, but it's over."

She put her hand up like a stop sign. "Wait, you're confusing me. It's over?"

"I ended it. I don't want to live this way. We have to hide at home, and if we're together here in the open, our parents will find out."

"You gave him your V card?"

I nodded. "Weeks ago."

She rose from her bed and began pacing the room. "Let me see if I get this straight. How do you go from him bullying you around and treating you like crap to fucking him? Explain it?"

"It just happened. He apologized."

I couldn't honestly explain it because it didn't make sense. I tried to put all the puzzle pieces together, but we fell in love, and it didn't seem to matter anymore.

"He apologized? He ruined your summer, and he had his friends join in his little torture fest."

"Excuse me, but aren't you having sex with one of those friends?"

"Remy didn't torture me," she pointed out. "He tortured you."

"And I'm your best friend!" I cried.

"So we're both at fault. So, he fucked you, you two fell in love, and now it's over, is that it?"

My heart is broken into a billion pieces.

"That's it," my voice broke.

I began to sob. My body shook as I cried, and Clover sat on my bed to embrace me.

I ANTICIPATED the pain of going to trigonometry class. I missed Gideon, and we'd been broken apart for less than a day. His chair was empty when ee entered class, and it stayed that way as Mrs. Ordonez began attendance.

"Jaxson, where's Gideon?" I whispered.

He shrugged. "He didn't come to English class this morning. I'm not sure where he is."

I bit my lip and fixed my eyes on Clover. Something was wrong. Gideon wouldn't miss class without a good excuse.

"Miss Bedford, do you have any idea where Mr. Berne is?" Mrs. Ordonez asked.

By now, everyone at the school knew we were stepsiblings.

"No. I haven't seen him all day."

She tapped the attendance screen on her tablet to probably mark Gideon absent. I couldn't pay attention as I worried all class. Once it was over and we rose from our seats, Clover whispered into my ear.

"It doesn't mean anything."

I bit my tongue to force the tears back. Spanish was much the same. Mrs. Dolan asked if I knew where Gideon was and marked him absent, too. I started to debate between going to history and wanting to get back to the dorm to check if he was there.

Clover tried to soothe me during class by holding my hand, but it did nothing to allay my fears. Gideon was responsible, and even though he had early acceptance to Yale, he wouldn't blow off classes for no good reason. When class was over, I shoved my tablet and book into my backpack.

"Calm down," Clover said.

"For what little I know about my stepbrother, something is wrong."

She leaned into my ear. "Something is wrong. You two had a breakup. If that's not wrong, I don't know what is."

Clover looped her arm in mine after we pulled on our long coats, and we hurried back to Beckley Hall.

"You think we should be together?" I whispered.

"You were happy with him. I know you were, even if he is an asshole."

I almost tripped over my own feet as we got into the lobby

and silently cursed at the elevator for taking so long. We had company, so I didn't say anything. When we got off on our floor, I shoved my backpack in Clover's hands and ran to the boy's side.

Gideon's door was closed, and I couldn't see any lights coming from underneath. I knocked as Remy came out of his room wearing Bancroft football sweats.

"I already knocked," he said. "He wouldn't miss practice. Something isn't right. He was fucked up when he got back yesterday." Remy narrowed his eyes at me. "Did something happen at home? He told me your parents are home."

I swallowed hard. "Nothing I know of." I wiggled the doorknob, and the lock held, but from inside. I heard groaning.

"Gideon," I called.

More groaning.

I was bordering on hysterical as seconds passed. Gideon would answer the door if he were able.

"Remy, get the RA! He's in there."

He took off running down the hall, and I kept calling Gideon. His groans turned to a series of hacking coughs. The RA came back with the master key a minute later and opened Gideon's door. He was lying in his bed, as white as the sheet that covered him.

A couple of empty Gatorade bottles littered the floor, along with a spilled bottle of aspirin. I ran to him and touched his head. He was as hot as a blazing fire, and his body trembled beneath the covers.

I looked up at the RA. "He needs to go to the hospital. He's burning up."

Daniel began dialing for emergency services on his phone. I sat on the edge of the bed and stroked Gideon's sweaty hair from his forehead. A crowd had gathered at Gideon's door, but Remy pushed them out.

"This isn't a sideshow," he growled.

We stayed with Gideon, and I held his hand until emergency came and took him to the hospital.

"I should call your parents and let them know he's sick," Daniel said.

"I'm his sister; I'll do it," I replied.

I hurried down the hall, my hands shaking as I hit the contact for my mother.

"Avery, this is a surprise," she answered.

My voice was barely audible as I said, "Mom, Gideon is sick. He went to the hospital."

"Oh my God, when?"

"Right now. You have to come up here."

Her voice became as shaky as mine as she responded, "Let me get off. Payne is at the office. We'll be up as soon as we can. Keep us updated."

She hung up, and Clover came to meet me as I sniffled back tears.

"Do you want me to drive you to the hospital?" she asked.

I did, but if my mother came, she would find out Clover went to Bancroft.

I shook my head. "My mother."

Clover frowned. "Enough of this shit. This is an emergency."

"I can drive myself. I should be fine."

She put her hand on my shoulder. "Are you sure?"

The tears were threatening to fall, but I pushed them back.

"MISS BEDFORD?"

I looked up as Dr. Wong, who was taking care of Gideon, came to talk to me. Our parents still weren't here, so I was his only family.

"How is he?" I asked.

"Gideon has pneumonia. We're treating him with antibiotics

at this time. He asked to see you. I would assume your parents are on the way?"

I nodded. "They should be here soon."

"You can go in, Bay 5."

I hurried down the hall, slid the glass door open, and then closed it behind me. Gideon had two drip bags attached to his arm by a tube and an oxygen mask on his face. He opened his eyes when I entered.

"Avery," he rasped.

I put my hand over my mouth as tears spilled over my bottom lids. "You had me scared half to death. You weren't in class."

Gideon gave me a weak smile. "I'm sorry."

"Why are you sorry?"

He held out his hand, and I took it, dragging a plastic chair to his bedside with my foot. I sat down and smoothed the wrinkles out of his blanket.

"I'm sorry for everything."

"Now is not the time to discuss it."

I reached up to smooth his hair back and touched his forehead. He felt much cooler. I was relieved.

"I don't want to lose you," he croaked.

I was about to answer when our parents came through the door. I stood up and went to my mother while Payne went to Gideon. He gently hugged him, and I started to sob again as my mother embraced me.

CHAPTER 33

Gideon

After a few days in the hospital, I went home on Friday afternoon. My father and Renata stayed all week in one of the fancier hotels in town. He spent the time conducting business before he told us he'd take everyone home for the weekend, including Avery.

I still felt like crap, but it would be nice to sleep in my bed. I settled into the bench seat opposite Watkins with Avery next to me.

"I'm sorry about the Spanish project," I said.

"Not a problem. I picked something, and I'm almost done translating. We can decide who does the speech later—it'll be you."

I smirked. "Me?"

"Well, it's only fair since I did all the other work."

I chuckled, which set me in a fit of coughing. I wouldn't be playing football for a couple of weeks, but our backup quarterback was pretty good. We won the game on Friday by twenty points. If it were me, I think the spread would've been bigger.

My father and Renata were discussing something on the other bench seat, so I slid my hand over to Avery's, linking my pinkie with hers. It wasn't over. It couldn't be. She glanced up at me.

"We should talk later," she said.

I nodded. Part of the reason I got sick was that, on top of not sleeping, I'd spent three hours running in the rain trying to figure out how to work it out between us. By the time I saw Avery in the elevator, I was soaked and coughing. Come Monday morning, my chest felt like a vise was sitting on it, and I was blazing hot.

My breathing got worse as the day went on, and by the time I was found, it felt like I was trying to breathe through water. I was grateful Avery came to find me.

I NAPPED MOST of the way home, and once I was settled in bed, Renata had Avery bring me chicken soup and crackers. Rina, one of the maids, had stocked the small refrigerator in my bedroom with Gatorade and water.

"I'm glad you're getting better," Avery said after she set the tray on my bed.

She turned to go, but I stopped her.

"Can you stay with me?"

"I can, but I don't want to talk tonight."

I smirked. "Okay. So you just sit here, and I won't say anything to you."

She scowled. "That's not what I meant."

"I know what you meant."

I spooned up some chicken soup and moaned when the flavor hit my tongue. The hospital food was horrible.

"I'm having a burger tonight," Avery said.

I dropped my spoon into my soup. "How can you torture me with this information?" I asked.

She grinned and looked at me with her big doe eyes. "Call it payback."

"For what?"

Avery sat on the bed next to me and stroked my face. "It would take me all night to tell you."

"Don't break up with me," I whined.

"Gideon, we agreed not to talk about this tonight."

I shook my head. "I want to. Indulge me."

"You know how I feel. It's bad enough I spent all freaking week hiding Clover from my mother. Now you're asking me to hide my boyfriend for however long?"

I winced. "I'm in the same boat. I have to hide my girlfriend."

Tears threatened, and I saw them brimming on her bottom lids, waiting to fall over.

"This whole relationship never should've started."

I pushed the tray off my lap and took her hand. "I needed you, darling Avery. We're two tortured souls. Do you get that?"

Avery knitted her eyebrows together. "How so?"

"We both lost our parents and became irrelevant to the others."

She sighed. "Gideon, I wasn't irrelevant to my mother after my father died."

I caught her gaze. "But you are now. Your mother has been seduced by Bernc money."

"Maybe."

"No, not maybe. It's the truth. We were destined to be together, and you can't deny how you feel about me."

She averted her gaze, looking at my duvet cover. I could almost imagine her thoughts. She'd almost escaped from me and was home free, but I pulled her back, and this time, I would fight for her.

"But…"

I put my finger on her lips. "Sleep with me tonight. I missed you in my bed."

A look of worry crossed her face. "Suppose your father checks on you?"

"He won't if I tell him you're sleeping on the chaise."

"I'm not sure my mother would allow it."

"She will trust me."

ONCE I WAS SETTLED in bed for the night, and our parents made sure we were comfortable, Avery climbed into bed with me. She put her head on my shoulder and her arm around my waist. My chest still hurt, and if it did by Sunday, I wouldn't be going back to school for the upcoming week.

"Giddy?" Avery voiced.

"Yes?"

"You're not letting me go, are you?"

"No. I can't."

She was silent for a moment. "I love you."

My heart swelled with the overwhelming feeling of love, one I only had when she was near. When I began to cough, she raised her head, backing away.

"No," I said in between coughs. "Don't leave me."

"Gideon, I'm not leaving you. I don't want to lie on your chest if it gives you a coughing fit."

I finished and sipped at the orange Gatorade sitting on my nightstand. It soothed my throat.

She stared at me. "Did you take your antibiotics?"

"Yes. I have another round at midnight."

Once I was settled again, Avery put her head back on my shoulder. I hoped this would be a restart for our relationship. But outside forces were working against us, which gave us a slim chance of success. I could almost feel that I would lose Avery.

END – Book 1

Want to find out how it all started with Gideon and Avery?
You can get the free prequel by clicking below.
Beautifully Inappropriate

If you want a taste of what's in store for Beautifully Wicked Book 2 – see an excerpt below and purchase here on Amazon or read for free in Kindle Unlimited:
Beautifully Wicked

BEAUTIFULLY WICKED

AVERY WAS LEAVING and I dreaded losing her for any amount of time, but my weakened body wasn't strong or healthy enough to live on my own. I would have to be without her for a week which seemed like an eternity. Never in my life did I feel this way – with anyone.

"Come here," I said as Avery backed away.

"No, Giddy. Watkins is waiting."

I pushed the covers off and a chill rippled through me even though the room was warm. I was still running a slight fever.

"Don't make me come after you."

She sighed and came to the bed, pulling the covers back over me and tucking them under the mattress. I couldn't resist stroking her golden hair. I had so much love for my stepsister, hell, I was fucking deeply in love with her. When she told me it had to end, I nearly fell apart.

"You don't have the strength to be pushing me against walls and making threats," she said with a giggle.

I did have the strength to pull her onto the bed and bury my face in her sweet scented hair.

"You could stay home. Bancroft has an emergency leave of absence."

Avery looked up at me with her big doe eyes, the gray blurred by the tears forming on her lower lids.

"Don't make this any harder than it already is. I have to go back to school. We can't give them any signs we're together."

By them, my stepsister meant our parents, friends, servants. Anyone who could out us. This couldn't end between us.

"Avery, I love you," I whispered into her ear.

She ran her soft fingertips over my cheek. "I love you, too. It's only five days. I'll be home on Friday afternoon right after class. I promise."

I caught her gaze. "Friday isn't the problem, it's the other days I won't see you."

She pressed a soft kiss to my lips. I wanted to deepen it, roll her under me and strip her clothes off, but I didn't have the strength. Avery broke it and rose from the bed.

"No more. I have to go. Get some sleep."

I huffed. "I sleep like crap when you're not with me."

"Get used to it because it's five days before I come back."

I glowered. "Don't remind me."

"Get some sleep, Giddy."

Avery left my room with only her lingering floral perfume to remind me she was mine.

~

I slept most of the day, waking up every half hour until I received a text from Avery.

I'm back. Friday will be here before you know it.

Don't take this the wrong way but fuck you.

LMAO. I love you too, Giddy.

My father spoke with the school, and they would be sending homework as well as recordings of lessons. I was thrilled. I tossed my phone on the bed and flicked on the television. I was still tired but on the mend. As I dozed, a knock on the door woke me.

"Yeah," I rasped.

My father opened the door. "Gideon, how are you feeling?"

I wanted to tell him I felt like shit, but I glossed it over. "Better. My chest still hurts."

He sat on the edge of the bed. "Too bad you'll be out for the game this Friday."

I frowned. "Why?"

"Coach Leary had some time to watch you play."

I gritted my teeth. "Dad, I'm not interested in college ball. I don't need a scholarship and my time will be taken up by classes and homework."

He pursed his lips. "I asked you to think about it. It's good discipline."

"And I have thought about it. The answer is no."

We'd had this conversation so many times and I had the same answer each time. He kept pushing me. Sometimes I wished my knee would give out and that would be the end of the argument. It would always be a no. Once high school ball was over, I would be done with football.

"I don't understand why you keep asking when you know my answer."

I began a deep bronchial coughing fit, holding my aching chest. He waited for me to catch my breath which was hard when breathing felt like a bunch of razorblades slicing through your lungs.

"Because I want you to be well rounded. Enjoy all college has to offer. Maybe you can join a fraternity."

I wiped my mouth. "A fraternity too? Why don't I just look forward to D's?"

"You're a smart boy. I know you can handle everything. I'd like you to work with me this summer."

I groaned. "You mean nine to five in a suit with a long drive to the city and back to Westchester?"

"Gideon, you'll take over the company one day. I want you to learn the business."

I wanted to tell him we would never work together. My trust fund was earmarked for making my own way in the world. I had my last name and that was enough to get my foot in the door. Plus I would have Remy, Jaxson and Xavier by my side. We would take on the world.

"Suppose I don't want that?"

My father knitted his eyebrows together. "And what do you want to do? Live off your trust fund like one of those spoiled brats on television?"

"No," I said quietly.

"Then what?"

I shrugged. This conversation was exhausting me.

"Dad, can we talk about this when I'm better? I'm really tired."

He rose from the bed. "I'll let you get some rest."

I turned on my side and went back to sleep. I dreamed of my mother and how she would take care of me when I was a child. She was my rock and when she died, I was lost. I don't think my father knew how to react to her loss and he immersed himself in work. I needed him but he wasn't there. Chef Hawkins became like a second father to me. He was there more than my father.

MY WEEK WAS full of naps, bowls of soup and light meals, classwork and homework. I was feeling better but still a little weak. I couldn't wait to get back to school, practice and the weight room. And I was excited for Avery to come home. The phone and text weren't satisfying my need for her.

I wanted to fell her in my arms, press my lips to hers and bury my face in her floral scented hair. I missed her.

"Where are you?" I asked.

"Almost home. Would you stop calling me!"

I heard the blinker clicking.

"Are you getting off the exit?"

"For fuck's sake, Giddy, you act like you haven't seen me in months."

I laughed. "I feel like I haven't. I missed you this week."

"There was a time you couldn't stand seeing me."

"Darling Avery, that was never true. I always wanted to see you."

It was true. From the first time I saw her, I wanted her. I became infatuated and then fell in love.

"Can I hang up and concentrate on the road?"

"Where are you?"

"Near Huston Street."

My stomach churned with excitement. I couldn't wait to see

her after a few days apart. I hoped Avery agreed to go to Yale. I had it all planned out.

"That's only a mile away. You can talk to me until you pull in the driveway.

Avery laughed and it was like music to my ears.

"Do you want me to stop for anything before I come home?"

"Hell, no! Just get here."

I heard beeping as she punched the code into the driveway gate.

"I'll be in soon."

She hung up on me before I could answer. I jumped out of bed and ran to the bathroom, giving my teeth a quick brush. I hadn't shaved in a few days and my dark stubble was thick. If I knew Avery, she would only want to sleep and that was unfortunate, because I was full of lust. I want to ravage her sweet, little body until she passed out from exhaustion.

I climbed back into bed and waited what seemed like an eternity. The minutes ticked by and when she didn't come upstairs, I opened my door to find her lugging her duffel upstairs with Renata trailing behind her.

"All I'm saying is that I bought you a suitcase set and you don't bother using it. It has an overnight bag," her mother complained.

"You're home this weekend?" I growled.

I had to keep up the act to throw our parents off the scent. If they had any inkling of our relationship, there would be hell to pay.

She licked her lips to tease me. "I see you're feeling better."

"I am. Hi, Renata."

My stepmother trailed me as she followed Avery into her bedroom. I felt bad for my girl but worse for me because I wanted to see her so badly. I stepped back into my room and listened to the muffled voices next door. Once I heard the door close and Renata's footsteps in the hall, I slipped through the passage which connected our closets.

I found Avery pulling off her sweatshirt revealing a green t-shirt underneath. It rode up on her stomach and she tugged it down as I stepped into her room. She rushed into my arms and embraced mc. God, I loved this girl.

"Is Renata in a mood?" I asked.

"She's annoyed I'm not using the Louis Vuitton bags she got me. I never asked for them," she said into my chest. "How are you feeling?"

"Much better now that you're here."

"Giddy, I missed you this week even though it's so hard to be together."

"We have all weekend and our parents are leaving for the city soon."

She looked up at me. "I just got home."

"They're having dinner with one of my father's business associates. I'm sure they'll be home late tonight. We have the house to ourselves."

Avery clung to me and I kissed the top of her head. "I love you."

"Did you practice your speech?" she chuckled.

I knew it was only fair that since she did all the translation of the speech for Spanish, I would be the one to stand in front of the class and deliver it. At least she was responsible and I didn't have to fight with her about getting it done.

She was perfect in cvcry way and I wished I knew her before our parents came together. I realize I was spinning in circles, using girls for my entertainment and pleasure, but there was still the problem with control. I needed it and she didn't want to give too much.

"Of course. I have the perfect accent."

"You can try it in bed tonight."

"I can't wait," I said huskily.

She broke from me, unbuttoning her jeans and my dick more than stirred as she shucked out of them.

"We're not having sex, just sleeping. You need to rest."

She turned and opened her bag, taking out a pair of gray sweatpants. I went to her and stroked her ass, exposed by the powder blue thong she wore.

"I love your ass," I said.

"Knock it off. You're make me hot."

I moved the hair from her neck and kissed her, running my lips up to the emerald she wore in her ear.

"I need to fuck you tonight. Don't deny me," I whispered.

Her nipples pressed against her shirt and I reached up to cup her breast.

"Stop, Giddy," she moaned.

"You don't want me to stop. Did you come this week? Did you touch your beautiful pussy?"

Avery leaned her head back against me, dropping her sweatpants on the bed.

"Stop teasing."

I licked the rim of his ear. "You didn't answer my question? Did you touch yourself?"

She whimpered. "Would it matter?"

"If it doesn't, then answer the question."

"I did. I had to."

I smiled against her ear. "And what did you think about when you did it?"

"You. Always you."

By now my dick was so hard my balls ached with need for relief. Thinking about her plush, pink pussy and how wet it must be by now was making it worse.

"I want to play tonight," she moaned.

I was just about to answer when the doorknob rattled. I shot into the closet as Renata burst through the door. Avery whipped around.

"Mother! Don't you know how to knock?" She snapped.

I hid behind the island and prayed she wouldn't come in.

"I've seen you naked before, so your underwear is nothing special. I like those on you but they're inappropriate to wear for school. What happened to the white panties I got you?"

"I changed before I came home. Would you like to look through my dirty laundry? You'll find several pairs of boring white panties."

"Suppose there was a windstorm and your skirt blew up? You would be flashing everyone your ass."

"Mom, is there a reason you're here?"

"We're leaving for dinner. Chef made Wagyu sliders and fries for you and Gideon. Try to get along with him."

Oh, she's going to get along with me, especially when I slip my aching dick into her tight, little cunt. Don't you worry.

"I always try. He's the one who acts like a jerk."

I heard Renata sigh before she exited the room and as I rose from behind the island, Avery stepped into the closet.

I chuckled. "I don't always act like a jerk."

She smiled. "Sometimes you do."

I slapped the top of the almond granite. "You know, this is just the right height to fuck or eat that tight pussy of yours. Want to try?"

"Dinner first."

Beautifully Wicked is available on Amazon or free on Kindle Unlimited. Get it now by clicking below:
Beautifully Wicked

Made in the USA
Middletown, DE
13 November 2023